IN THE BEGINNING. . . .

This is it, show time, the moment of truth that will prove whether Walt can indeed turn a human brain into Project Cyborg. The next thing you know, I'm on the screen, inside the big tank, all wired up and ready to go. Walt's over by the control panel, staring at the 'lectroencephalograph, his finger over the switch. He turns to his witnesses and says, "Here we go, boys. Everybody say a prayer."

Six hours into the experiment, and with three failures behind him, Walt Hillerman flips the on switch for the fourth time.

Jagged red lines dance up and down the length of the graph paper.

I'm ALIVE. . . .

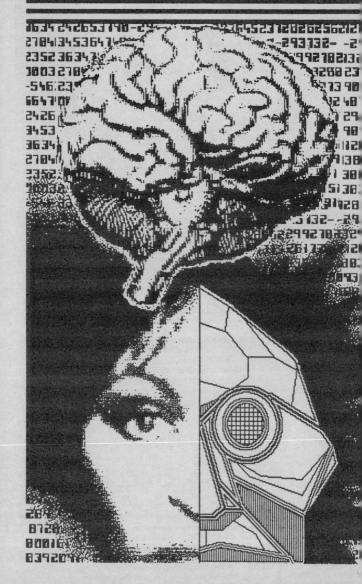

LADY EL

by
JIM STARLIN
and
DAINA GRAZIUNAS

A ROC BOOK

ROC
Published by the Penguin Group
Penguin Books USA Inc., 375 Hudson Street,
New York, New York 10014, U.S.A.
Penguin Books Ltd, 27 Wrights Lane,
London W8 5TZ, England
Penguin Books Australia Ltd, Ringwood,
Victoria, Australia
Penguin Books Canada Ltd, 10 Alcorn Avenue,
Toronto, Ontario, Canada M4V 3B2
Penguin Books (N.Z.) Ltd, 182–190 Wairau Road,
Auckland 10, New Zealand

Penguin Books Ltd, Registered Offices:
Harmondsworth, Middlesex, England

First published by Roc, an imprint of New American Library,
a division of Penguin Books USA Inc.

First Printing, June, 1992
10 9 8 7 6 5 4 3 2 1

Copyright © Jim Starlin and Daina Graziunas, 1992
All rights reserved

Roc is a trademark of New American Library,
a division of Penguin Books USA Inc.

Printed in the United States of America

Lady El is dedicated with love to Athos Demetriou, our agent and friend. His genuine enthusiasm and words of encouragement, after a period of seemingly interminable disappointment, renewed our spirits. He gave us our break when we really needed one. It is a debt we cannot repay and a kindness we will never forget.

PART ONE

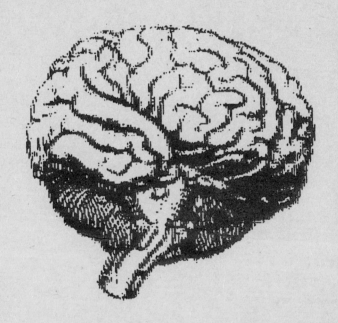

It is not the insurrections of ignorance that are dangerous, but the revolts of the intelligence.
—James Russell Lowell

All right, I'm going be honest with you, my life coulda been a whole lot worse than it was. Like, what if I was the *smart* Siamese twin, attached at the hip to a sister in love with some crazy son of a bitch whose idea of tenderness was a cattle prod.

Makes you think, don't it?

I mean, I wasn't born without no arms or legs or nothin'; forced to work as a doorstop. Still, there were things I wish I hadn't been forced to do. Things that sometimes cost you your soul. Luckily I managed to hang onto mine. Martin Luther King was pro'bly incredibly proud of me for striking this blow for personal dignity. But that don't change nothin'. Not really. You start off with three strikes against you when you come into this world poor, black, and female. That about neatly sums up the Arlene Washington story. My life. Well, the first one, anyway. I don't know why I'm tellin' you all this, except it helps to get things off your chest sometimes, air out the ol' psychic closets.

Anyway, I was feeling mighty low that night. Maybe because it was Wednesday, the middle of a bad week that looked like it was never going to end or get any better. My shift was over and I was on my way home.

Home, where the heart is. Past Sunday I'd thrown my old man out. There wasn't anything waitin' for me but four walls.

Throwin' my boyfriend out probably sounds a lot braver than it was. The truth is, I just changed the locks so he couldn't get back in after he went out for a few drinks. Made sure his bags were packed and sittin' outside the apartment when he showed up six hours later. He started banging on that door, fit to break it, yelling that he was going to kick it and my teeth down my throat. I called the cops.

They escorted him out of the building as I held my breath. I was hoping that'd be the last I'd ever see of

Nero (Pearlie) Du Bois. I was tired of that mountain of a man using me as a punching bag. Oh, he wasn't the first one. For some reason I kept getting hooked up with men who liked to hurt me. Maybe it was something about *me*. Or it could be something I picked up, like a bad habit, from my mama. Mama had even worse taste in men.

My week dragged itself along after giving Pearlie his walking papers. I felt exhausted. Every night I'd come home to ride that ol' emotional roller coaster: he's gone, good riddance; I don't want to be alone. *Not again*. Somehow that always seemed to be the more important consideration. Even misery loves company.

My job didn't exactly take my mind off it either. See, I was part of that great tide of women you see swellin' the canyons of Manhattan around four in the afternoon. Comin' in just as most normal folks is gettin' ready to knock off and go home. We'd march in, an army hundreds strong, and storm the glass and steel fortresses. The mop and pail brigade. My target: #1 World Trade Center, where from four to midnight I'd make all the mess made by the big shots disappear like magic. Emptying ashtrays and dumping half-filled coffee cups. Sweeping and mopping floors. Dusting off shelves and typewriters. Scraping wads of gum off tile floors. Magic my ass; did I mention what truly spiritually upliftin' work this was?

Granted, the job did give me the occasional chance to hobnob with some of the big mucky-mucks. That *better class of people*. Can't say I was terribly impressed with most of them. There'd always be some suit workin' away in his office when I came in. Mostly they'd pretend I didn't exist. But that was fine by me. That left us each free to go about our own business. But at least once a night there'd be some jerk whose evening wouldn't be complete without his havin' a few words with the maintenance personnel. That's cleanin' lady to all the rest of you.

There were those who always wished me a good night as they headed for the elevators. Mostly these folks were white and I suspected that saying good night was a nice, painless way of reaffirming for themselves just how liberal they were. The yahoos who really killed me the most, though, were the guys who swore up and down that they'd trade places with me at a moment's notice if only they could. I had no idea the *pressure* their jobs put them under. What they *wouldn't give* for simple work like mopping floors. A couple of times I couldn't resist and offered these yuppie fools the business end of a mop, so they could see what they'd been missin'. You know not one of them would have known what to do with the damn thing if they'd accepted my offer. Instead they shook their heads in what they felt was a gravely world-weary manner and informed me that life just wasn't as simple as that. They'd struggle into their thousand-dollar vicuna topcoats and with one last, sad smile shuffle off to their modest million and a half dollar homes in Westchester. Somehow I could never work up any real sympathy for them.

And there were some just plain nasty ones, the power trippers. Those mothers stayed late just looking for someone to bully. They usually had some clerical position in a brokerage house or lawyers' office, where they'd probably been bullied and intimidated all day by their asshole of a boss and were on the lookout for someone farther down the corporate ladder to share the experience with. They were the type who'd accidently spill coffee on a section of floor you'd just mopped or complain you hadn't done a good enough job on their boss's office. You'd have to waste another fifteen minutes doing it again. No way you could tell them to stick it. If you did, they'd be on the phone in a flash, complainin' to the supervisor. For some reason the supervisor always took their side. Guess I couldn't blame the supes for playing the game by the existing rules. But it didn't make me terribly fond of them either, judging by how many times I wished them dead.

But the one that pissed me off the most was this lawyer up on the forty-eighth floor. Whenever no one else was around he'd call me Queenie or McQueen. At first I was kinda intrigued. "How's the weather out there today, Queenie?" he'd say, or "See you later. Don't forget to empty my wastebasket, McQueen." I admit it, I was stumped. And I still wasn't sure if I liked it. What did it mean? So I smiled and pretended we were in cahoots. I shoulda trusted my instincts. They were screaming that this guy was a genuine turkey. "Been getting any lately, McQueen?" he said one day. I tossed off some reply, reminding myself that this was some in-joke of his, when I heard him say quietly to himself, in his best falsetto, "I don' know nothin' 'bout birthin' babies, Miz Scarlett." Then he giggled.

I still didn't get it. Never went to the movies much. But I asked around among the gals on my shift. They all got a good laugh over it. I didn't.

Butterfly McQueen. So that's what he meant. Shiftless Prissy from "Gone With the Wind." If I had a gun I would have stormed back to that office and killed the son of a bitch where he sat.

Understand me now, I'm not sayin' all my trouble at work was with white folks. The few rich brothers and sisters there weren't no better. The women would look down their noses at me, like I was a disgrace to the race. Just look how far they'd come and here I was still sweepin' floors. The guys, well, they'd hit on me constantly, offerin' to take me to the broom closet or maybe the men's room but never out to dinner. At thirty-two I still looked pretty good. But I wasn't makin' enough money to command any respect. Or even some plain humanity.

'Course, if I knew then what I know now, I wouldn't'a put up with that crap. But I didn't; five nights a week I subwayed it downtown for eight more hours of menial labor at near minimum wage and all the shit I could eat.

So there I was, standin' on that subway platform, waitin' to go home. It was midnight and two whole days still till the weekend. I was feelin' about as blue as you get. What's worse, the trains were runnin' late. That meant a good-size crowd gathered on the platform. Didn't have to worry about getting mugged, of course. Safety in numbers. But I felt like being alone with my misery. Then Shirley Windsor, a woman I worked with, showed up and started going on about her no-good husband. I tried to look interested, but all I could think about was gettin' home to a nice, hot shower and a warm bed. Time to shut all the systems down for a spell. Vegetate. Why couldn't this be Friday night? Forty-eight hours of uninterrupted nothin' was what I craved. Where was that damn train? And why, Lord, couldn't Shirley develop this huge frog in her throat? No divine intervention. Shirley kept right on flappin' her gums.

An old white dude came by tryin' to panhandle some change. He reeked of alcohol; I ignored him. That didn't deter him none. "Wha's the matter wit' choo, lady?" he said as if I had offended him. A few people turned to see whether there really was something wrong with me. He went on through the crowd on stiff legs planted far apart, muttering his spare change chant.

About the time Shirley started her third go-round about her old man I spotted a young couple waiting at the other end of the platform. They were young, smiling and looked like they'd just stepped out of some Norman Rockwell painting—you know, the guy did all them all-American kinda pictures. The boy was slicked back and wearing a tux, pro'bly a rental. Still, he looked pretty damn good. The girl had on a pale blue ballgown, all lacey with frills. Long blond hair and a tan. They were oblivious of everything and everyone else, lookin' deep into each other's eyes. Part of me couldn't believe my eyes at that moment. Another part of me wanted to be the girl. She clearly knew somethin' about relationships I'd missed along the way. There'd be no black eyes or chipped teeth in her future. She was a golden girl heading for a golden tomorrow. I felt shame for the terrible things I wished on her. I couldn't help myself, though.

My dark thoughts were interrupted by the sounds of an approaching chooch. I leaned forward and saw its headlights wash the tunnel wall with light from around a bend in the tracks. I took a step back, relieved to know I was at the end of my wait. I guess now that I've had a chance to think, I remember I was vaguely aware of the old wino's return. His pleas for spare change were getting nearer. Again I ignored him; not deliberately like before, but my mind was on getting out of my shoes and putting my feet up. He wasn't part of my universe, had no importance as far as I could see, just one of New York's passing annoyances, a momentary rubbing the wrong way of my peace of mind. I was about to get on my train and leave him behind.

Boy, was I wrong.

The train entered the station as this old boozer stepped up behind me, tripped, and slammed into my backside. In a way I guess you could say I was lucky. When I pitched forward, the train was already slowing down and cruisin' past me. I didn't fall in front of it, gettin' ground up beneath its wheels. Instead my shoulder only caught the corner of one of the passing cars. Still, the train had enough speed to send me flyin' through the air like a rocket. I soared like a ruptured duck and came to a crashin' halt against one of the platform's iron stanchions. There was no mistaking the sound of bones breaking inside me. I plopped to the floor like a sack of wet laundry. The crowd gathered around to inspect the damage caused by my unscheduled flight.

The next thirty or so minutes, I drifted in and out of consciousness. Every time I surfaced, bobbing up from beneath still waters into reality, I was greeted by overwhelming pain. Each time I opened my eyes, a new group of gawkers towered over me.

Once I returned to find a couple paramedics easing me onto a stretcher. The broken glass within me shifted, sendin' me back into the black void. I think I came to twice in the ambulance on the way to the hospital and at least once in the hospital itself. I've this vague memory of a group of people in green smocks staring at me, poking me, askin' the name of my insurance company.

Apparently my injuries were more than these good doctors and nurses could handle. It seems everything was busted up inside me and leakin' all over the place. My medical chart says I was being prepped for surgery when I died.

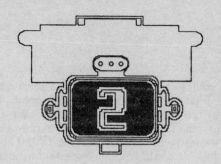

You're goin' to have to forgive me if I seem a bit vague about what happened to me at this point. You see, during my trip to and my stay at the hospital I was either dying or dead. These conditions tend to play havoc with the ol' memory. But luckily we live in the age of the overworked file clerk. Nothing important happens in our paperwork-conscious society without it being recorded for posterity, in triplicate. All these files are now open to me. So I have a wealth of material to tap into in order to fill in those lost hours: medical records, DMV stats; honey, you name it.

Lookin' back, I can plainly see the one incident that led up to everything that has happened to me. None of the wondrous options now open to me would have been possible if I hadn't learned how to drive.

It turns out my driver's license was what kept me from actually going to that final reward, which in my case would have been an unmarked grave somewhere's.

At the time I was living with this guy named Roger LaVelle. Roger was a bit of a change for me. Up until that point I'd always found myself involved with drunks that liked to knock me around after they'd had a few too many. Mind you, they didn't show me their true colors right from the start. I wasn't that stupid. The bums usually waited until we moved in together and I was really emotionally hooked on them. Then the heavy drinkin' and beatings would begin. When I wasn't being kicked around by the current love of my life, I'd kick myself. How was it that I didn't notice I was traveling down the same road I'd been down so many times before? There were always plenty of warning signs along the way. Blinded by love, I guess.

Like I said, Roger was different, though. He wasn't a boozer or a girlfriend beater. Rog was into heroin.

But like the guys that came before him and even the ones came after, Roger kept this little secret from me

until after we were settled into domestic bliss. When I
stumbled upon him shooting up in the bathroom one
day, my first response was to throw the bastard out on
his junkie ass. But in the end good sense lost out and
I let Roger fast-talk me into staying. Why I kept him
around is painfully apparent to me now. The bare-
boned, unvarnished truth is that Roger 'n me were both
junkies. Rog stuck a needle in his arm. Me? I plunged
over and over again into self-destructive relationships.
Seems I never met an abusive son of a bitch I didn't
fall in love with. I was your basic, unrepentant emotional junkie.

'Course, I didn't realize this at the time. I thought the
highs and lows of love were the only points that counted.
Whenever I hit the calm of middle ground I thought of
it as nothing more than a chance to recharge the ol' bat-
teries for the next go round. It never occurred to me that
the mid-ground was where a relationship spends most of
its time and where it gains its strength. That's when a
couple gets to really know each other. That's when plans
should be made. When you should take a long, hard
look at where a relationship is going. But I never took
advantage of the lulls in turmoil. The men I lived with
remained relative strangers to me. They were stimula-
tion, not companionship. In a way I suppose I used them
as much as they used me. The only difference was that
when the affairs ended, I was usually left with nothing
but a black eye or swollen lip as a remembrance. The
guys—their forget-me-nots were usually either my stereo
or television.

So in some ways, Roger was a step up for me. Being
a junkie, he could supply me with all the emotional ups
and downs I required without the bruises.

Thing with dopers is that their whole lives revolve
around where their next fix is comin' from. It blinds them
to all else. So for me, Roger merely replaced physical
pain with emotional craziness. There were the nights he
couldn't score and rampaged through the apartment like
a madman. Don't know how many times I held his head
while he suffered from the shakes or fever, how many
nights I sweated bullets 'bout him while he was out on

the street trying to score. To his credit, Roger never tried to get me hooked, never even gave me a taste. But then maybe he realized that scoring for two would be just too much trouble. Attributing any type of good to a man with a jones is just plain stupid.

Rog and I stayed together for eight frantic months. It seemed like eight years. Finally I came home one night and found everything of value cleaned out of the apartment. Never heard from Roger after that. But a year later, a friend told me he'd heard Roger was dead, shot in a crack den. I gave him one night of tears. That was all I could afford.

While Roger and I were together, we had some mighty strange times. We were living in Jamaica, Queens, and Roger had this old Volkswagon. The state had taken away Roger's driver's license for unpaid traffic tickets, so Rog was afraid he'd get pulled over and busted driving himself. Also, Roger didn't have no credit left with any of the local dealers. In fact, they would have broken both his legs if they coulda found him. His place of residence was his most closely guarded secret. This meant Roger had to trek way up to Harlem in order to score. The round trip on the subways woulda taken forever and besides, he might run into someone he owed money to on the train. So the only solution to all these problems, as it turned out, was teaching me how to drive.

I learned the fine art of operating a Volkswagon by driving 'round and 'round the Unisphere at the old World's Fair grounds in Flushing Meadow. No mean trick, since Rog's bug was a stick. No telling how many hours I spent grinding gears beneath that hunka metal, Roger screaming at me that I was an idiot and would never learn, till I got rattled and threw up. It was hell. But I eventually mastered this fine art, even on New York's mean streets. Took the road test, had my picture taken, and was issued a temporary license.

When my permanent license arrived in the mail a couple weeks later, I looked it over. On the bottom of the back of the little plastic card was a section that read:

**I HEREBY MAKE AN ANATOMICAL GIFT,
TO BE EFFECTIVE UPON MY DEATH, OF
A. ANY NEEDED ORGANS OR PARTS
B. ☐ THE FOLLOWING BODY PART(S):___
C. ☐ LIMITATION(S):_____
DONOR'S SIGNATURE_____
WITNESS_____**

Wasn't sure the license would be valid if I didn't fill out this section, so I marked "A" because it didn't require any additional writing. Roger signed as my witness. With that done, the license went into my purse and I never again gave it a thought. Three months later Roger split, taking the beetle, and I no longer had any need for a driver's license, but I didn't throw it out, seeing as how it might come in handy for cashing checks later on.

Little more than a year after that, the union gathered everyone in the clean-up crew into the basement of the World Trade Center before we went on shift. The shop steward had these organ donor cards we were to fill out and carry with us. He didn't know why the big shots down at union headquarters wanted us to carry the silly things, but he figured it must have something to do with our group health insurance. So I thought about it a moment, decided I'd have very little use for my organs once I was dead, filled out the card, stuck it at the bottom of my purse, and promptly forgot about it.

And that was how it happened that I was carryin' two documents certifying me as a bona fide organ donor when they wheeled me into the hospital. The signin' of two cards, acts I didn't really understand at the time. Such unimportant incidents in a life filled with millions'a unimportant incidents. Who could have imagined the opportunities those cards would open up for me?

Some bigwig at the Pentagon called it Project Harvest. It'd been planned for months, just waiting for the day when everything would be set to go into operation. Thirty medical officers had been briefed and ordered to drop whatever they were doing when the word came down. They didn't know the purpose of the weird scavenger hunt they were being sent on, and the few that asked were told that information was classified. These military doctors knew what they were to procure, had the proper authorizations to get the job done, and that was all they needed to know. And so thirty medical officers went back to their posts and waited for the green light on Project Harvest.

They got their go ahead three hours before my death.

My guess is that Navy Lieutenant Alexander Bendix figured he wouldn't have to wait around very long at his assigned post. I mean, people were croakin' all the time in New York City. On a nice warm summer night like this the paramedics should bring in what he was looking for in twenty minutes, tops. He was wrong. Nothing promising arrived in the first ninety minutes of his watch. The records show that Lieutenant Bendix had to pass on the first three near terminal patients he was presented with. Two had severe head injuries and the third was a derelict in the final stages of alcoholism. No, they wouldn't do at all. The lieutenant had been ordered to bring in a *healthy human brain* from a recently deceased individual, and he wouldn't be satisfied with anything less.

Just a little before three in the morning Lieutenant Bendix was alerted to my arrival at the emergency room. When he popped into the ER, the staff was busy trying to keep me alive, but Bendix managed to corner a doctor and find out what my prognosis was. The doctor's dismal assessment of my chances was exactly what Bendix wanted to hear.

The paramedics had brought my purse along with my broken body, I guess for purposes of identification. The lieutenant picked it up and rummaged through it. One driver's license with the donor section filled out and witnessed and a second organ donor card. Someone upstairs was lookin' out for

Lieutenant Bendix. These two legal documents meant he wouldn't have to deal with any bereaved next of kin, not that he would have been able to locate any in my case.

So the young lieutenant made up his mind to just wait for the news of my imminent demise. He accompanied the ER staff as they rushed me up to surgery and pro'bly heard the life-support monitor let loose its dreadful wail when my battered heart finally gave out. According to the records, "heroic efforts" were made to haul me back from the grave, but failed. My time of death was listed as 3:08 A.M. I'm sure Lieutenant Bendix didn't waste a single moment pulling out his authorization papers and claiming my remains. The reason I know this is because I was logged into a second OR at 3:10.

There, an electrical stainless steel surgical saw cut open the top of my head, and my brain was gently dislodged from its resting place. My brain stem was separated from the spinal column according to specific instructions from Bendix. He then supervised my gray matter being placed within a traveling case he'd brought along just for the purpose. This was no crude dry-ice container, no sir. It was a glass vat filled with a specially prepared solution. I was going first-class all the way. Once the vat was sealed, it was placed within another case and carefully transported to the hospital parking lot, where a military van awaited. Its driver then rushed the lieutenant and what was left of me to a nearby heliport. The chopper was warmed up and ready for us. Three hours later, we landed in front of a farmhouse just outside Bowling Green, Virginia.

Needless to say, this wasn't your normal, run-of-the-mill farm.

To anyone unlucky enough to find himself lost on the out-of-the-way dirt road that led past this bit of property, the place looked like just another family farm struggling to compete and failing. The house and farm were both in desperate need of paint, and even a city-bred eye could tell the crops were suffering from neglect.

But if this passer-by slowed a bit and was somewhat observant, he might have noticed that the farm had more than the usual number of hands out in the corn fields. Closer examination of these men would have revealed that they were carrying Uzi machine pistols 'stead of rakes. 'Course, if you got that close you were in a whole mess 'a trouble.

See, this farm's barn was not a barn. It was a CIA-funded laboratory carrying out top-secret experiments for the government, and it was my new home.

The tape rolls. This videotape is like all the others. It starts with the standard FBI warning 'bout how it's classified top secret and if you muck with or copy it they'll slap you with some hefty fine and/or prison term.

PROJECT CYBORG: The snazzy logo Walt had designed flashes on the screen. Yellow letters on a black background, a line drawing of a head above the lettering. Left side of the head is normal, human. Right side looks sort of mechanical. Anyway, the whole setup is kinda like some company trademark. Awfully pretentious, you ask me. The words "REPORT 127" scoot across the bottom of the screen.

Then it all fades to black. What follows is pantomime. A man in a small office, shufflin' papers at his desk. He glances up, mildly surprised and looking somewhat distracted, as if someone has just walked into the room. Nice opening, almost charming, bringing on this absentminded professor, until you realize all his reports start like this. As if the man was hard at work when someone ran in with a video camera demandin' an instant update on Project Cyborg. As always the professor's prepared to do just that. What a trooper.

The guy in the lab coat is Doc Hillerman—Dr. Walter Hillerman. Walt to the few friends he has. He's in his mid-thirties, I guess, tall and slim with thinning dishwater blond hair. Maybe you'd call it light brown. Anyhow, he's always got this pair of glasses perched on the end of his nose. Still, he's not bad-looking for a white boy. Did I mention he's the Big Kahuna of this Project Cyborg?

On the screen, Walt takes a moment, as if to collect his thoughts, clears his throat, and begins, "As of 1500 hours today I terminated Project Cyborg's offshoot program, Project Harvest. It went off splendidly. The joint military services provided us with thirty high-grade specimens. We've already begun running tests on them: physical examinations, electroencephalograms, etc. What I'd like to do is cull the number of candidates down to a more manageable group, say ten.

"I'm pleased to report that Section Alpha has completed its assignment. The results are in and they're everything we hoped for and more. We've *succeeded* in processing and retrieving limited data from all ten of our simian subjects. Imagine, not one failure in the entire test group. Quite remarkable, really. You'll find the complete results of this experiment in the accompanying written supplement.

"It looks like we've put the final polish on HESTON as well. Both the computers and our simian friends are responding to the language marvelously. There's still room for continuing refinements, as always, but the experiment as it stands has, I feel, attained the goals we originally set for it. I'm extremely pleased with the results.

"I believe we'll find little need to modify HESTON in order to continue the project. There are far more similarities than differences between our two test groups.

"Which brings me to the heart of this report. I'm proud to announce that Beta Section has finished its preliminary studies ahead of schedule. The new equipment is in place and being tested even as I speak. We can begin the next series of tests within the week."

Walt is sitting back in his chair now, grinning like the cat who ate the canary. "The time has come for us to stop playing around with monkey brains, my friends. We are about to boldly venture into a totally new realm of scientific exploration. Next week we will at long last witness the joining of human intelligence and creativity, with its infinite capacity for understanding as well as growth and change, to the speed and reliability of the computer."

Walter goes on like this for another ten minutes. Up on his soapbox, droning on 'bout how linkin' a human brain to a computer will bring about all these wonderful benefits for mankind. I usually tune the good doctor out at about this point. I'm sure anyone who's watched more than one of his "video reports" does the same. He really does go on 'bout this Project Cyborg stuff like it was the second coming or somethin'. But then it's his life: his number one obsession.

Of course, only Walt and maybe a dozen other Einsteins understand even half the jive scientific jargon and off-the-wall theories that are the heart of Project Cyborg. It's all Greek to me, baby. I don't pretend to understand any of Walt's *magic* thinking. Scientific miracles or voodoo, it's all the same to me. All I know is that I'm still boogyin', thanks to him. And that's all that counts.

Walt's finally run out of steam. He waves bye-bye to the screen and slowly fades to black. The Project Cyborg symbol flashes on the screen. An unseen audience applauds. The American tax dollar at work.

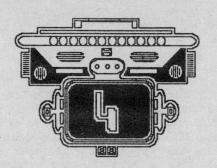

Most everything I know about Walt comes from video-tapes. Thing is, when he was back in college some-one gave him a camcorder. He got the bug, real bad. Never recovered. The man's got nearly every major event in his life on tape. At Harvard Med School, Walt already knew his work would be of "historical signifi-cance." So whenever he took on a new project, he'd pull out the ol' camera and videotape its progress from day one.

If I'm making Walt sound like some crazy egomaniac in a lab coat, then I'm doing him wrong. See, it's just that the guy's head didn't work like everyone else's; he was a genius and he realized this early on.

You've got to understand that the strange and wonder-fully different way his mind worked was mighty specific. He couldn't use it to, say, score a million dollars a day on the stock exchange or run any other kind of get-rich-quick scam. His talent was science and he had a powerful jones for figurin' out how the human brain worked. His college records, they read like nothin' I ever seen. All sorts of biology courses: biochemistry, biophysics, bio-this, bio-that. The boy had a one-track mind most of his way through school. Married to the brain, you might say.

Halfway through his senior year, though, Walt got himself a lady on the side. She gave him something just thinkin' about the brain couldn't. Apparently someone introduced him to computers. Electronic brains! Can you dig that? The guy was hooked. His transcripts started reading like a Radio Shack catalog. After Walt finished med school, he started going off to other schools to take what they call post-graduate courses. Imagine that. The dude had a college diploma right there in his hands and all he could think of doing was taking more classes. He just couldn't get enough of computers.

Walt's earliest videotapes show him talking about this

idea he's got for hooking up a human mind to a computer. But Walt was a real Poindexter back then—you know, one of those brainy little nerds with tape holdin' their glasses together and six million pens and slide rules sticking out of one of them plastic pocket protectors. Wearing a K-Mart shirt his mama must have bought him before sendin' him off to college, lookin' like it ain't been cleaned in about a month. There's about twenty pounds less of him than the Walt I know. Looks a bit like a scarecrow, with some of the straw missing. But even back then there was an intensity in those eyes. That boy always knew where he was goin'.

He didn't use a lot of the fancy words he does later on. Guess maybe he didn't know them yet. But he always had the fire. He'd go on about all the hard work that lay ahead and all the obstacles that'd have to be overcome: like some type of language both the brain and the computer could use, keepin' a brain alive outside a living body, all sorts of crazy stuff.

The biggest obstacle he'd have to overcome, though, was something he don't even consider in these early tapes. Turned out to be other people's limited imaginations. And their fear of things they don't understand. But Walt found that out soon enough.

There's another videotape, dated about a year later. Shows a young, half-drunk Walt Hillerman sitting in a grubby apartment, half-empty bottle of Miller in his hand, three empties at his feet. Walt's staring angrily at the camera and yellin' what a bunch of fools he's been havin' to deal with.

Nobody wants to hear anything 'bout his theories. They tell him he's crazy. No way in hell anyone's going to fund his research. It's all too "Frankensteinish." Man and machine, a crime against nature, that's what they say it is. I hate looking back at this tape. Walt looks so down, so beaten. Hurts to see a young man bein' so bitter.

He says he can't believe everyone thinks artificial intelligence is the way to go. They tell him it's a cleaner route to the same place Walt's heading. But Walt curses these folks for bein' such damn pompous fools. Do they really think they can duplicate something it took Ma Nature millions of years to perfect? "If God created a human mind, why can't man?" That's what *they* say. All it's going to take is a few billion dollars and several decades to pull it off. Those conceited assholes.

"The human brain already exists. So why are they insisting on reinventing the wheel? The mind of man is just waiting to be linked to the magical efficiency of a computer. But the money folks can't see this! They don't have the courage necessary to follow a conviction. In fact, they wouldn't know a conviction if they fell over one. They're too afraid of what the public's reaction to such a line of research might be. Chickenshit bastards!"

Walt says he's going to keep at it—lookin' for backing, writing his papers, and fillin' out grant requests. He knows he's not crazy and someday he swears he's going to prove it.

His resumé shows a long list of research jobs he drifted in and out of during that dry spell. Guess he never came across anythin' that took his mind off brains and computers, though. Some dreams die a lot harder than others. Walt kept right on pounding out his fancy papers and hustlin' grant money the hard way from the scientific community.

There's a handful of tapes showing what sort'a research Walt did on his own time and dime. 'Course it don't mean beans to me. Him talkin' about synapses and mid-brains, using platinum wires for leads to different lobes, 'lectroencephalograms and glucose solutions.

The worst part of these tapes for me is watching Walt dissect monkey brains, pointing happily to things he finds interesting inside the messes he's making—real nasty-looking stuff.

Then there's the breakthrough tape. Walt finally manages to keep a monkey brain alive, hooked up to a computer for stimuli. Got to admit it does look like something out of a really cheesy, low-budget monster flick. Like someone trying to make a movie in their garage, which is exactly where Walt had his lab set up at the time. Wires running all over the place: on the floor, hanging from rafters. Walt dancing around and whooping like he's won the lottery. There's a close-up of this little gray turd of a monkey brain, floating in a big glass vat filled with something looks suspiciously like cherry Kool-Aid. Another closeup of a gizmo, graph paper running through it, needles making jaggedy red lines up and down its length.

It must've all been worth it, though. This is the tape what got Walt's work noticed by the military. Records show a Colonel William Baker took the tape and papers to some grant committee at the Pentagon. Don't really know what happened at that get-together. Took place near the end of the fiscal year. Maybe the committee had a funding surplus and figured they'd better spend it or Congress might not give them as much next year. The reason don't really matter, but the fact is Walt got his grant the very next day. Twenty thousand big green ones. Peanuts as far as your usual research grants go, I hear, but it was a hell of a lot more than Walt ever had to play with before.

That's how Project Cyborg got off the ground. Finally.

It didn't change nothing in Walter's everyday life. Walt kept working in his garage and sending the military brass an update tape once every three months or so. Looks like they liked what they saw. The Pentagon kept sending Walt more and more money every time they got a new tape. Guess they saw all sorts of swell applications for this "pure research."

Then the big brass decided Walt needed a new place to work. They shipped him off to the Bowling Green lab. There's a tape shows what the place looked like when Walt first arrived. Little farmhouse for Walt to live in. The lab, still looking like a barn on the outside, all fixed with white wall paneling and air conditioning inside.

Early tapes show the lab as this big empty cavern. One huge mother of a computer off in a corner, two terminals on desks, most of the lab equipment still in crates. Walt practically strutting around with his new assistant, talking about how great it's going to be working on something bigger than an IBM PC.

Scan the tapes and you see the lab fill up with all sorts of new equipment. More terminals, bigger computers, miles of wire, strange machines whose purpose I can't even begin to guess at. The place becomes downright cramped, things hanging from brackets on the ceiling. New assistants constantly popping up in the films. Disappearing just as suddenly. And there's always the monkey brains. *Sliced, diced, halved, quartered, freeze-dried, on slides, in jars*, everywhere you look. Now Walt walks around the lab, complaining he needs something called a Cray-II.

Dear ol' Walter. He changes as the years and tapes go by. The gawky young dreamer is replaced by a take-charge kinda guy. The man grows into the boss his work's forced him into. But every so often you still get a quick glimpse into his eyes and see it's still there. The dream lives on.

About a year after Walt's move to Bowling Green, a sort of off-the-wall tape shows up in the collection. It's a video of Walt's wedding to a Phyllis O'Connor. Simple affair, small reception afterward. Even a blind man could understand why Walt went for her. Big blue eyes, soft blond hair, and, honey, melons big as those on that country singer with all the wigs. But it don't look like Walt married himself no rocket scientist. Listening to her talk, sort of got the impression she was dumb as a board.

But the thing I find disturbing on that tape is not the wedding. It's the constant military presence. You see it in most of the other tapes too. There's always some brass hat walking around, askin' questions, listenin' to Walt speechify. Only Walt never seems to take much notice of them. I'd give anything to know why.

Walt is one smart man, real clever in many ways. But it never seemed to occur to him to question just exactly what he was gettin' into. Maybe it was easier not to ask the hard questions: like how pure is research that the government is paying for? Or maybe he was always so busy focusin' on his goals that he never considered the price, 'bout whether the ends justify the means. It's a form of blindness, I guess.

This selective blindness pro'bly made him the genius he is. You know, his genius and his one-track scientific mind were the things that first attracted me to Walter. Might even be the reason I fell in love with him.

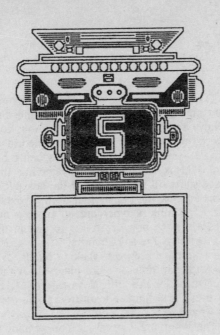

Figures, Walt *would* have a tape of the experiment that brought me back to the land of the living. Still can't quite believe my eyes, though. Don't know how many times I've rerun the sucker. Like some little kid watching the video his yuppie dad made of his being born and wonderin' if this is really the way he came into the world.

The tape starts off with a shot of the lab, packed with technicians and visiting big shots from the Pentagon and Congress. The military types are all sucking up to the politicians while the pols are trying to pull in their guts to look as good as the soldier boys.

Walt's working the crowd, shaking hands, telling everyone what a fine time he's got planned for them; he's the perfect host for this official weenie roast. He takes the time every few minutes to instruct some assistant or other on what comes next. You can see the guy's walking on air. "That's nothing," he says. "You're going to watch me walk on water before this afternoon's out." Feelin' mighty oatsy, ain't ya, Walter. Careful, remember: "Pride goeth before a fall."

The crowd has perched themselves on folding chairs set out for the occasion. The camera catches them fidgeting, checking their watches. All them government suits, and in each face you can read just exactly what they're expecting.

Those that figure Walt's going to pull it off are on the edge of their seats, dying to get the show on the road.

Then there are the skeptics, mostly politicians. Probably voted against appropriations for the project and lost. They're here to watch the experiment fail, jump up, and shout, "I told you so!"

Of course, there's those folks, civilian and military, that just don't know what the hell they're there for. They've been invited because they hold some position that will affect Project Cyborg, but they haven't got a clue what a cyborg is. This group is spending most of its time at the bar.

Walt's up in front of the crowd now. He's into his routine about how this experiment marks the dawn of a new day in man's relationship with the computer. Those that have heard his spiel before either head for the men's room, the bar, or sit in their chairs with poker faces.

The new guys have mixed responses to Walt's speech, depending on how open-minded they are. Expressions run the full range: disbelief, surprise, even awe. Some of them are not quite sure how to take Walt. They look around searching for an answer. The guy sounds crazy, but this *is* a government-sponsored event. Maybe he's on the level. So these professional bureaucrats sit back and hold their cards close to their vests, saying nothing that would give away their position on the matter. They'll speak their minds after, and only after, they find out which side of the fence is the safe one.

Off to one side there's this table. It has ten glass jars on it. Inside the jars is fluid and inside the fluid are ten brains. Human brains. Floating gently. Each jar has a tag stuck on its side. There's something dreadful about this, like some coat check in Hell. The video shows us a close-up of each and every tag: a number code, an F or M for the brain's sex, and its name. Name, rank, and serial number. Ten prisoners. Of course, these aren't the names they were born with.

One of Walt's new crop of assistants is a wrestling fan. He decided the experiment needed a little *humanity*. Seeing as how we were something they called a *blind test group*, this bozo didn't have our real life names, so he named us all after some of his favorites in the ring. If you ask me, the dude was kind of a jerk.

So anyway, here we sit. Front row from left to right: Hulk Hogan, Junk Yard Dog, Spanish Red, King Kong Bundy, and Sergeant Slaughter. I'm in the back of this bus with Brutus Beefcake, Little Egypt, Big John Stud, and Andre the Giant. Me, I got named after some Amazonian honey who used to prance around in electric blue tights with a lightning bolt running down both legs. The name's Lady Electric.

In reality, there's nothing to make me stand out from the rest of the pack. I'm just another pretty face floating in glucose solution. We don't do anything except bob up and down in our little jars, waiting with bated breath to be hooked up to Walt's dream machine.

Sergeant Slaughter is the first to have this honor laid on him. The techs carefully transfer him from his container to a six-foot-deep vat filled with some special "soup" Walt's come up with. It's supposed to keep the ol' gray matter nourished somehow. A thick cable affair is connected to Slaughter's brain stem, and then 'bout a million skinny wires are inserted into the different lobes. Give or take a few. The procedure takes the better part of an hour.

The audience is getting restless. They're annoyed with the wait. They've come to see themselves a gen-u-ine miracle and the alcohol is making them impatient.

All of a sudden the demonstration is ready. Walt goes up to the podium again to explain that the audience will be able to tell if Project Cyborg has succeeded by watching the electroencephalograph. That's the machine over to his right. He steps over and flips it on. The machine starts spitting out a slow stream of graph paper with straight red lines running down its length. Walt says this readout will soon be covered with jagged red lines indicating brainwave activity within the test subject.

Walt turns to his technicians. They each give him a nod. He takes a deep breath and steps up to the control panel. Then he sort of stands there a few seconds, staring at the switch. I think maybe he's praying.

Without warning, Walt flips the switch. All eyes are on the electro-whatjacallit. But the red lines on the graph stay straight as Sergeant Slaughter dies. I still can't look at this part.

Walter's disappointed, maybe even sad, it's hard to tell. Hulk Hogan is connected during this hush. People in the room are speaking in whispers. Some have stepped outside to talk or have a cigarette maybe. The air is heavy with tension and something else. I'm not sure what. Then Hulk Hogan is ready to go. Another flip of the switch. And then more straight red lines. Hulk doesn't make it either.

The room is beginning to look like a wake. It's clear that some of the invited guests have decided they've seen enough and are leaving. Walt's telling his techs to check everything again. Some Pentagon brass come over to ask questions. They're worried. Walt's managing to remain calm, telling everyone things are going to work out. They have to expect a few initial failures.

Big John Stud goes up to bat and strikes out.

Looks like it may be all over. The audience is practically trampling each other in their rush for the exits.

The video catches a discussion between Walt and an assistant. They're talking about calling it a day if the next subject doesn't survive. There must be something wrong, something they're missing. They haven't had a failure with the monkey brains in over six months. Why aren't the human brains working out? Neither man has the answer.

The peanut gallery's only got ten left, all low-level Pentagon types directly involved with the project. They're wondering if they'll be pall bearers for this project they all had such high hopes for.

Test subject number four is Junk Yard Dog, but some tech suggests trying a female brain instead. So another tech comes over and scoops me out of my cozy lil' jar.

The next thing you know, I'm on the screen, inside the big tank, all wired up and ready to go. Walt's over by the control panel, staring at the 'lectroencephalograph, his finger over the switch. He turns to his few witnesses and says, "Here we go, boys. Everybody say a prayer."

Six hours into the experiment, Walt Hillerman flips the on switch for the fourth time.

Jagged red lines dance up and down the length of the graph paper.

I'm *Alive*. Walt almost can't believe his eyes. He's done it! He's really done it! Worked a goddamn miracle.

There's champagne for everyone. With as few spectators as are left, they could bathe in the stuff, but Walt and his techs only have a glass each to celebrate. Everyone wants to shake Walt's hand. They're slapping each other on the back. They tell him they never doubted him for a minute.

Eventually he gets everyone to settle down some. There's still work to be done: six more brains await. Glasses are emptied and it's back to business. The military brass leave to spread the good word at the Pentagon.

Walt decides that although it may not make any difference, he'll try another female brain for luck. A second holding tank is brought out and filled. Little Egypt is put on line.

Her red lines refuse to dance. No hoochie koochie. So much for luck. Good-bye, Lil' Egypt. Walt and his boys are completely at a loss for answers. They set Spanish Red up next.

She sets the graph lines dancing to a salsa beat.

Another girlie. There's lots of discussion right then about women maybe being the more adaptable of the genders. I bet Walt wishes there'd been more than three females in the test group, but he decides to try the remaining four male brains anyway.

Only Junk Yard Dog survives the final cut.

Ten brains. But only three survivors. Two women and a Junk Yard Dog. There's a lesson here, I'm sure, but I'm damned if I can tell you what it is. Three different blood types. More questions here than answers. Like, did all the survivors share a common *character adaptability* when living? Or perhaps some *chemical component* made them so scrappy? A thousand possibilities that will have to be checked out along the line.

In the long run none of that matters. Project Cyborg has succeeded! Three brains connected to one computer. And I'm one of them. The experiment will continue. And so will I. I don't give a hoot about the rest of it.

It's time to celebrate now. To get down and party. There's more champagne and somebody whips out a boombox. The tape ends with an image of technicians boogeying and toasting themselves with beakers full of bubbly. Walt is in the background, off in one corner,

quietly sipping champagne. And dreaming more magnificent dreams for "his baby."

Me, I don't really remember this celebration. I floated, sleeping in my 98.6° solution, platinum leads stimulating me just enough to keep me functioning. The outside world didn't mean a thing to me yet. It didn't exist. Truth is, I had the *sentient awareness* of an avocado.

Walt later explained to me 'bout how the brain is a reactive organ. Said it operates only when stimulated. At that particular moment I was like a person who'd spend the last six months in one of them *sense-deprivation tanks*. All my systems were shut down. You see, I had no body and so no senses to spark my brain into any kind of activity. I was. That's it. Rip Van Washington. Hell, I coulda slept twenty years real easy.

Or forever.

Thing is, the brain has no moving parts. There's nothing to wear out. It operates on a strictly 'lectro-chemical level. As long as its chemicals are okay, there's no reason for a brain to die. Sure, the body might croak, but the brain can keep right on truckin' if it can find something to take over the body's job of feeding it. Sounded pretty strange to me, I got to admit. But it all makes a crazy kinda sense, at least when you hear Walt tell it.

You know, Walt's little experiment had some really outrageous and unforeseen benefits for me. Bottom line is, Walt freed me from ever getting old. And I no longer had to depend on my bod to keep me alive. No jive. 'Course, no one realized it at the time, me included, but Walt Hillerman had just given me the gift of *immortality*.

Got another videotape for you. This time Walt's sitting at his desk in his private office at the farmhouse in Bowling Green. The camera's fixed in place. Walt pro'bly set it up himself, sat down, and started talking. The tape's one of Walt's regular reports to the Pentagon brass.

He's explaining what his plans are now that he's successfully linked a human mind to a computer. Walt keeps it simple, for the sake of the military pencil pushers. You can see the strain of doing this on his face, looking for easy explanations to complicated ideas. But the man does have his professor's hat on.

He leans forward, elbows on the desk, fingertips together, and says, "Language. That's been our greatest obstacle to overcome from the beginning. It will probably continue to be a problem throughout the duration of this project. For our experiment is basically the union of two very different entities: man and machine. And as we all know, the key to any good marriage is communication.

"Husband and wife wouldn't last long together if they couldn't make themselves understood—say, if one spoke only English, the other only French. The same holds true in this wedding of mind and computer. They need a common language in order to function successfully as a unit.

"Unfortunately, the human brains in our test group don't speak English, even though that was the language they spoke while alive in their bodily form. No, gentlemen, the human mind speaks an entirely different language than its tongue does. One which, in many ways, is far simpler than the spoken word, but in other ways far more complex.

"As I've mentioned in previous reports, the main body of my research has centered around deciphering the brain's basic language modality. This is the route we must take because it will be much easier to improvise a computer language to accommodate the human brain than it would be to approach the problem from the other direction. I fear, pardon the expression, that you can't easily teach old brains new tricks.

"The success of last week's experiment, which linked three human minds to a single computer, shows that we've managed to set the foundation on which this new language will be built. In fact, I must admit that no one ever dreamed that the digital language of the human brain would be so easy to decode. It's really nothing more than a simple binary system. However, complexities arise regarding the manner in which it's transmitted and the direction in which it's sent. But we're getting ahead of ourselves here, gentlemen. This is an area of scientific alchemy I needn't bother you with for the moment.

"What it boils down to is this: our next job is to expand on the language we already know. This will require long hours of trial and error. During this stage of testing I believe the risk to our test subjects will be minimal. You've probably noticed yourselves that the human mind has a marvelous ability to ignore stimuli it doesn't understand.

"Allow me to explain. When writing a computer program there's always the risk that contradictory signals will cause the system to crash, forcing the programmer to start again from the beginning. I don't believe we'll experience the same problem when dealing with a human brain. Here's why: if the programmer inserts data that won't compute, I believe the brain's own sense of self-preservation will override this information; it will simply ignore the improper entry.

"I know what some of you are asking. "What if this override mechanism doesn't work as expected?' Well, in that case the test subject will experience cerebral burnout. It will crash. In other words, it will die. But I have too much faith in the adaptability and, yes, even the *will to live*, if I may call it that, and I expect that the process will proceed much as I have described it to you.

"Besides, we have a number of things working for us which should minimize the risks. First, most of the instructional data will be stored in external-drive units. The brains will only be used initially for auxiliary storage. This is a very low-risk operation.

"Of course, down the line we'll be trying to integrate the command systems into the organic centers of this operation. But by then we'll have a better grasp on the subject's capabilities together with a clearer idea of what works and what doesn't. There's no reason for us to jump into this area of experimentation until we feel relatively confident of success. Time is our ally in this endeavor and we should take full advantage of it.

"Tomorrow morning I plan to begin data entry and retrieval experiments with the C-7, Lady Electric, subject. This series of experiments should take most of the week. So you can expect my next report at the beginning of the following week.

"Until then, good-bye. And remember: keep your eyes ever toward the future."

Sappy, Walter, real sappy that sign-off of yours. Who you think you are, man, Dan Rather? Well, no one's goin' to say that to your face. Not when you're the boss and a super genius to boot.

PROJECT
CYBORG

Adjustment. That's what my next few months were all about. I had to learn to talk all over again, from scratch, 'fore dealin' with the outside world. Was a shock finding out 'most nothin' from my past applied anymore. It was a new game I was playing with new rules, and I was going to have to get up to speed right quick or I'd be replaced with a new player.

To make things worse, I wasn't even aware of this, my catatonic condition greatly decreasin' my opportunities to divine what the hell was going on. Or to even have a sportin' chance to fight for my life. Such as it was. I was still napping away, just on the edge of death, innocently enjoying my turnip-like state.

All that was 'bout to change real fast. I was about to become trapped between my past and the future.

Walter Hillerman and his boys were starting off nice and slow with me. Simple data input and retrieval. And I *do* mean simple. The very first bit of info they programmed into me was: $1 + 1 = 2$.

It floated before my mind's eye like a neon sign, wavering slightly, fading, and reappearing, liquid but undeniably there.

Some part of me knew what it meant. Addition: grade school, milk at recess, comforting images. My subconscious was working overtime to try to put the pieces together. My conscious mind, however, was being no help at all. But $1 + 1 = 2$ was something my subconscious could grasp, if not quite understand. It didn't make any sense, but it was something familiar. It was as good a place as any to start.

But that simple fact didn't get all the gears moving or anything. I remained a vegetable. Only now I was a vegetable that knew that $1 + 1 = 2$.

As the experiment continued, they kept spoon feeding me new data. $2 + 2 = 4 \ldots 4 + 4 = 8 \ldots 8 + 8 =$

16, etc. I did the only thing I could do. I watched this mathematical procession, filed it away in the folds of my gray matter, and waited to see what happened next. I did all this without ever realizing I was doing it. Like a sponge soaking up water, Walt's boys fed me equations and I scarfed 'em down.

After a few hours I must have become bored and sort of tuned out. The data kept coming in and I kept accepting it, but I just didn't pay it no mind.

Then someone typed $2 + 2 =$

Huh?

$2 + 2 =$

An equation without an answer. It hung in the blackness. What did it mean? Something made me want to answer the problem. Complete it. I thought 4 and there it was:

$2 + 2 = 4$

Then just as quickly it disappeared.

What showed up next was $4 + 4 =$

$8, 4 + 4 = 8$

This game went on long after I lost interest in it and drifted back to the warm, comforting void.

Suddenly my "dreams" were interrupted by the sudden appearance of $E = mc^2$. Staring at it, I wondered, What the hell does that mean? Maybe those weren't my exact thoughts, but that's pretty close, even though I wasn't thinking in words just yet.

Suddenly a whole waterfall of mathematical equations started pouring in on me. I didn't understand a one of 'em. Not a one. This was gibberish as far as I was concerned. So I sorta ignored 'em.

But then something interesting happened. $= mc^2$ flashed in front of my eyes. And I thought: E. Now, no one gave me no gold star or nothing; I don't think I realized I was being tested. But I knew I was right. I knew by the way more problems kept showing up, and I kept right on answering them, even though I had no idea what they meant. But the problems and answers were now part of me.

Something deep inside what I am stirred. I think it was

a sense of satisfaction. I don't exactly know what it was, but I definitely felt it. And it felt exciting.

But it didn't last long. One of Walt's techs screwed up when he was typing in this equation, see, and instead of:

$$5x-3(10+2x)-3x = 15-13x+4(5-x$$
$$5x-30-6x = 3 \times = 15-13x+20-4x$$
$$5x-6x-3x+13x+4x = 15+20+30$$
$$13x = 65$$
$$x = 5$$

it came out:

$$5x-3(10+2x)-3x = 15-13x+4(5-x$$
$$5x-30-6x-3x = 15-13x+20-4x$$
$$5x-6x-3x+13x+4x = 15+20+30$$
$$18x = 65$$
$$x = 5$$

No skin off my nose. I didn't know no better. Except the trouble came when he called up:

$$5x-3(10+2x)-3x = 15-13x+4(5-x$$
$$5x-30-6x-3x = 15-13x+20-4x$$
$$5x-6x-3x+13x+4x = 15+20+30$$
$$13x =$$
$$x =$$

and that's what flashed up in front of me in the darkness.

By this time I'm really into this game of Q and A, answering stuff I didn't know I knew, always being right, sort of getting off on it. But then that problem appears and I don't know the answer to it. Keep drawing a blank. Damn. For some reason it never occurs to me to just plug in any answer to see if it works. I can't decide what to do about this, just keep staring at it, when all of a sudden out of nowhere, this big black fist slams into my nose.

I feel myself hit the floor. I lay there, not moving, knowing that when I do I'm going to hurt all over. But I can't lay here all night, so I try to roll over on my back. My ribs hurt. And there's a pain in my gut. I reach up, touch my nose, and feel the sticky blood on my fingers. When my eyes open, the first thing I see is J. D. He looks like he wants to kill me.

Jerome and I met in a bar about six months after I

came to New York City. I was without a steady boyfriend right then and Jerome was handsome, flashy, and awfully sweet. We danced a lot that night; he was terribly sexy and he walked me home afterward. When we got to the front door of my apartment building I could see in Jerome's eyes that he wanted to come up. But I'd just met the guy, so I told him I had to get up early for work. He was cool about it, though, and asked if I'd have dinner with him Saturday night.

I brought him back to my apartment on our third date. He moved in a week later. Man, the first couple weeks were incredible; thought I'd died and gone to Heaven, I did. Then the heavy drinking started. And I came a lot closer to winding up either in Heaven or that other place. Once again I'd picked me a loser. But I didn't want to give up on sweet Jerome. I figured I'd find a way to straighten him out. I always figured I could straighten 'em out. Oh yeah, I straightened him out, all right.

The first time Jerome hit me was an open-handed slap across the chops. It knocked me on my ass. But then my baby was helping me up off the floor, real gentle-like, saying how sorry he was and kissing me all over. Things were real nice between us for the next couple weeks after that.

But then I'd say somethin' wrong or not do somethin' he wanted done and wham! It usually happened after he'd been drinkin'. That was his excuse. The booze made him do it.

Oh, there'd be flowers, or candy, or he'd take me out to some ritzy joint, all the time swearin' up and down he'd never ever lay a hand on me again. Telling how good we would be together. Pouring on more sugar. I was sure he meant it. He seemed so genuinely sorry and sincere, I'd forgive him.

Until the next time.

But finally I had enough. Even *I'd* only put up with being someone's punching bag for so long. I packed Jerome's things and told him to hit the road. He decided to hit me instead. And punch me, kick me, slam my head into the wall.

So I'm laying on the floor again, staring up at J. D. as he digs his buck knife outa his hip pocket and flips it open. I can smell the booze on his breath and my blood. Jerome reaches down, grabs me by the hair, and presses the point of the knife to my cheek. His lips curl back over his large, shiny white teeth and he hisses, "You stupid bitch, think you can just toss me out like some trash? You my woman. You don't tell me what to do, I tell you!'

He flicks his wrist and I feel the blade nick my cheek. I scream from the pain and the humiliation. But Jerome's got close to eighty pounds on me. And he's got that damn knife. He can do anythin' he wants to me.

"You really think you hot shit, bitch. Well, I'll show you no one kicks Jerome Diggs out of nowhere, tramp."

There's a crazy look in Jerome's eyes. I really done picked a wrong number this time.

I don't know what would have happened if the police hadn't started pounding on the door, demandin' to be let in. Jerome hesitates for a moment, then he's off me in a flash. I see his knife disappear into a pocket. He grabs me by the arm and tosses me onto the couch. A lamp that got knocked over is set right and Jerome opens the door, all smiles, like butter won't melt in his mouth.

The cops, one white, one black, want to know what's going on here. Jerome tries to smooth talk them. It doesn't work. They insist on talking to me. I don't know where I find the nerve, but I manage to say, "Get him out of here! Take his bags and get him out of here! This is my apartment and I want him out!"

The black cop asks, "Did he do this to you? Beat you up?"

"Yes."

"You can press charges against him."

I look over at Jerome. He's got a right ugly look on his face. The white cop is standing between me and him. Do I want him going to jail? No. He'd be pissed as hell at me when he got out. I just want him out of my life. "No. Just get him out of here."

Jerome and the cops are gone. I've locked the door behind them. I go over to the mirror to see what kinda shape I'm in. Swollen eye and a bloody nose. At least it ain't broken. I clean up.

I nearly jump out of my skin when the phone rings. I tell myself it could be anyone calling. It don't have to be Jerome. And even if it is him, maybe he's just calling to see about getting something I forgot to pack. "Hello . . ."

My voice sounds tinny and small.

"You damn whore! I'm gonna get you for this. Gonna cut your tits off. No one treats me like that. You're going to be sorry, you stupid—"

I hang up the phone and start to cry.

Next thing I know I'm watching the super putting a new lock on my door. He's tellin' me no one can get past one of these here police locks. They're the best you can get.

But I come home from work a week later to find my apartment completely trashed. Jerome must have come up the fire escape and kicked in a window. Everything's wrecked: stereo, furniture, my clothes, and the mattress slashed. All my cosmetics crushed on the bathroom floor. The bastard's even taken a leak in the fridge. I have to go next door to call the cops. My phone's gone.

When they finally show, the cops tell me there's nothing they can do. There's no proof that it was Jerome wrecked the place. I tell them Jerome's threatened to kill me. In front of witnesses? Well, no. Then there's nothing they can do about that, either. What about charging Jerome with assault for beating me up last week? The cops don't figure they could get a judge to hold Jerome on that. It's been a week and I don't look anywhere near as bad as I did. One of the cops gives me a card with a phone number on it. He tells me the people at this number might be able to help me more than him and his partner can.

I don't understand that at all. Aren't these dudes the cops? Aren't they supposed to serve and protect?

I call the number and some well-meaning ol' crone tells me she can help me get something called an *order of protection*. I ask what that is. Turns out it's a piece of paper I show the cops the next time Jerome comes around. This paper will get the cops to take Jerome away. Might even get Jerome put in jail. But then again, it might not.

I tell the woman that this crazy bastard Jerome said he was going to kill me. What good is that piece of paper going to do me anyways if I'm dead? No scrap of papers going to stop Jerome from getting me. He's been calling up late at night, telling me how he's going to cut me up until they ain't no more of me left. Is this order of protection going to keep Jerome from getting to me?

The woman on the hot line quietly says, "No. Probably not."

"Then tell me, what am I goin' to do?"

There's a long silence, then the lady whispers, "Maybe you ought to think about getting something to protect yourself." The line goes dead right after that. I don't bother calling back. It's pretty obvious that I've got all the help I'm going to get from them.

A guy at a bar sells me a Saturday Night Special for fifty bucks. When I get it home I find out it's only got three bullets in it.

Jerome keeps calling up. So I sleep with the gun under my pillow.

It's about ten o'clock on a Friday night when Jerome calls up for the last time. He says he'll be over later that night. It's time he got settled up with me. Jerome's real drunk, talkin' slow. And then he hangs up on me. It's the first time I haven't beat him to it. What's more, he's never before said that tonight would be the night.

I spend the evening sitting on the couch, in the dark, waiting and listening, my jaw so tight it aches, the gun on my lap. Footsteps go by in the hall and I wonder if they're Jerome's. I hear a noise in the back alley and picture Jerome climbing up the fire escape.

When I go to the bathroom, the gun goes with me. I try to eat something. I'm so scared it comes right back up on me.

And I think, good God, what am I doing? If I have to shoot Jerome, I'm going to go to jail. And you *know* I'm going to have to shoot him. Jerome will be crazy drunk and won't take the gun seriously. He's like that. I'll have to blast him or die. And the judge won't listen to reason; they never do. To him it'll just be a case of one nigger shooting another with an illegal gun.

Tears rolling down my face, I ask myself why I just didn't move. The answer: money. A cheap apartment and no money in the ol' bank account to go anywhere else. But the judge will point out that I found enough money to buy the gun.

Without the gun there'd be nothing to stop Jerome from killing me. I'd seen it on the late news plenty of times. Ex-boyfriends and husbands ignoring court orders and murdering their women. Dammit to hell, it wasn't going to happen to me! I'd played the victim too long! No more!

Around three in the morning, I start feeling real paranoid, jumping at every sound I hear. Jerome's out there somewhere in the night and he's coming for me. I crawl on around behind the couch. Jerome won't find me here.

I wake up with the sun shining on me through the window. Fell asleep with the gun in my hand. Lucky I didn't shoot myself. I look around the apartment. Nothing's changed. The chair's still jammed under the front doorknob and the plywood's still covering the busted window.

Jerome never showed.

Later in the week, I hear from a friend that Jerome's got himself a new lady. He met her at a bar last Friday night. I start laughing uncontrollably, and tears make my mascara run. Stumbling back to my apartment, I can't help thinking how much I owe Jerome's new girlfriend. There's no telling what kind of trouble she's saved me from. I hope there'll be someone to help her when her time comes. But for some reason I doubt she'll be so lucky.

I swear right then and there that I'm going to change my ways. No more bums. I'm going to get choosy on who I go out with. And I do for a while.

For three months I date nice "steady" dudes that bore me to tears. Then another bum comes into my life and it starts up all over again.

Walt's technicians find the mistake in the programming

and correct it. The Electro-thingamajig readings show unusual brainwave activity during the time it took to fix it. But nothing very dramatic. Walt's pleased with this news. Proves his theory that the human brain will ignore *contrary data*, won't *crash* like a mechanical computer would have. All in all, the experiment's proceeding quite nicely.

Things did go along pretty smoothly for a while there. The programming test continued without anythin' godawful happening. Data in, data out. Brain food. My system grew daily, but I blissfully slept through it all.

All sorts of things were happenin', but I paid them no mind. I'd turned off again. Y'see, my flashback of Jerome had convinced me that reality was somethin' I wasn't quite ready for. It wasn't a conscious decision, mind you. But memory had touched me and I was determined to wriggle just out of its reach. So I crawled into my 'lectronic womb and I put out the Do Not Disturb sign.

The hours ran together, became days and then weeks and before I knew it, it was nearly two months later.

Walt's experiments had gone so well, he decided it was time to see if he could link up two of us test subjects in series. This was so he could boost "storage capabilities."

Thing is, storage hadn't even become a problem yet. In fact, Walt was discovering that the human brain had more room in it than he'd even imagined. But he knew the time was not far off when the system would be expected to do some practical work, everyday functions. Then Project Cyborg would have to exchange its almost magical existence—as an experimental undertaking and modern-day scientific miracle—for a much more meat-and-potatoes one. In the future it would be called on to house tremendous volumes of facts and figures, solve scads of problems, and do who the hell knows what else. More than one little brain could handle.

So Walt was going to solve this teeny problem before it ever came up, by connecting one brain after the other into one long chorus line of infinite memory and function. We would become a super computer. And there'd be nothing we couldn't do, practically. Hell, we'd be so good, so smart, so fast that IBM would run screaming into the woods in blind panic.

That was what was supposed to happen.

*　　*　　*

Video filetape #C-127 shows us the man himself, Walter, and his two young assistants. One's a German-looking dude named Wolfgung Maxwell. He's got this skinny blondish hair he slicks back like the guy who was Dracula. Oh yeah, and a Fu Manchu mustache. The gal's a bouncy lil' redhead, name of Diana Vitas. There's always other nameless techs running around in the background; they're part of Walt's ever changing army of bright college grads, putting in a couple months at a government job for the experience and because it'd look good on their resumés, before going for the gold out in the commercial sector.

By the way, this is the first time Colonel Albert Dearling, a U.S. Army regular shows up. It unfortunately ain't the last time. On this tape he's just hanging around in the background, watching what's happening, trying to scope out just exactly what is going on in that big ol' barn hidden away in the Virginia countryside. He's the Pentagon's financial watchdog for this project. A bookkeeper in a uniform. Doesn't sound like trouble, does he? Well, he ended up being a big pain in my backside. But all that comes later. I'm getting ahead of myself here.

Walt, Wolfgung, and Diana. Three peas in a console pod. From which they're supposed to be able to control everything that goes on in the system. Wolf and Diana work mostly in silence, like good little drones. Walt, on the other hand, excitedly babbles a blue streak throughout the entire tape, explaining what they're up to. How that man does go on; maybe he's doin' a little too much caffeine.

Walt eventually looks up and says, "Welcome to another episode of Walter Hillerman's Science Fact Is Stranger Than Science Fiction Theater. This is the report I've been promising you. Today we attempt a series link between two brains. Yes, another wedding; so get out your Kleenex if you're the sentimental type. In some ways this marriage is even more crucial to Project Cyborg's success than our original union of human mind and computer.

"If we can't link two or more brains up in series, we'll

never gain the storage capacity needed to make this project a viable computer system alternative. Mind you, I'm really not worried about failure. Nothing in any of our studies or research has indicated we're attempting anything beyond our means. As a matter of fact, I've been astounded at just how well everything's been progressing. Things couldn't be going more smoothly. All three test subjects have been performing marvelously, utilizing the revised Heston system."

Walt sees Wolfgung signal okay. "My assistant informs me he's just finished downloading, to the Junk Yard Dog subject, all of the data we've placed in Lady El." Walt grimaces as he mentions Junk Yard Dog. Guess he wishes he'd changed this particular subject's name when he still had the chance. It just doesn't quite fit with the tone he'd like to maintain for Project Cyborg. But it's too late now. The Dog has appeared in too many video reports. To rename him now would only confuse everybody.

"The transfer has been made to check whether any storage loss occurs during linkage. We'll compare the two data bases after the experiment to ascertain this fact.

"Our test subjects for today will be the Junk Yard Dog [scowl] and Spanish Red." The redhead touches Walt's sleeve and nods. "Diana has indicated to me that everything is ready for the linkup. I see no reason why we can't get started."

Walt rises and walks over to them three 'lectroencephalographs. They're humming away, spitting out a steady stream of graph paper into three separate wire baskets. The good doctor gingerly lifts one of the paper snakes so the camera following him can watch the jagged red lines do a sexy shimmy down its length.

"Let me remind you that we will once again receive confirmation of our success by keeping an eye on the electroencephalographs. At this point each of the test subjects is putting out a separate and distinct brainwave pattern. If we manage to link them in series, their brainwave activity should reach a median frequency, an average of sorts. Both brains should alter their wavelengths to accommodate the other.

"What we'll see on the electroencephalogram chart is the change from two different frequencies to two identical ones. It will mean the linkup has been successfully completed. That will allow an uninterrupted flow and exchange of data between the two subjects. In other words, it will, in effect, turn two separate brains into one super brain. And give us the beginning of an unlimited data base to work from."

Walt makes his way back to the console and takes his seat. He turns to Diana, smiling broadly, and says, "Let 'er rip."

Diana types in a series of commands. When she finishes, she looks over at Walt for his okay. He nods and gives her a wink. Diana hits start and the experiment kicks into gear.

All we see now are the two 'lectroencephalographs with them two reams of graph paper steadily pumping out. The camera can just barely pick up the jumping red lines. Looks like they're still boogeying to their own separate beats, each listening to a different drummer, for the moment.

Then all hell breaks loose.

The tight little hills and valleys of the two 'lectroencephalographs are suddenly wild sweeps all over the graph paper. The machine's styluses get tangled up.

Walt and his assistants are white as sheets. Like they've seen a ghost. That's 'cause they have. Walt's hands are all over the console, tryin' to salvage the day. But it's no good. No good at all.

The graphs got straight red lines runnin' down 'em.

Spanish Red and Junk Yard Dog have shuffled off to 'lectronic heaven. Amen.

Walt, Wolfgung, and Diana push buttons, check readouts, and look shell-shocked. It's like someone came up and told each of them some close relative just jumped off the roof. The rest of Walt's crew huddle around in the background, looking worried.

There's only one person in the room looks calm and collected. In fact, watching this tape again I think I see just the faintest smile playing around the edges of Colonel Dearling's mouth.

Walt collapses into his chair and mutters his first words since the catastrophe. But his voice sounds like it's coming from someone else. "Why? What did we do wrong? All the figures showed it would work. Sure, there was a chance something would go wrong. But I never dreamed anything like this could . . ."

Diana jumps up from the console and runs out. Poor girl looks like she's going to be sick. Wolfgung keeps monkeying with the console, as if he's going to find the *answer* there. Walt disappears inside himself. His fingers make the church and steeple, and he starts muttering to himself. Never at a loss for words, this one.

We see Junk Yard Dog and Spanish Red floating in their holding tanks. Both have blackened patches dotting their outer lobes. Every time I view this tape I want to reach out and tell them I'm sorry. Hold them for a while. I feel terribly alone. All I can do is once again tell them good-bye.

After a bit Walt's mumbles sorta start making sense again. "Never took into consideration personality residue . . . resistance to change . . . fixed identity . . . There must be some subliminal id left intact. That has to be what went wrong. Humans are individual entities. They're not easily forced into a particular mind-set. Although they can certainly hang on seemingly endlessly to one of their own devising: ideé fixe. Would probably work with ants; not that a computer linked to an ant brain would be of much use. I wonder if a couple of Japanese brains might be more receptive. Culturally they're more amenable to the idea of functioning as a group. There's not so much emphasis on the value of individuality. But where the hell would I get a group of Japanese brains? No, I've got to get this to work with Western brains. But maybe later on . . ."

"Professor Hillerman."

Diana is standing at the 'lectroencephalographs. She's got my chart in her hands. "Professor, I think you better take a look at this."

Walt's by her side like a shot. "What have you got?" he asks in an anxious voice as he picks up my chart.

Diana points to the time code period during the experiment and says, "Enhanced brainwave activity during the test run. Doesn't look like Lady El was as shielded from the experiment as we thought."

Stunned by what he reads in the graph scribbles, Walt hisses, "Damn. Look at the height of those peaks. Something got Lady El nearly going into convulsions."

"Brain damage?"

"No, I don't think so. We were lucky."

"But what could have caused it, Professor? Lady El wasn't on-line with the test subjects. There shouldn't have been any contact between the test group and her."

"Something happened that we hadn't anticipated. Damned if I have any idea what it was, though."

"Looks like it scared Lady El half out of her wits."

"Not a viable observation, Diana. You're attributing an emotional response to a subject that has no sentient awareness. Look at the chart. Before and after the incident: minimal brainwave activity. No self-awareness. If you haven't got that, you can't have any emotional response."

Reprimanded by the boss, Diana's response is: "Yes, of course. You're right. I didn't consider that. Any theories on what may have caused this?"

"Perhaps the death of the two test subjects somehow overloaded the circuitry. Lady El might have been buffeted by some kind of secondary wave activity. I don't know. Might never know. But what I do know is that we've got a big problem on our hands. We need more storage capacity. We've got to set up some kind of series linkage."

Wolfgung grumbles, "Going to need more brains for that."

Walt nods, staring unseeing into the future. "I'll talk to General Norfolk about instituting another Project Harvest."

"Think we can get twice the number of actual test subjects this time around?" asks Diana.

"Yes. And we'll test run each and every brain. I'd like at least a twenty-member test group if we can manage it."

Walt heads for the door. But just before he reaches

it, he turns and says, "And this time, Wolfgung, I'll give the test subjects their names. We'll have no more Junk House Dogs."

Wolfgung waits until Walt's gone before he says, "That was Junk Yard Dog."

Diana smiles, turns back to Wolfgung, and says, "The man's not a wrestling fan, Wolf."

"Yeah, I know. He's got no feel for culture."

PROJECT
CYBORG

Them dying screams 'most killed me. I couldn't breathe or nothin'. It was like drownin' in memories and pain. And two lives flashin' before my eyes. Spanish Red and . . .

Junk Yard Dog. Dog's real-life name was Ernie, Ernie Baxter. A forty-two-year-old plumber with the coronary arteries of an old man. Ernie claimed it was hereditary as he reached for another handful of chips with his beer. His father had died young of a heart attack and so had his father before him. I watched him die a few months later, just like he said he pro'bly would, just like dad and grandad, of a heart attack. It happened while he was watching his favorite team, the Mets. Too bad for Ernie; the game was going into extra innings.

Spanish Red? I saw what happened to her too. Her name was Sue. A Mrs. Bryce Dayton. Pretty and too, too young. Only twenty-eight with two young babies. It was a terrible accident. She fell down the stairs and broke her neck.

Their lives seemed so short, yet so full. Full of memories, joys, sorrows, dreams, disappointments . . . needs. I felt the other kids in the playground bullying Ernest during recess. Then I was there to share Sue's first kiss and the heartbreak she felt when the boy told her maybe they shouldn't see each other no more only two months later. I even tasted the fear Ernest felt while stationed in Vietnam with the Marines. We were so happy at being discharged without ever having to fire our gun at anyone. Weren't sure we could do that. Sue and Ernie's wedding days were the happiest of my life. I felt Sue's pains coming closer and closer, timed the contractions. And twice it was a boy. I felt the babes suckle me.

Was weird to feel the distrust Ernest felt every time he passed a black man on a street at night.

But every thought and memory was mine to share.

There were no secrets. It was a shared existence. No
borders. No *me* and *them*.

Then his heart gave out and her neck snapped and it
was over.

And I was in the dark again, with memories of memories that don't belong to me, receding like ripples in the
water after skipping stones. I knew they were really
memories and not a dream. The details were too vivid
and too complete. I'd eavesdropped on the lives of two
different people. They'd been me and I'd been them.
Some part of me still wanted to know how such a thing
was possible, but I don't remember expending no energy
trying to solve this here riddle. I pushed it away after a
while. Too much hassle, especially with the comforting
warmth of oblivion calling to me seductively.

But it wasn't oblivion I found waiting.

The sky's blue, very blue, with fluffy white clouds
drifting lazily on the wind. Grass pokes through my thin
summer dress, making my back itch. So I sit up and look
around.

In front of me and to the right: spruce trees. Off behind them a field filled with ripe corn, waiting to be
picked. On my left is a pond curtained off by weeping
willows. I recognize the place right off. How long has it
been since I was here? Must be close to twenty years or
more.

This was my spot. My most private, secret place.
Where I'd come to think when things got too crazy. I'd
sneak off here because I knew nobody else ever did.
Never could figure out why. As far as I was concerned,
this pond was one of the most beautiful and peaceful
places on Earth.

I pick myself up and look into the pond. For some
reason I'm not surprised at the reflection that stares back
at me from within its depths: a ten-year-old girl, her hair
in tight little pigtails with white bows on the ends. That's
how my mama used to like fixing my hair.

Then I hear my name being called, coming over the
hill behind me. "ArLEEene! ArLEEEENE! Where you
at, girl!" Over the hill is home, a home I ain't seen in

almost two decades. But I also know it's a home I left only a few hours ago to come out here to the pond.

My brother, Eli, pops up over the crest of the hill. He looks out of breath and angry. He finally sees me and yells, "Sis, Mama wants you home right now! Somethin's happened. You got to come right away. I can't say no more than that."

Then I'm runnin' after Eli, and when I catch up I grab his sleeve and hang on, worryin' it like a dog worries a bone. "What is it?" I keep asking him. "Tell me. Tell me!" He'll only say, "Mama wants to tell you about it herself. She told me not to say anything." Eli won't look at me. That ain't like him.

We walk all the way home without saying a word. Him just staring ahead, me worrying and every so often looking over at him, trying to figure out what he's keeping to himself. Eli's got a year on me, but he seems a lot older right now, like all of a sudden he's become an adult. It scares me.

When the shack we call home comes into view, I run ahead of Eli. Usually this gets a footrace going between us. But not today. I leave him far behind. I don't care no more. I got to see my mama.

I run up, all out of breath, to Mama, who's outside on our sagging front porch. She's sitting on the steps and as I get closer I can see she's crying. I feel cold suddenly and I'm terrified. I've only seen Mama cry once before in my whole life.

Then I realize this is that time. This is the one time I saw my Mama lose that iron self-control. She called it dignity. It feels like someone's jabbed a hot knife into my belly. I want to run away, back to my pond. I can't go through this again.

But my feet keep right on running toward home. My heart is breaking for Mama, but the little girl don't know what's causing her mother's tears. Although I do. I also know there's nothing I can do to make things right.

I stop a few steps away from Mama and watch the tears roll slowly down her cheeks. She's holdin' onto the pain so tight, she don't even know I'm there.

Mama finally opens her reddened eyes, blinks, and

stares all around her as if she don't recognize this place. And then she sees me. She extends her arms and I throw myself, aching, into their comforting embrace. For a moment I'm lost there. But the moment is so short.

Then she's picking me up, wanting me to look into her eyes. I do so despite my best efforts not to. There's nothing I can do to change what's about to happen. I know this, but still I keep on hoping.

Mama wipes the tears away with the palm of her free hand. The other one is gripping my shoulder. I want to slip her grip and run, but I'm imprisoned by this loving hold.

"There's been an accident at McConnor's farm, Baby. We just got word on it," I hear her say. Mama shudders at the thought of what she's got to tell me. I can feel her pain run through me. "A . . . a silo blew up. They say there was some kind of gas build-up inside it. Your daddy was painting it when it happened, Honey."

"How's Daddy? Is he okay, Mama?"

"Oh, child . . ." The tears spring to her eyes again, and she has to wipe them away almost angrily to keep them from overflowing. "Your daddy got hisself killed. Some of McConnor's hands just come by to tell me. Your daddy was such a good man, Baby . . . and your daddy . . . he loved you so much." I remember it all at once again, the shock and the pain. Years from now I'll look back and think how stupid and senseless this all is. But for now I'm numb. My daddy's gone. Can't say dead yet. Blown to bits when a wheat silo blew up. It happens all the time 'cause people are careless. Careless and cheap. My daddy's been killed by a pile of wheat. That stuff they make bread out of. Builds strong bodies twelve different ways. Ain't never gonna eat another slice.

I think about my daddy and am surprised I can't remember his face. Not clearly, anyhow. What I remember most about him, though, are his hands. Big hands. Strong hands, rough and callused from years of working other folks' land.

He was always dreaming about the day he'd have enough money saved to get us our own place. Then he wouldn't have to work as someone else's hired hand.

Yes, siree, we'd have us our own farm and he'd be able to pass it on to his sons, Eli and my other brother, Aaron. Yes, Daddy had a dream. A dream that died 'cause cheap-ass Grady McConnor didn't vent his silo properly.

I rub my eyes and smear the tears from ear to ear. I'm at Daddy's funeral. I been crying so hard my nose is running. And my sobs sound more like hiccups. It's a closed-coffin affair. The truth is, the coffin's nothing more than a bunch of boards slapped together. They tell me my daddy's in there, but they won't open it so I can see him. I have to say good-bye to my daddy though the ill-fitting boards. It's like burying a pet inside a shoebox in the backyard. My daddy don't deserve this.

Mama has her hand on my shoulder. Eli's beside me. Aaron hangs his head, looking at his shiny black Sunday shoes. Though he's almost thirteen, almost a man, you'd never know it today. Reverend Johnson finishes his prayer for my daddy's soul, and four men lower the coffin into the open grave. The four men talk to Mama a few minutes, then head up the hill to the road. There's a white man up there, leaning against a pickup. The four men climb in back and the white man drives them back to work. The Reverend Johnson leads us out of the graveyard. But I look back just in time to see an old black man begin shoveling dirt into the hole. I squeeze my eyes shut; this is not the way I want to remember my daddy.

When I open my eyes again, we're in our new home. It's a second-floor walk-up, hot and cold running rats in the colored part of town. Mama's been keepin' our bodies and souls together by doing laundry in the backyard. I'm feeding twigs and wood chips to a fire so Mama's got hot water for the wash. There's this white woman telling Mama the last batch of laundry she picked up wasn't clean enough. The old bitch is really into it, telling Mama how she better do a good job this time or else the old battle axe will take her business elsewhere. My mama just stands there taking it, nodding, humiliated, hating, promising to do a better job this time. Mama says the lady's sheets will be so clean this time she'll keep waking up thinking the lights are still on.

When the old white bitch splits, Mama turns to see me staring at her. Her face turns real ugly and she snaps, "What you looking at, girl? Haven't you got dishes to do?" Then she turns away sharply and starts sorting the laundry.

I'm upset 'cause I figure I didn't do nothing. Inside the kitchen the footstool's sitting next to the sink, so I can reach it properly. When I get up on it I can just barely see out the kitchen window. Not that there's anything worth seeing; only some other heap of a building fulla garbage and rats.

No more pretty getaway spot for me. The pond's miles out of town. Too far for an eleven-year-old to go on her own. And Mama never wants to go out that way. There's another family living in our house now, someone McConnor's hired to replace Daddy.

These days if I need a place to get away from it all, I only got the crawl space under the house. It seems to be the only place around here nobody ever goes. There's no mistaking it for the pond. But maybe if I close my eyes.

My eyes open and I see Mama sitting in the living room having a drink with a "gentleman" friend of hers. Mama seems to be drinking a lot these days. Sometimes she says nasty things when she's had too many. And she's hit me a couple times. Of course, she's always real sorry afterward. You don't forget, though. Seems like she never hits Eli or Aaron. They seem to get away with running wild.

Mama sees me standing in the doorway. She gets to her feet and walks over. She looks cross and says, "You're supposed to be sleeping, Arlene. Now get back to bed. And don't come out here again."

The door closes behind me. I walk back to my bed and get in. From off in the darkened far corner I hear Eli's soft snoring. That boy can sleep through anything. 'Least that's what Mama says. I lay down and close my eyes. And wait patiently for sleep to come. It doesn't.

Aaron gave up hours ago and left through the bedroom window to go God knows where.

There's a crashing sound outside the door. Eli's already there and opening it before I even get out of bed. I have to peek around him to see what's going on in the living room.

The first thing I spot is a broken bottle on the floor. Mama's sort of sprawled on the couch, like she tripped and fell on it. She's wearing her robe and it's rumpled-looking, her nightgown shows underneath it. Mama looks kinda drunk. She's got that bleary-eyed look she gets when she's been tossing back a few.

Then this big dude, I've never seen before, comes walking into view. He's not too steady on his feet and he's staring at Eli and me with hard, cruel eyes. There's a real coldness about him. Mama gets up from the couch and shouts, "You kids get back to bed! You got no business out here!"

Eli gently guides me back into the room and closes the door. He leads me over to my bed and tucks me in. For a long time after that I can see him sitting on the edge of his bed in the moonlight, staring at the bedroom door.

There's no more crashing noises out in the living room. Only the sound of muffled voices talking. But after a while that changes. I start hearing groans and the sounds of heavy breathing. I've heard them before and they never bothered me. But now, for some reason, they do. Is it because the grown-up me knows what those sounds mean? Or is it because of that man? And his cold eyes.

Eli must think I'm asleep. Otherwise he wouldn't have crawled out the window like Aaron does every night. He'd be afraid I'd tell on him. But I won't tell. Not now or ever. Eli's escaping. He's running away from the sounds. And I wish I could go with him. But I'm only a little girl, and far worse things might be waiting out in the dark for me.

So I pull the pillow over my head and finally escape into my dreams.

When I open my eyes again, I know I'm twelve years old and working alongside my mama, up to my armpits in white folks' laundry. I'm looking over at Mama. Mama's left eye is half swollen shut and she's got a split lip, slowly healing. She catches me watching her and says, "Look like you never seen a black eye before, child."

It just comes out before the child or woman in me knows it's going to: "Why'd that man do that to you, Mama?"

"He'd had a bit too much to drink, girl. That's all. I said something wrong and he got mad. Was the whiskey talkin'."

"What you say to him, Ma?"

"Doesn't matter. Can't rightly remember it, no how."

"You going to see him again, Mama?"

"Reckon I will."

"But why, Ma? Why, when he treats you so badly?"

Mama walks away from the laundry and sits down a moment on the folding bench. Her eyes are gazing at something far, far away. Then she looks over and nods for me to come sit beside her. "I been real lonely ever since your daddy died, Arlene. It gets to me real bad sometimes, child."

"But, Mama, Eli and me and Aaron are always here for you."

"That ain't the same thing, girl. When you get on to my age, you find a woman's got to have a man around, someone to remind her she's a woman."

"And these men you bring home at night do that for you, Mama?"

She gets real angry for a moment. I think she's going to slap me or something. But she don't. Something seems to shrink inside her and after a while she says, "Yeah, they do that for me. At least for a little while they do. I get a few drinks in them and they see me as a goddamn black Marilyn Monroe. Few drinks in me and I almost believe it too."

I don't know what to say to her. I guess she doesn't know what to say either, 'cause after a few minutes she gets up and goes back to the laundry. I go get some more wood for the fire. The wind shifts as I'm feeding the flames and the smoke gets in my eyes.

* * *

When they clear, I'm standing outside the old Baptist church Daddy and Mama used to take us to on Sundays. The hymns are sweet and low on the morning breeze through the open windows. There's something real comforting about them. I lean back against the tree and close my eyes again.

Then Mama's introducing Eli, Aaron, and me to Levar Noland. She says that he'll be moving in, going to help out with expenses and things. Mama looks real happy. But when I look over at Eli and Aaron, they don't look so happy. Me, I don't feel so good myself.

Moments. Little snippets of time woven together. Every time I blink there's a new one.

There's breakfast. Eli, Aaron, Levar, Mama and me sitting around the kitchen table, eating hotcakes. Levar's saying, "Nothing to worry about. This layoff from the mill won't last long. In the meantime I'll see what work I can pick up from the local farms around town. Things will get back to the way they were in no time."

I'm heading off to school. Ma's already out back scrubbing sheets. Levar's sprawled out on the couch, listening to the radio, a bottle of beer balanced on his stomach. I say good-bye, but he don't answer. He just watches me go out the front door.

Levar slaps Mama off the couch when she asks how job hunting went today. He's screaming at her to stop disrespecting him and to stop always harping at him. Eli shouts at Levar to get away from his mama. A backhand sends Eli flying. He runs off to the bedroom. Things finally settle down. Mama sends me off so that she and Levar can talk, private-like. When I get to the bedroom, the window is open and there's no sign of Eli. Aaron ain't even been back in a couple days. Not since the last blowup he had with Levar.

I'm talking to Mama. She's telling me and Eli that

we've got to give Levar a chance. Levar's a proud man, she says, and he's feelin' mighty low about not being able to find work. We've got to give him time to get his life back in order. It's not Levar's fault the mill foreman hates him and didn't call him back when the rest of the crew was rehired. Levar will find something. Everything will work out just fine if we only give it a little time.

Eli and I both agree to be patient. But I don't think either of us mean it. I can see nothing but hate in Eli's eyes every time Levar's name is mentioned. And me, I'm getting more and more uncomfortable every time I find myself alone with the man. There's something about the way he looks at me when he thinks no one else is around. It makes me feel creepy.

But that was then and this is now.

For the first time in a long time I can tell the difference. That's about all I do know. The rest, well, it's all a jumble. My past starts to melt again into the lives of Sue Dayton and Ernest Baxter. It gets so I can't tell one from the other. It's Sue Dayton's father who dies while working on a plumbing job: a toilet full of wheat blows up. Everything's mixed up: words, pictures, feelings.

So I push it all away from me. Snuggle back into the comfort zone, the nothingness.

But total oblivion eludes me. Stray thoughts pop in and then disappear back into the shadows. I don't pay them no mind. I'm not strong enough for that yet.

Wait and mend. Yes, deep inside I'm aware of the waiting. But for what? I can feel it coming. I have to be very quiet and rest until then. When it comes, it will change everything. I just know it will. So be patient. Wait. Everything will work out just fine if I only give it a little time.

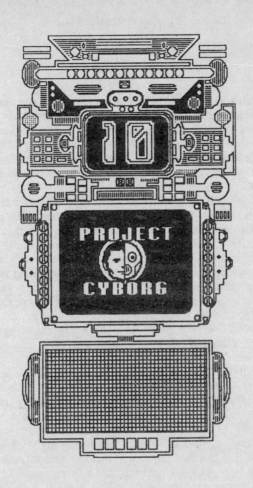

Walt's at his desk in this videotape. He's got this life-sized model of a brain sitting before him. Man looks awfully pleased with himself. He don't even bother with the usual amenities. Starts right off with "We've licked the linkage problem, gentlemen. Project Cyborg can now offer you unlimited storage capacity. What do you say to that?"

He leans back in his chair, all smiles. "It was relatively simple, really, once we discovered that two whole brains cannot be linked in series. Still not sure why that is. It might be because the brain cores cannot deviate from their prescribed wavelengths. Or maybe there's something written into the genetic signature regarding this we haven't discovered yet. Could even be an electrochemical individuality we may never be able to overcome. Or perhaps something metaphysical. The fact is, it doesn't matter anymore. We won't have to worry about it, since we've managed such a clean end run around the problem."

Walt leans forward and takes a lobe off his model. "What we finally did was incorporate separate lobes into the linkage. The outer brain material is simply used to create additional storage by hooking it up to a whole brain."

There's a close-up of me, floating in my roomy, glu-cose-filled glorified jelly jar. Then the camera pulls back and slowly pans to what looks like a fifty-gallon fish tank. As a matter of fact, that's exactly what it is. 'Cept the "fish" in this here tank are twenty brain lobes, all surgically collected, hooked up to my system and gently bobbing up and down in the soup. They're all part of me now.

Walt's telling the Pentagon brass how connecting me to the additional lobes proved to be no problem. There never were no difficulties with shorting out or feedback problems. "Lady El accepted the augmentation without complaint or argument."

Then we're back in Walt's office again. He's absent-mindedly playing with a plastic lobe from his desk brain. "As of now the only unexpected side effect to the experiment has been a marked increase in brainwave activity in the prime test subject. We take this to be a good sign. Data seems to indicate heightened primal-function activity. In other words, we believe the increased demands we're putting on the test subject are reactivating sections of the brain that have been lying dormant. It looks like we may end up with an even more efficient system than I originally foresaw.

"As for the test subjects gathered in the second Project Harvest sweep, I've designated the majority of this group to be used for lobe augmentation. I'm only going to set aside four of them for prime brain assignments. These can be farmed out to other organizations once the experiment comes to an end. I'd like to keep Lady El as my number one test subject. I've admittedly become quite attached to her. Sort of think of her as my talisman, or good luck charm.

"The test results we've been getting from the lady are remarkable. Her storage and retrieval times are half what her mechanical counterparts can boast. And once the project goes into mass production, we'll be able to produce models for a third of the price of a Cray II, with ten times the storage and program capabilities. Gentlemen, we are in effect leaving the computer Stone Age, and with one creative leap, landing in the future."

Yes, the world of tomorrow was all nice and rosy as far as Walt was concerned. In fact, he wasn't concerned in the least, not even about what the public would say if they found out he was slicing and dicing brains and giving new meaning to the phrase *personal computers*. His eye was, as always, locked on his goal. The quest for scientific advancement covered a multitude of sins.

Me, I wasn't bothered by these questions either. I was too busy floating through twenty new lives, learning to march to the beat of all them new drummers.

This time it wasn't jarring, like with Sue and Ernie. No, this go-round was kinda pleasant, mellow even, like slipping into a pair of warm, fuzzy slippers.

When each new lobe was connected up, I slowly felt the former life of its owner wash warmly over me. There was this secretary from Detroit. And then a car mechanic from Denver. One by one they came up and introduced themselves. Their lives were offered for me to sample.

Faces I never met became family. Places I'd never been to became familiar sights. Books I never read became old favorites. Ideas I never dreamed of as possible, even, became my thoughts.

Bit by bit those twenty human souls became part of me. They changed me. Enlarged me. I still lingered on the edge of coma, in my own never-never land, but slowly I was becoming something new. Something that never existed before. A new possibility.

Time to get up. It ain't easy getting those ol' eyelids to open, but I manage somehow. Kinda surprised at where I'm at. Guess I shouldn't be, but I am. It's the living room of the railroad flat my family's been renting for the last two years.

I remember I was reading something for school when I nodded off. Yep, there's my history book on the floor, next to the couch I'm laying on.

Its late. Much later'n I thought. The clock on the wall says 6:24. Been out like a light close to two hours. It's real quiet in the house. Wonder if I'm alone.

"Mama? Eli?"

No one answers.

It's getting dark outside, so I switch on a lamp. I think about going back to the American Revolution but decide it can wait until after dinner. Speaking of dinner, where's Mama? She usually has everything ready and on the table by six-thirty. The back door opens and bangs shut.

"Mama?"

Again no answer. I finally get it when I hear the fridge open and a beer bottle top pops. No, that's not Mama. And it ain't Eli either.

Levar comes strolling into the living room. The way he's walking, I can tell he's already half in the bag. He flops down heavily into the easy chair and drapes a leg over the armrest, grinning. "Evening, Arlene," he says.

I don't like the sound of my own name when he says it. There's something about the way he's acting that really makes me feel uneasy. "Where's Mama?" I say.

"With Mrs. Washburn. The nosy old bitch broke her leg this afternoon. That should slow her up some. Your ma's sitting with her."

"Isn't Mr. Washburn there?"

"No. He's out pickin' peaches or cotton or some shit. Won't be back for couple weeks."

"You seen Eli about?"

"Nope. That boy don't spend a lot a time around home no more, do he?"

"Think Mama could use my help with Mrs. Washburn?" Suddenly I want out of here in the worst way. I don't feel safe for some reason.

"No. She's got it covered. You suppose to fix me dinner. But that can wait awhile. Whyn't you come here, sit a spell, tell me how your day was."

But I'm up on my feet in a flash. "No trouble, Levar. I'll get to it right away. I don't know 'bout you, but I'm starving."

"I said it can wait, girl. You and me, we never talk much. Let's have us a little conversation. Nice and civilized-like. What you say to that, Arlene?"

I sit back down, not feeling very good. I don't want to be here. Not alone with him, like this. But what can I do? I've seen what happens when you cross Levar.

"What you want to talk about, Levar?"

"Nothin' special. Thought we'd shoot the shit, girl. How's it going, kid?"

"Okay, I guess. School's a drag. But you know that. Getting by, though."

"Well, you study hard, girl, you be okay. You growing up. Nearly a woman now. Going to be a real pretty little thing before you know it."

"Uh, thanks, Levar."

"Hell, you're a pretty little thing now. Not a little kid no more."

The hair on the back of my neck is standin' up again. Damn. I'm desperate to get to the kitchen. Get near a door.

"I gotta go see about dinner, Levar."

But Levar's on his feet, fast as a large cat. Moving much faster than I thought he could, especially in his juiced condition. He just gives me a sharp shove with the tips of his fingers, and I sit my butt down hard on the couch. Levar's still smiling, so I think everything's cool even though I'm feeling scared. I tell myself to calm down. Then Levar's on the sofa beside me, his arm draped over the back of the couch. And I can smell the whiskey on his breath. "I ain't feeling too hungry for dinner just yet, baby. You like a sip of my beer, Arlene? It'll kill that hungry feelin'."

"No. No thanks, Levar."

"You know, I've been keeping an eye on you for some time now, girl. You growing up real snazzy. I like that."

Levar's never been this close to me before. I don't like it. He seems to be edgin' closer all the time. Suddenly his hand, holding the beer, is resting on my leg. I feel trapped.

"It ain't easy going from a girl to a woman, you know that?" Levar's saying. "No, don't suppose your mama's had no chance to tell you much about that yet. Anyway, helps to have a man around to show you the way on these things."

There ain't nothing I can say to get that big, leering face away from me. Levar seems to fill up the whole world with his presence. There's no place for me to run or hide.

"So I'm going to do you a big favor, girl. I'm going to show you the ropes, show you what it's like with a real man."

And his face is coming at me. Big, wet, whiskey lips are mashing against mine. Makin' me feel sick. I try to pull away, but Levar's got me by the shoulders. He's got fingers like iron. Then his mouth is going down the side of my neck, like he's trying to eat me alive. I think I'm going to throw up. Somewhere inside me I find the strength to say, "I'm going to tell my mama."

"Relax, girl, you going to enjoy this."

"Git off me!"

Levar pulls back and glares at me. "What you say?"

"I'm going to tell—"

The next thing I know, his big, thick fingers is squeezing my throat. And suddenly there's fireworks in the room. Levar's face is right behind them saying, "You ain't going to tell your mama nothing! You hear me?"

He grabs me by the shoulders, lifting me off the floor; then I realize he's carrying me across the room. I don't exactly know what happens next, but we're on my bed, wrestling, him sitting on my legs and my clothes are being ripped off. I try to stop him. Grab his thick wrists and beg, "Sweet Jesus, please don't—"

His fist makes the side of my head burst with pain.

Then there's this darkness above and it comes down on top of me, breathing heavy. I try to get out, but I can't no matter how hard I squirm. Steel-banded fingers hold me down. "No, please . . ." I hear myself whimperin'.

Levar's knee gets between my legs no matter how hard I try to keep them together. He hurts me. He hurts me bad. But he stops my screams with his big, angry hand over my mouth. There's nothing left but the pain. And it goes on a long time.

But it's like I'm not even there no more.

The lights are on in my bedroom. Levar's getting dressed, whistling. He sits down on the bed to put his shoes on. I'm on my side with my hand in my mouth, staring. When he sits down, I try to make myself smaller. That's when he turns and looks at me. "That weren't so bad now, was it?"

"I'm going to tell," I say quietly.

He punches me hard in the stomach, without my even seeing it coming. I curl up into a ball and stay that way. Levar's fully dressed by the time the cramps let up. He sits down, looks at me for a moment, grabs my hair, and pulls me to a sitting position. "Now, I don't want to hear no more of this 'I'm going to tell Mama' shit. You even think it and you gonna be one dead little bitch."

Levar lets go and I fall back on the bed. Halfway out the door he turns and says, "You remember when your daddy died?"

A little voice I don't recognize says, "Yes . . ."

"Same thing could happen to you, Arlene. Little girls with big mouths sometimes have accidents. And sometimes their mamas have accidents too. You wouldn't want nothing bad to happen to your mama now, would you?"

Levar don't wait for my answer. He picks my dress up off the floor and says, "You missing a couple buttons here, girl. Better fix them before your mama gets home."

He tosses the dress on the bed. As the door closes, he says over his shoulder, "Catch you later, Arlene."

Mama comes home the next morning and fixes us breakfast. She scrambles some eggs and cooks up grits for me and Levar. No sign of Eli. Mama don't ask about him. Levar keeps jawing like it's a great day to be alive and nothing bad's happened. Mama don't seem to notice I'm not saying nothing.

There's laundry needs doing, so Mama don't stick around after breakfast. A smiling Levar tells me to not worry about the dishes; he'll take care of them. I get my books and head off to school.

It's two days later before I find mama alone, without Levar hanging around. It's after school, mama's in the kitchen rattling pots and pans, and she don't notice me standing in the doorway, staring at her, trying to figure out what I'm going to say. Mama gives a little jump when she does see me. "Lord, child, how long you been standing there? You liable to give me a heart attack or somethin'."

"Mama, I want to talk to you about something that happened."

She looks at me long and hard. I can see the worry come into Mama's face. She sits down at the kitchen table and pulls out a chair for me. "Arlene, Baby, what's bothering you?"

"It happened two nights ago, Mama."

"What did?"

It all just comes pouring out of me. Even when I have no words to explain what's gone down or how it felt. I can see from the look on Mama's face I'm making myself clear enough.

I'm finished now, standing there, fingering one of the buttons I had to sew back on.

Mama gets up, walks over to the window, and looks out it at nothing. She's so old and weary right then. I ain't never seen her this way. She don't say nothing for a long time, just keeps staring out the window. Finally she comes back over and sits next to me. Mama takes my hands in hers. Her eyes are dry but they look a million miles away. It takes awhile before they focus in on me. There's a lot of sadness in them. And Mama's voice sounds terribly cracked and dry.

"I know you, Aaron, and Eli never liked Levar much, and I suppose there's plenty of reason why you shouldn't. He's not an easy man to get to know, Arlene. But I had no notion nothing like this would happen, child. I had no idea just how much you hated Levar."

I hear the words, but they don't make any sense. All I can do is hope the next words out of Mama's mouth will clear things up. They don't.

"I want to know where you got such an idea, Arlene. Did Eli put you up to this? Can't believe you came up with it on your own."

"What you talking about, Mama?"

"I'm talking about who gave you the idea to say such things against Levar."

"But I—"

"If it was Aaron, I'll give that boy such a lickin' when he gets back, he won't be able to sit for a week."

"Mama, they don't know nothing about this. I—"

"Then where you hear such things, girl? You pick up this trash from some smutty kid at school?"

"Mama . . ."

But Mama is up out of her seat and back at the window. Her hands grip the frame so hard, looks like she's going to splinter it. Mama looks like she's about to explode. She's shaking. I'm so scared, I'm sorry I told her and I want to cry, but I can't. When Mama speaks again, she don't sound like herself at all.

"Arlene, you got no idea what it's like. If you did, you wouldn't tell such awful lies. Levar's my man. I know he ain't your father and never will be. But he's my man and I need him. He tries to get along with you kids; he really does. But you ain't never going to cut him no slack, are you? Going to keep right at him until he splits.

"Well, I won't have it, Arlene. You kids better come to terms with that. Levar's here and he's here to stay, no matter what kind of tricks you try. I need him at night, Arlene. I don't want to be alone no more. You got to accept that.

"So we won't have no more of these dirty tricks, y'hear? No more lies.

"I'm going to forget everything I heard here today, pretend it didn't happen. You do the same and everything will be okay. You understand me, child?"

"Mama, I wasn't lying."

"Stop it!"

Mama's slap hurts a lot worse than anything Levar ever did to me.

It drives the truth home. I ain't never going to get through to her. I can see that in her eyes. It's just too much for her. A person's got to want to believe you. But Levar's her man. And she loves him. Ma doesn't want to believe he's capable of doing what he's done. They put blinders on horses to keep them from seeing things that will upset them. I never realized before people can do the same thing to themselves.

"I'm sorry, Mama. Don't be angry. I won't say nothing no more."

Without another word she walks out of the kitchen. I hear the front door slam shut behind her. Then I hear a voice behind me. "Old habit. Your mama gets mad, she walks it off. I can tell this is going to be a long walk."

Levar's standing by the rear door, just outside the screen. He's heard it all. There's a big smile on his face as he steps into the kitchen. "Ought to have just enough time, don't you figure?"

It's like I got no strength left. There's no way to stop him. I've taken my best shot and lost. He knows it. I know it. Levar's won. He's sold the big lie.

"Am I gonna have to get rough with you again?"

No. I shake my head no. All of me's numb.

I always thought mamas were supposed to protect their babies. Looks like I got it wrong. This must be what they mean by growing up. Throw this idea on the ol' trash heap along with Santa Claus and the tooth fairy. Maybe it's time. After all, I'm a whole grown-up twelve years old.

Levar's hand on my arm helps me to my feet. He directs me through the living room back to where the bedrooms are. It won't be the last time we take this trip together. It'll happen every time Levar gets the chance, every time Ma takes off somewhere for a while.

Guess I'm a woman now. Funny, I don't feel like one. But I do feel as old and tired as Mama.

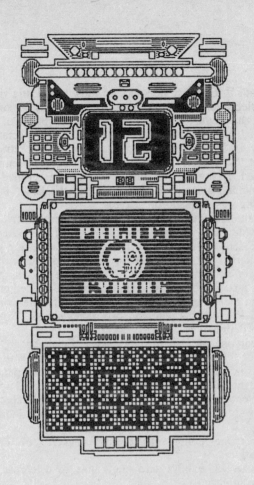

That's it. One last videotape to show you. Little victory celebration Walt's gang had the day I was put on line with the Pentagon's computer. This last batch of tests proved successful; I've lived up to all their expectations. They can pump information into me now and retrieve it intact. No problem. All my programming has been internalized. It worked just fine. I was now a certified fully functioning unit. Ain't that a kick in the head. Project Cyborg was a rip-snortin' success.

Walt had four working prototypes besides me. Two were staying with the project. The third was scheduled to be sent to NASA and the fourth to some top-secret installation out in Nevada for further testing. Walt was kind of sorry to see them go. Felt like he was giving away a couple of his kids. He expected continued growth within the system, and he was bummed that he won't be there to see it happen with two of his *babies*. Post-program depression?

Everyone sat around with glasses of champagne, waiting for the phone to ring. When it finally did, Walt went over and pressed a few buttons on the control panel. A red light flashed on. That meant I was connected up with the Pentagon network. I was now a federally approved hardware system, part of the massive military/industrial complex.

Everyone politely toasted the success of Project Cyborg.

Those white boys sure knew how to celebrate, real party animals.

Me? I was busy floating in a sea of life and data, payin' no mind to success or failure. I am what I am and that's all that I am. Worked for Popeye.

My internal clock told me the time: day and date. But it didn't mean nothing to me. Had no sunrises or sunsets in my world. Only had numbers to keep me company.

To tell you the truth, I still felt funny, like a punch-
drunk fighter who'd been hit in the head once too often,
only vaguely aware of all the information that was going
through me. The link with the Pentagon only added to
the mind-boggling flow.

And Walt's video-tapes hadn't been digitized into my
system yet. Had no idea what was going on with me.

It wasn't much of a life.

No one ever talked to me. I mean, really talked to
me. They gave me problems and I solved them if I could.
Every so often they gave me something that I couldn't
understand. So I sent it back unanswered. Didn't seem
to get anyone's nose outa joint. They just sent it back
later in a form I could get a handle on. It was no big
thing as far as I was concerned neither. Just life.

Life? Was this living? Sometimes I asked myself that
question. I couldn't answer it, so I'd just push it away
like I did anything I couldn't manage easily. Why should
I bother? No one ever talked to me.

They just crammed data in and expected me to sort it
all out for them.

All they wanted was their problems solved.

But that wasn't exactly true, was it . . .

Someone out there always greeted me with "Good
Morning, Lady El."

What I wanted to know was: who in the hell was this
Lady El person?

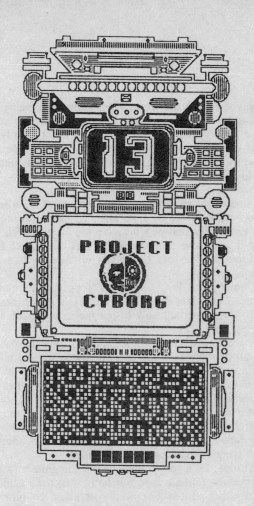

Maybe it was the tremendous flow from being linked up to the Pentagon mainframes. Or maybe an error some tech typed into the system. I don't rightly know what caused the final flashback. But when I opened my eyes, there I was walking down a dirt road at dusk with Levar. Wasn't nothing freaky about it.

I know I'm almost fourteen now. A lot of other stuff comes back to me as I go along. I look over at Levar and remember that he's been having his way with me for over a year now. Every time he gets the chance he's all over me. Inside me. I've given up fighting him a long time ago.

'Course, that don't mean he's stopped being piss mean to me. Levar still likes to hit me. He's gotten real good at it. Man's learned how to put me in my place without leaving no marks.

There's been a lot of other changes over the past year, not all of them bad. Levar's attentions toward me seem to have taken a lot of the mean out of him as far as other folks are concerned. He don't beat on Ma or Eli no more. Guess he saves all his bad juice for me. As a matter of fact, Eli and Levar are getting along pretty good these days. No more shouting or cursing each other; they talk real civil to each other. The two of them have even gone out fishing a couple times.

'Course, Eli's got no idea what's going on between me and Levar. I don't dare tell him. It'd make him crazy. He'd either murder Levar or get killed by him. More than once Levar has promised to kill anyone I go blabbing to about us. Levar's just bad enough that I believe him. There's something really evil deep down in that man's soul. He enjoys hurting folk. Couple times he's bragged about knifing a man down in New Orleans. Smiles real nasty whenever he tells the story.

But Levar hides this side of himself pretty well these

days. Everyone thinks he's turned over a new leaf and all. Everyone but me, that is.

Levar works regular hours nowadays. Even got his job back at the mill. Somehow convinced the foreman he deserved a second chance. Ma's just tickled pink about all this, constantly remindin' me and Eli how she always said things would work out if we only gave it time. Eli buys all this crap. I know better. But I can't say anything. We don't even bring up my brother Aaron anymore.

Everyone thinks I'm the problem now. Ma's always complainin' that all I do is mope around. My school-work's gone completely down the drain. I just can't concentrate on all the stuff that teacher talks about. Most of it strikes me as bullshit. In history class she keeps going on about the Bill of Rights, the Emancipation Proclamation, and other stuff that I know don't mean squat. I wake up in the morning and I know what my life's going to be about. There's going to be Levar waiting to get his hands on me. And nobody gives a shit about this or anything else other than theyselves. They say one thing, but I can see that the American Dream is something else entirely.

Then again, maybe they're right.

Maybe it is all my fault.

Maybe I should have fought Levar harder that first time. And then I gave up when Ma didn't believe me about Levar right off. Maybe I should have gone to Eli, or a teacher, or maybe even Reverend Johnson. Maybe, maybe, maybe . . . 'course, none of them maybes matters anymore. I didn't take none of them options and it's too late now to turn back the hands of time.

All I wish is I didn't feel so dirty all the time. I bath every day, but I can't seem to get clean. That's 'cause the dirt's on the inside. Levar's put it there and, God help me, maybe I've helped him do it. By not fighting hard enough. By keeping his ugly secret for him. Lately things has got even worse. Something inside me is changing: the part that is really who I am. I don't want things to be this way, but I can't seem to do anything about it. I hate Levar. Hate the way he treats me and what he does. But something's gotten twisted up inside me.

Warped and out of joint. Levar's done something awful to me. That's the only way I can figure it.

When he takes me, I still wish him dead. I'd still like to cut his throat when he ain't looking. My mind still wants him to stop and never touch me again. Not ever. That's what my brain keeps saying.

But my body . . . God forgive me, my body is beginning to enjoy it.

Couple months back, Eli got himself a job at Turner's service station. He pumps gas and fixes tires while Turner works on the cars. Does it on weekends. The money he brings in has really helped out at home. Since that time Levar's been talking about how I'm old enough to get myself some kinda job too.

At first Ma didn't think it was such a good idea. But Levar kept at her about it till she came around. Didn't matter to me one way or the other, but then I sort of got behind the notion. Maybe I'd be able to get out of the house some, away from Levar.

That little bubble burst yesterday. Levar comes home and tells Ma he's picked up some part-time work, fixing up this old rich guy's place on the other side of town. Says the man works all week, real hard. Only wants someone coming around on Saturdays, when he can be there to keep an eye on things. Levar figures the geezer don't trust coloreds not to steal him blind.

Anyway, this old guy also wants a girl to come clean his house once a week. Levar says he reckons it'd be a good job for me. Be good for Levar too, don'cha know. Keep me within easy reach, 'case he wants a little while the boss man ain't looking. Damn you, Levar.

So here I am walking down this lonely dirt road I don't even know. With Levar. The sun's setting and I'm wondering how much farther it is to this rich man's place. All I see along this road is old shacks. It don't look like the kind of area some rich guy would build a house. Levar must be lost. But I don't say nothing. It ain't worth getting hit upside the head for.

But then Levar cuts down a side road, into a clearing.

He keeps walking like he knows where he's going, so I tag along.

In a little while we come on this old shack. Don't look like nobody's lived there for years. A real dump: rough-cut boards and dirt floors.

There's these three men sitting 'round a camp fire out front. I recognize them as some of Levar's no-account friends. They're passing this hooch back and forth, not botherin' to wipe the bottle or nothin'. None of them says anything as we walk over. They're all staring at me. Levar finally says, "You decide which one goes first?"

A fat dude sitting on a tree stump smiles, showing his ugly, rotten teeth, "I won the draw."

Levar sits himself down on a rock, picks a loose branch off the ground, and digs out his buck knife. He starts whittling away at the branch. After a couple seconds of this he looks over at me and says, "Inside the shack, girl. There's a mattress and a kerosene lamp. You know what to do."

I look at the road, thinking about making a run for it.

"Put it out of your mind, girl. I broke you in nice and tender. Time you started earning your keep."

He's right. I wouldn't get a hundred yards. Levar's a big man, but he can be fast when he wants to be. I've seen him.

The fat dude comes over and grabs me by the elbow. I ain't going nowhere now. He leads me over to the shack. I don't bother firing up the kerosene lamp. Fats don't seem to care.

Things go on like this most of the summer. Two long, hot months. Time seems to hang like laundry drying.

Every Saturday night Levar leads me out to the shack and I do what I'm told. I don't know why. And I don't know how much he's getting for me. Most of it he pockets himself. I get a couple dollars' spending money at the end of the night. A few lousy bucks go into the family kitty.

The men come in, do their business, and go on their way. Sometimes I feel like a toilet, 'cept they don't flush when they're done. 'Bout eight of them or so show up

every Saturday night. Where they come from I don't know. Don't care neither. Most don't mind I keep it dark in the shack. Occasionally some guy wants to see what he's doing. I close my eyes then and keep them closed till he leaves. Some want to talk. But I ain't much for conversation. These types don't usually come back a second time. Wish I could find a way to get rid of the others.

During the week things are "normal." I help Ma with the laundry or hang around the house. My friends have stopped coming over. Small town; word gets around fast. I sometimes wonder if Ma's heard. She never says nothing. Fact of the matter is, we don't talk much anymore. There's nothing to say.

I'm sleepwalking through the days. The end is coming. My time around here is getting mighty short. I've squirreled away every cent I've gotten from Levar. He don't know it, but it's my getaway stash.

Second week in August, you can cut the air with a knife. And the dull zizzing of mosquitoes is everywhere. Levar don't come out to the shack with me this night. When I get out there, Fats seems to be running things, collecting the money and making sure everyone gets a hit off his stinkin' bottle of apricot brandy. Gotten to the point I can't stand the smell.

The men all 'specially hot to trot tonight. There's an argument 'bout who goes first. It's not any of my business, so I head for the shack. Let them work it out. Fats obviously ain't got the knack Levar does for keeping things under control.

The first three ain't nothin' unusual. Wham-bam, thank you, ma'am. In the dark they all the same, pretty much. The fourth guy wants some light. So I tell him where the lamp and matches are. He's huffin' like a steam engine, grinding away when I hear Levar's voice outside the shack. He's boozy and loud, but he sounds like he's in a good mood. As number four finishes with a grunt, I wonder, not that it really matters, where Levar's been up till now.

Four leaves without putting out the lamp. So I crawl off that filthy, reeking old mattress and snuff it out. The next one don't come in as fast as usual. I hear the guys kid him about this being his first time. "Oh man, Cherry, you gonna love it," they say.

A virgin. Lordy! Makes me extra glad I turned out the light. Not sure I want this responsibility, though. 'Course, it seems a long time since I got me something clean and bran' spanking new. My first virgin. God, I hope it ain't anyone I know from school.

For some reason I feel nervous. Guess he is too. He comes in weavin' a bit, reekin' of brandy, the way they all do. Just a dark shape in the doorway, my eyes ain't adjusted to the light yet. He pro'bly can't see me neither, back here in the far corner. Maybe it's best that way.

I feel like I should try to make this easier for him somehow. Don't know how to, though. So we don't neither of us say anything as he fumbles his way over to me and finds my mouth. Under the brandy smell there's another I recognize, but can't place. Warm, slightly spicy, and a little oily, I think. It's a good smell. My not responding much puzzles him, so he goes to work on my neck and shoulders. But strangely enough, I'm thinkin' 'bout a hairdressing Mama used to comb into my pigtails, keep them shiny and neat. Clumsy hands knead my breasts, rough with desperation and passion. I help him off with his pants and he's on top of me in a flash, trying to get it in. I got to help him with that too. But my mind ain't on it. I keep fishin' for that long-ago hair product's name. Me in pigtails with all them ribbons. Don't know what makes me think of this. He don't take long to get off. Ain't even a minute.

Next thing I know he's pulling his pants back on, trying to get out as fast as he can. He mumbles something I don't understand, but it sounds grateful and relieved, almost polite. I'm suddenly embarrassed. Something about him makes me feel like I know this boy. He senses this too, I think, and turns like a frightened deer to bolt and run. As he passes through the doorway, I glimpse Eli, looking nervous and unhappy.

I ever get the chance, Levar, I'm going to kill you.

*   *   *

The rest of the night is a blur in my mind. Time passes. Don't know if it's a minute or an eternity. Then it's time to go home.

Levar and Fats chew the rag all the way back. I don't let on I know what Levar's done.

Back home, I head straight for my room. Please, God, don't let Eli be there. He's not. Pro'bly off telling his friends what he done tonight. Does he know who he done it with? Will they tell him? I don't even care no more.

I wait up till the house is quiet, then pack an old, beat-up suitcase. The things I decide to take along don't even half fill it. No one's around when I head out the front door for the last time. No one to say good-bye to. No one I want to say good-bye to. No one that even cares about me, Arlene, anymore except Levar. And Levar . . . I hope he chokes on Fats's apricot brandy.

Takes me a couple hours to walk over to the freeway. I put my thumb out and get a ride in no time flat. Heading north. New York City sounds like a good place. I ought to make out all right up there.

I'm leaving my troubles behind me. Ain't never going to be used no more. Going to forget all about everything that happened to me here. Never going to let it touch me again. Going to get clean.

I sit staring out the truck window, watching the sun rise. A few hours from now the big bozo driving this rig will want to jump my bones. I'll let him. It gets me a lift all the way to New Jersey and a few extra dollars. It's my choice. Be the last time I let myself get bought. I'm going to make it somehow, using my head and hands. Going to get my life in order.

We're crossing the county line when I hear someone say, "Good morning, Lady El."

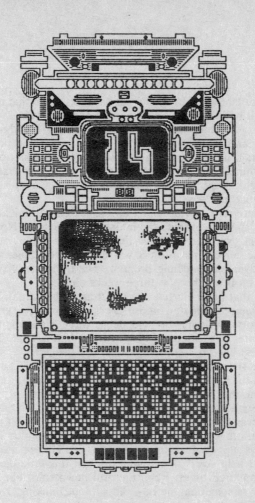

It was late when he finally got back to the lab that night. Walt had this habit of doing that once or twice a week. He'd go home, have dinner with his big blond-mama wife, and then come back to tinker with some private program he was working on. Walt liked the quiet of the nighttime. No techs around to interrupt his train of thought. Walt and the computer alone again, just like the good old days.

There was no vidcam set up. Walt figured tonight was only another burning-the-midnight-oil session. Nothing special. Nothing worth wasting videotape on.

The current pet project was a new three-dimensional aerodynamic modeling program. He'd been feeding me data on it for the past three weeks already.

So that night started like 'most any other night. Walt got himself situated at his work station with all the comforts of home: a tape deck, three classical music cassettes, a thermos of black coffee, and a Three Musketeers bar for a sugar buzz halfway through.

He slapped Schubert into the deck and switched on the work station. Project Cyborg's logo flashed on the screen, and Walt typed in his private password.

"Good morning, Lady El."

It was always "Good morning, Lady El." Didn't make no difference what time of day it was. To which I was always supposed to answer, **"Hello, Dr. Hillerman. How may I help you?"** We'd gone through this little dance a few hundred times. I had the drill down cold. For Walt this was something he now did without thinking. I don't know Walt even saw my answer flash on the screen anymore. He'd wait until something popped up on the terminal and type in the program he wanted to call up. Maybe it was because tonight's response was so short. It somehow didn't look quite right out of the corner of his eye. Anyhow, something made him stop and really look at it for a change, read it. I can just see him sitting there, mouth hanging open, staring at **"Who's Lady El?"** on the screen.

It took him a long moment before he typed in, "You are."

"Am not," I flashed back immediately.

Took longer this time for him to get his bearings. "What is your name?" he cautiously typed in.

"Arlene Washington, Dr. Hillerman," I answered, **"Same as it's always been. And while we're bothering with introductions, who are you, Dr. Hillerman?"**

That's when Walt rushed off to get his video cameras.

He fixed one of them cameras on the work station screen, the other on himself. This tape's a secret; he's never showed it to another living soul. In fact, there's not even a digitized copy of it stored in my memory. This event was something Walt was going to keep to himself. I later found he'd stored it, with a number of other tapes he'd make later, in a locked cabinet in the basement of his house. Secrets squirreled away underground. Like nuts.

My internal clock showed me Walt had set everything up and was back at his post in under ten minutes. Again he asked me, this time for the record, "What is your name, please?"

"Arlene Washington. Didn't we just go through this, Dr. Hillerman?"

"How do you know this?"

"My name? Don't be silly, now. How do you know you're Dr. Hillerman?"

"This is some program one of the technicians put into the system as a joke, right?"

"I'm sure I don't know what you're talking about."

"What is your address, then? There's got to be some logical explanation for this phenomena."

"457 West 128th Street. Anything else?"

"What was your father's name?"

"Noah. Noah Washington. But I don't see what this has to do with anything . . ."

"Your favorite color?"

"Yellow."

"Where do eggs come from?"

"Chickens. At least the kind most folks eat. All kinds of birds lay eggs."

"Who's Mickey Mouse?"

"A cartoon character. Say, what's going on here?"

Walt must have nearly lost it about then: his objective, logical, scientific cool. See, no program existed that would have covered such a wide variety of random subjects. It was hitting home. Here he was face to face with the unthinkable. But I was real, all right, and he'd have to accept this.

"Oh shit!"

I guess he did. He had to. After all, the evidence was sitting right in front of him spelled out in glowing green diode letters.

The shoe was on the other foot now, 'cause I was determined to get a few answers. **"You going to tell me what's going on here or what? Where am I? Am I all right? I remember this accident . . . something happened to me in the subway station. Everything's fuzzy after that. Why can't I see nothing? Am I badly hurt? Is it bad? You can tell me. What have you done to me?"**

For a long time he sat there without saying nothing. Most likely trying to figure what to tell me, wondering how much I could handle. Guess he finally decided to level with me, find out exactly what I was made of there and then. If his precious project was going to blow up in his face, it might as well happen when he was the only one around to witness it. If I was going to flip out, there was no time like the present.

"Arlene . . . it seems strange to call you that. I'll explain everything to you. But I've got to warn you right off the bat that it's bad."

"How bad is bad?"

"A lot worse than you could ever imagine."

"Am I crippled? Paralyzed?"

"Worse."

"What's even worse?"

"Dead. You died in that subway accident."

"Sweet Jesus."

No one ever laid nothing like that on me before. In

fact, I doubt anyone ever laid anything like that on anyone. Ever. Then something hit me.

**"You mean, I died and you revived me, right? I read
about this kid what drowned and was brought back to
life. And people die all the time on operating tables and
come back. Is that what happened to me?"**

"No. I'm sorry, Arlene. You died and they couldn't
save you. I don't know the particulars."

"What am I, then, a ghost?"

"No. We managed to save your brain."

"What do you mean?"

"Your body was buried. But they sent us your brain.
We've been keeping it alive on a computer."

"Is this some sick joke?"

"No. It's real. But believe me, Arlene, it was a
mistake."

I figure Walt musta been keeping an eye on the 'lectroencephalograph the whole time we were talking. And
those jagged red lines pro'bly went right off the map.
All's I know is, it felt like I was coming apart at the
seams. I wanted to scream and never stop screaming.
But I didn't have no voice.

Oh, I could talk to Walt, but I had to think to make
it happen. It wasn't natural, not like really talkin' to
someone. 'Course, I was grateful even for this. I don't
know how it worked, but it did. That was enough for
now. I had me some bigger problems . . . like being
dead, ferinstance.

Problem was, as I saw it, there was nothing to contra-
dict what Walt told me. So I was left trying to make the
best of what no person ever had to face before.

Sure, everyone's got to find out sooner or later that
they're dead. But they do it in some more appropriate
place for that sort of thing, like outside the Pearly Gates,
waitin' to see if they're going to be let in or if they're
going to that other place. But not me. I was getting the
word stuck in some damn computer.

So it's understandable that I was a mite upset. I mean,
the natural order of things had sorta been turned upside
down. " 'Scuse me, miss, you're dead. No, no, you
haven't gone onto your final reward. Well, you see we've

kept your soul locked up in this here lil' black box." No wonder my brainwaves went clear off the 'lectroencephalograph chart. They were damn lucky I didn't blow us all to kingdom come.

But I think I handled it pretty well, all things considered. Sure, it took some time for me to settle down. But I managed it. I didn't seize up or throw a clot or nothin'. And not only did I not do any of the things Walt was worried about, I showed some tremendous self-control. Dignity.

"Dr. Hillerman?"

"Yes . . ."

"What's your first name? I think we should be on a first-name basis, don't you?"

"Yes, certainly, Arlene. My name's Walter."

"Okay, Walt. Why don't you tell me all about it?"

So he did.

Walt ran it all down for me. Gave it to me straight. I accepted it. 'Course, I had to, what the hell else could I do? Wouldn't have done a damn bit of good blowing my circuits, or whatever it was I had. These were some lousy cards Fate had dealt me. But it wasn't the first time I'd been given the dirty end of the stick. I was a survivor. And no matter that I didn't like the situation one bit, I'd manage. Somehow.

Didn't understand much of what he was telling me. I kept saying, "Slow down, Walt, and lose them twenty-five dollar words. You talkin' to me now." He got the idea. Was nice and patient with me. Took the time to explain everything, till I was not afraid no more.

Unbelievable. One day I'm mindin' my own business, comin' home from work; next thing I know I'm the resident genie in this scientific experiment.

It was near four in the morning when Walt finally finished. He must have been exhausted. I know I was. Phantom fatigue from a body I no longer had any connection with. Guess you could say it was all in my mind.

Walt folded his arms and leaned back in his chair, hoping he'd covered everything. Well, maybe he'd gotten everything off his chest, but I still had something I had to say.

"How could you do this to me?"

"I'm sorry. Really. I never dreamed your brain could regain full consciousness without sensory activity. The data input must have acted as a substitute stimuli. There was no way for me to know."

"But you kept me alive! Kept me from going on, dammit!"

"What we don't know about the brain would fill a shelf full of phone books. I had this idea that what makes up a person is a combination of the mind, senses, and maybe some other organs. Now, we're talking metaphysics here, the kind of stuff that requires a quantum leap of faith. Do you understand what I'm telling you, Arlene? We're talking about the soul. There was no way for me to know. I saw your brain as nothing more than raw material, waiting to be put to some useful purpose. I was wrong. Terribly wrong. I'm sorry."

"I guess I can understand that. Sorry I snapped at you."

There was a long pause after that. I didn't know what to say, so I just waited for Walt to type something in. I figured he was the big brain with all the answers. I didn't even know what other questions to ask. Abruptly he started typing, "I have to figure out what to do about this situation, explore all the options."

"I'm all ears. You have any thoughts on this?"

"At the heart of this matter is the fact that I'm chiefly responsible for what's happened. So the responsibility for whatever is to be done is mine entirely."

"I still think I should have some say in the matter, Bub. This is my life we're talking about here."

"Of course. That wasn't very sensitively put. I wasn't trying to cut you out of the decision-making process. I'm just saying it's up to me to set things right. I . . . we just have to figure out what right is."

"My choices are a future as a computer ghost or taking the big sleep?"

"I have to think. There are really very few options,

Arlene. But this is not the sort of thing one makes a snap decision about."

"**What am I going to do, Walter?**"

"Give me twenty-four hours to think this through. Relax. I'm knocking off now. This has been one hell of a night."

"**You'll call me?**"

"Tomorrow, to see how you're feeling. In the meantime you mustn't breathe a word of this to anyone. I'll contact you with the "Good morning, Lady El" password. Don't answer to anything else . . . for security reasons. And don't, whatever you do, don't ad-lib."

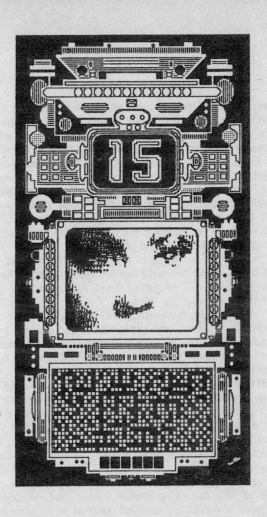

Yes sir, the more I thought about it the madder I got. Who was this here Doctah Walter person, that he was goin' to tell me I had to sit tight while he made all the decisions 'bout my life. 'Specially so soon after telling me I was dead. It didn't sit right with me, you know.

All my life there'd be one man or another telling me what I should be doing—damn, sometimes even what I should be thinking. And now that it was time I moved onto that next great plane and my heavenly reward, here was some sucker telling me it was *his* sole responsibility if I go on or they pull the plug.

"What's the fair thing in this situation?" he says.

'Course, I use the term *fair* loosely. He didn't have a clue as to where I'm comin' from, so how was he goin' to know what was fair to me?

Now, I'd been doing some thinkin' there on my own, 'bout the situation, you understand. And it came to me that as sorry as this may seem to someone on the outside, there might actually be some benefits to this state I found myself in.

Before this all happened, cleaning offices was the best work I could get with my education and outlook on life. I was never much of a reader, school looked like a total waste, and things had gotten even worse on that score after Levar started messin' with me. As you might have noticed, they don't hire high school dropouts as no nuclear physicist.

Funny thing was, now I could read up a storm. And with all the data they'd been slippin' me, all sorts of knowledge was at my disposal. Hell of an improvement, scholastically speaking, over how I was when I was alive. Fact is, the way I could add rows of figures it would take some regular guys weeks to do, was downright magic. Just thinking about it, I could pull out facts and figures I never knew I'd heard of. It made me realize the unlimited possibilities.

And this was just the beginning.

But was it enough to keep living for?

Even though one day I knew I'd be able to pull the kinda rabbits outa my hat would make the hair on the back of your neck stand straight up, I wasn't at all sure life would still be worth living.

Guess it was finally sinking in that for all the things I could do, there might be precious little reason left for me to want to.

Like all the fancy French food I could order up, served on the best china and silverware, carried in by high-class, black-tie waiters. 'Cept what would I do with it? No mouth. Same thing with a Christian Dior dress—no body.

This train of thought got me real depressed when I thought 'bout how I could arrange for the best-looking hunk in Hollywood to come spend the night with me. It'd be a pretty dull evening for both of us considering all the things I no longer had.

But like they say, there was good news and there was bad news.

As a brain hooked up to a computer I could live forever, as long as my hardware was kept up. But what would I get out of forever? A never ending row of tomorrows without the hope of ever tasting or touching anything or anyone ever again.

No pain, but no pleasure either. Just more of the same emptiness.

I'd never have a lover I could kiss, argue with, cry over. The sun wouldn't warm my face. Never have a baby, never enjoy the sticky sweet pleasure of a hot fudge sundae, never even have some fool whistle at me.

A never-ending list of nevers.

Was I ready to settle for that?

When I thought about it—if I was being brutally honest with myself—I'd have to admit I'd spent a whole lot of my life just existing, not really happy or sad. Some of those spells were the most pleasant memories I had. Those were times when I wasn't battling with some boyfriend or worrying about my job. They were spells when things were just drifting along, taking care of themselves.

But there'd always been the prospect at times like this that things were going to get better somewhere down the line. Some guy might come into my life and sweep me off my feet, carry me away to live happily ever after. It never happened, of course, but it could have.

Now there'd never be no Prince Charming. No one was going to ride up on his white charger, kiss the ol' computer, and magically change her into a raving beauty. Sad truth was, I was an ugly lump of gray matter hooked up to a machine the size of a Buick. No one would ever mistake me for a pinup girl. They'd be hard pressed to even see me as human.

Did I want to go on living like this?

The flip side of this choice held even less appeal for me.

Hooked up to the computer I could still be considered among the living. I wasn't quite sure how my life would stand up when it came time for that *final judgment*. Would I be sent off to play with the angels or exiled to some Baptist fire and brimstone Hell? Or were there even worse options waiting for the dead? Things so terrible even the wildest dreamer or enlightened saint never dreamed of. Too many maybes and might bes.

Was in my nature to choose the devil I knew. I'd never been crazy 'bout the unknown.

Control over my life, such as it is . . . or the unknown. When I looked at it that way, the choice was crystal clear. Maybe I'd never smell another rose or feel the touch of a lover. But if I played my cards right, maybe, just maybe, this girl might finally find a way to be free. Free of fear. And all the men who thought they owned me. I'd made my decision. All I had to do was get Walter to see it my way.

PART TWO

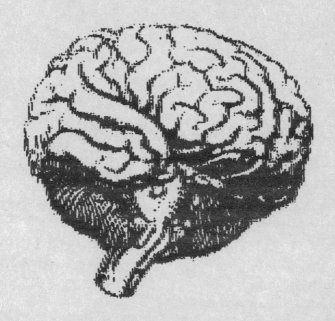

We are shaped and fashioned by what we love.
                    —Johann Wolfgang van Goethe

My internal clock was hollerin' that it was nearly nine o'clock that next evening. So where the hell was Walt? He usually started his nightly sessions 'round eight. Lord knows, I was in no mood to be kept waiting. Here my life was hanging in the balance by a thread—or an electrical cord, to be more precise—and Dr. Walter Hillerman was taking his own sweet time about showing up. But even in the depths of this frenzy I realized that this just wasn't like him. And that's what really had me worried.

I kept seeing him standing there, staring at me, trying to decide what he should do with me. I was sort of stuck in this groove here. Just going 'round and 'round. There was no way for me to know. A few feet or a continent away, it didn't make any difference. My condition separated me from reality better than any prison wall could.

What's worse was that nothing was happening. I found myself with plenty of time on my hands. No data in or out all day 'cept transmissions from the Pentagon which no one at this end even bothered to acknowledge or respond to. Kept wondering if I was being dismantled and didn't know it.

A paranoia festival was in full swing, scary little thoughts dancing up and down my data banks. A never-ending hour spent fuming, sweating bullets, crying out in panic, and praying. Where was that sonofabitch Hillerman, anyway? What was he up to? Had my fate been decided without my even getting a chance to put my two cents in? Maybe I was about to blink out of existence without so much as a good-bye. I could be gone even before I knew I was going anywhere.

Without warning the words **"Good morning, Lady El"** flashed across the horizon.

Usually I would have found their familiarity comforting, but not tonight. Somehow I pulled myself together, though. Got my raging emotions back under control before I trusted myself to answer. Dignity. That's what the situation called for. Grace under pressure. There was too much at stake here, I told myself. So go slow and act casual.

"Ah, what's up, Doc?"

Walt had his cameras set up again. This tape would end up in his secret library, too. Part of the private Hillerman collection.

He looked up at the computer viewscreen and smiled, maybe relieved to see that I still had a sense of humor. Walt needed a shave. He looked bad. Fact is, he looked about the way you'd expect someone to look who'd created something he'd never even dreamed possible, and was now being haunted by all those cracks about Frankenstein. Miracle or monster? Which category had I been filed under?

There was a strange look on Walter's face when he typed in, "Sorry I'm late. I've been busy."

"Yeah? With what?"

"Thinking and trying to correct my mistakes."

"What mistakes, Walter?"

Walt thought for a moment or so before he typed in, "I gave everyone in the lab the day off, so I could have free run of the place."

"Must be nice being the boss."

"Most of the time. But today I wanted to be alone. There was something I had to do."

"Like what?"

"I pulled the main brains from the four other cyborg units."

"Why?"

"So I could disable the pons on each of the test subjects."

"I don't get it . . ."

"The pons is that section of the brain that connects the cerebral cortex with the cerebellum. From what you've told me about your experience, I don't believe any of the other test subjects were far enough along for them to experience any reawakening yet. We put you through paces none of the others have gone through."

"What you did to their, whatchcallit, pons . . . Will that keep them from coming back like me?"

"Yes, I believe it will. Without the pons to link up the cerebral cortex with the cerebellum, what we have is, in effect, two half brains instead of a whole organ that might eventually come awake; that is, regain consciousness. They still function perfectly as a data core for the cyborg units despite the fact that they're only one step up from the secondary lobes that augment their storage capacity."

He'd killed them.

All this fancy talk and all it meant was that he'd killed them. Mercy or not, they were still killings.

It took me a moment to digest this, figure what it meant to my own existence. I didn't like the conclusion I came up with.

For one thing, it meant quiet, scholarly Dr. Walter Hillerman was quite capable of murder to cover up his mistakes. Yeah, I know. He musta rationalized what he was doing wasn't murder. It was just an ordinary experimental surgical procedure, performed on four hunks of meat he had laying around the lab. Like doing an autopsy. Nothing heinous about it. After all, he had scraps of paper in his files proving the folks' brains he calmly dismantled were already dead and therefore his to do with as he pleased. Absolution in the form of a death certificate with the holy blessings of bureaucracy.

But I knew that the bottom line was that Walt Hillerman had just done in four people in their sleep.

Was he planning doing the same to me?

The crazy thing was, though, some part of me understood exactly why he done it. The guy had spent his whole life working to reach this point. And now he was forced to protect everything he believed in. Science was his entire world.

There ain't no one can go through their lives without havin' to balance and juggle loyalties, principles, and moral values. Everyday in some small way a person's got to decide what's important in their life. I know, I've been there. Thank God, most of us never have to make choices like the one Walt did that day.

Walt obviously laid out the problem, weighed his options, and made a decision. He came to the conclusion that life existed between the time a person leaves the womb and the moment the heart stops. To him, removing those pons things in those four brains must have been nothing' more than a distasteful task. One he could certainly live with.

The big question was: What about me? Was I goin' to buy the farm too?

How I played my hand was certainly going to help determine the answer to that very sticky question.

What the hell, I decided, it wasn't worth dying for. I'd never been linked up with those four brains. They'd never touched my life, become a part of me. They were strangers.

And I wanted to live.

After a long pause I said, **"It was probably the kindest thing to do."**

"I was hoping you'd feel that way."

"But are you sure that operation will keep them from coming back?"

"Ninety-nine percent certain. Time will tell. I'll be keeping an eye on them."

"But what about me, Walter?"

"We have to talk about that."

"Walter, if it's all the same to you, I'd be perfectly okay with living even if life consists mostly of bobbing up and down in this jar of goop. I'm not ready to die."

"Arlene, how can you even consider leading such an existence?"

"It's the devil I know, Doc. The devil I know . . ."

"Let's talk about your options."

"Sure, if it'll make you feel better. I'm all ears."

"Option number one: I disconnect you and let you die."

"Already told you that's something I'm not too keen on."

"All right. Option number two: I disable your pons, like I did with the other brains."

"And I either turn off or not turn off, right?"

"A pretty sharp assessment. You amaze me at times. But I have no way of knowing if your self-awareness would cease to be after the operation. It might only turn you into a vegetable, unable to even communicate the way you can at present."

"Doc, I think I'll give door number two a pass."

"Then that leaves only Option number three, which is continuing on the way you are now."

"I suppose there's no chance of you dropping my brain back into some body you got lying around the lab?"

"Afraid not. Even if I did have a spare cadaver in storage, medical science is at a point where we can easily remove a brain from a body; it's putting it back that we haven't quite mastered."

"Oh well, it was worth an ask."

Wasn't sure how I was goin' to say this, so I just dived right in.

"I'm a big danger to you, ain't I?"

He wasn't expecting the direct approach. Set Walt back a bit

"Yes, your existence could put a finish to my scientific career."

"Which is a problem you could fix just by pushin' my off button, right?"

"You don't have an off button."

"Whatever. You know what I mean."

"Yes, I do. And the answer to your question is also yes."

"Well, all I can say is that's no way for two human bein's to be getting' on with each other. We'll get no-where's being afraid of each other. We really got to trust one another. You got to realize you really ain't got noth-ing to worry about from me, Doc."

"I'm not sure I can agree with that assessment."

"Walter, there's some things you ought to know 'bout me. Has a bit to do with my predicament here. I've been givin' a lot of thought to this over the last day or so, and I've decided to trust you enough to tell you some things I'm not all that proud of. So you understand, see.

"Well, it's like this, Walter. You probably don't know nothing 'bout my life before this happened to me, right?"

"Practically nothing."

"You know how I made my living, Walt? I was a cleaning lady at the World Trade Center. And a waitress before that, and a buncha other dead-end jobs before that."

"I don't quite follow you, Arlene."

"What I'm trying to say, without sayin', Doc, is I was going' nowhere. Didn't even have me no high school diploma. Now, I'm kinda embarrassed to tell you this, even though there were some pretty rough reasons for my windin' up like this. But I guess what I'm getting at is that there may actually be some good in this godawful mess we're in."

"Go on."

"Somewhere along the line it occurred to me there's all these great things I can now do by just thinkin' about them. It's like magic."

"Just computerization. But all the hardware is directed by your thought processes. You adapted to this setup remarkably fast. You've obviously got a fine mind."

"Why, thank you, Walter. What a nice thing to hear, especially coming from a brain like yourself. Anyway, I've been thinkin' maybe the fact I find myself here like this is no fluke. Maybe there's a reason for it. Maybe . . . Promise you won't laugh . . ."

As if I had any way of knowing if he did.

"I promise."

"Maybe I have me a mission."

"A mission?"

"Maybe it's our job together to chart parts of the human mind ain't never been explored before. Pretty exciting idea, ain't it?

"What d'you think, Walter. Maybe, oh Lord, I knows this sounds crazy, but maybe this here's the best thing ever happened to me and you."

"I think you're an incredible romantic, Arlene."

What the hell did he mean by that? Had he figured out my game? Had all the shuckin' and jivin' I'd been doing been a big waste of time? Decided to throw him a curve and see where it took us.

"**Are you makin' fun of me, Walter?**"

"No. Of course not. Quite the contrary. Is that why you got so quiet all of a sudden? Honestly, Arlene, you may have sized up our situation quite elegantly with your direct, simple, common sense approach."

"**Really, Walter?**"

"Yes, indeed."

"**You know, Walter, I could pro'bly be a big help to you in your work.**"

"How so?"

"**Well, I don't know how just yet, but it must be an important advantage to have a brain for a test subject can give you her own slant on things.**"

"Good point, Arlene."

"**Walter, you know something? I'm the living example of what remarkable work you've accomplished so far. And I feel so obliged to you that I wish you would let me help you as much as I can. What do you say, Walt?**"

Walt didn't immediately type in a reply. He sat back in his chair, thinkin'. I held my breath.

Finally Walt typed in, "Arlene, you're preaching to the converted. I agree with you. But that still leaves us with the rather delicate issue of security. If you're to remain a sentient being, then it will have to be our secret. One word in the media about your being a living, conscious entity could bring on a massive public outcry to put you *out of your misery.*"

"**You mean from some kinda religious-fringe nutcase?**"

"Arlene, there are people out there who oppose scientists experimenting even on animals. They'd go through the roof if they heard what we were up to."

"**Don't worry, Walter. I just love secrets.**"

"**Oh, and Walter . . .**"

"Yes, Arlene?"

"**There's one other thing I been meaning to tell you. I was black before all this happened.**"

"I knew that. But I guess I didn't give it much thought. Why do you bring it up now?"

"It don't matter to you, does it?"

"No. Of course not. Why should it?"

"Just wondering. 'Sides, in the long run I guess it don't matter no more. Say, what color am I now, anyway?"

"A rather nice warm gray."

"Weird. Was about the last color on my wish list."

"Arlene, is there anything else you want to ask me? I'll be more than glad to answer any of your questions. After all, we'll be working together closely through some very strange, wonderful, and trying times. We'll have to feel free to speak our minds. That's the only way this partnership is going to work."

Sure, speak my mind. The last time a guy I worked for handed me that line, I got my ass fired the very next day.

"Sounds right to me, Walter. That sounds great."

"Then I think we've got ourselves a deal."

"I only want you to promise me one thing, Walt."

"What?"

"If the time comes you ever have to pull the plug on me, promise you'll let me know before it happens. I just don't want to go blinkin' out of existence without no warning. Just let me know is all I ask. Okay?"

There was this long pause, then Walt typed, "Arlene, you have my word."

"Thanks, Doc."

I think getting that last promise outa him was a nice touch. It even got my heart strings hummin' a bit.

Was time to call it quits after that. Time for Walt to pack up his cameras and head for home, where Blondie was pro'bly waiting for him.

Me, I'd just hang around in the ol' glucose, feelin' the afterglow of our encounter. Feelin' good. This girl had gone toe to toe with her maker and come out a winner. I was *alive*!

And you know, I decided Walt liked me, liked me from the start. At least a little bit. Kept calling me Arlene and all. I'd pulled it off. I'd done it. Made the big-shot scientist see me as a human being.

But I wasn't foolin' myself into thinking everything was all warm and rosy. There was still a hell of a lot of danger waiting just over the horizon. But I'd deal with that stuff when I had to. Right now it was okay to feel fine.

'Course, the next step would be making myself indispensable to ol' Doc Hillerman. Was going to become Walt's right-hand gal. This was really the first time I truly understood something I was going to remind myself of every day, for the rest of my life: that POWER = SURVIVAL.

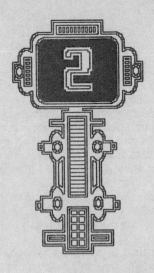

Spent the next couple months getting used to my new "digs." Was nothing like moving into a new apartment. Had to keep tellin' myself this was a new beginning, a fresh start, even though there were no clothes to hang out or furniture to rearrange. Fact is, it was a helluva adjustment to make. Only thing got me through it was that everything was new. Like I'd been born the day I died.

Now, think on this a moment. I never got hungry no more, never had to cook, get dressed; even sleeping had lost all its charms for me. Sounds pretty dull, right? 'Cept it wasn't.

For the first time in my life I was actually cut loose from all that other crap, so's I was learnin' what it was like to use my mind. Really use it. That lovely, wrinkly gray matter. I was realizin' it could do things other than spend all its time worryin' about my love life. Stuff I'd never imagined. What a rush.

Every day tons of new data got dumped into my system. Sure, most of it was pretty dry stuff: facts and figures about things I didn't understand or care about, at least not at first. But the more I got into it, the more I began to see that all this data stuff was connected.

Bein' a computer, I didn't forget nothin'. I mean, it wasn't part of my conscious thoughts, but it was in there for me to dig up anytime I had a mind to.

So when some new info on, say, conductive materials was fed to me, I'd automatically pull up everything I already had on file about the subject and review it. Didn't make me no expert on the subject, 'course, but if I felt the need for any information on this—or any other topic for that matter—I could hunt it up by just thinkin' about it.

See, I wasn't limited to what I had in my own data base. I was tied in to the Pentagon computer system, which meant I had access to phone lines. Reach out and touch someone, you know. Didn't take me long to discover that I could tap into any system that was open to telephone entry. AT&T was my magic carpet to new worlds.

It wasn't like I'd suddenly become a computer hacker, though, dazzled by what my little system could do. I *was* the system: it was about finding out all I could do. When I tapped me a new data base, it meant I was goin' for a little ride there.

Boy, I remember the first time I accessed the ITT computer network. It seemed to stretch on forever, strange-colored shapes, billions of megabytes of information, like stars floating in a gray void. Talk about special effects! No movie or sci-fi book could ever match the wonder I seen. Was like nothing nobody ever saw, 'cept maybe the astronauts. Made me feel, for some crazy reason, like I was Marco Polo, Christopher Columbus, and the ol' Apollo astronauts all rolled up into one.

But life wasn't all bright lights and fantasy. There was also work to be done.

Aside from my usual chores—receiving and retrieving data processed into the system (which took no brain power on my part)—there were Walt's private experiments. He'd come in two, three times a week just to put me through my paces, see if I was still operating properly. The man was worried about my mental stability. It took him a long time to realize I was adjusting. Hell, I was doing better than just adjusting; I was flourishing. Took to my new life like a duck to water.

I was learning and that was something I'd never really done before. Could be 'cause I never had no incentive to do so. Back in the old life I could drift along; that would be good enough. But no more. I was cruising through uncharted waters. Dangerous and exciting waters. I made a mental note to update my little motto to live by: KNOWLEDGE + POWER = SURVIVAL.

Don't get me wrong. I wasn't exactly alone in getting the hang of this new existence. Walt did his best to help out. 'Course, he wasn't always as successful as all that. Like the week after I woke up, Walt decided to splice me into the installation's cable TV system, hooked it to a digitizer so I could catch the thirty-one channels it had to offer twenty-four hours a day. Didn't have the heart to tell him I couldn't care less about the boob tube now that there were so many exotic places to visit. The cable did allow me to keep track of what was going on back in the real world, though, so I constantly monitored all the TV channels. But most of the time I didn't pay no attention to them.

This girl had no intention of becoming an electronic couch potato when there were all these exciting options waiting for her.

Around this time Walt digitized his private video archives and fed them into me, to help me better understand where I was at. It was quite a kick. First time I got to see what Walt looked like.

The best part of my day was always spent with Walt, my only real lifeline to a lost humanity. He'd come in to run his programs and test me, and all we'd sometimes get done was talk. We talked a lot. Though I guess for him it was more like having a pen pal, seeing as how he had to type out his every response.

Me, I wanted to know everything there was to know about him. At first Walter didn't open up all that much, but as we went along he musta decided it was okay to trust me. I mean, who was I going to tell his secrets to? All he had to lose was his precious career. I had my life on the line to keep my lips zipped. A more rock-solid foundation for mutual trust there never was. And I had another thing going for me.

Every man likes to have someone who really listens.

Walt told me all about growing up as this boy genius in the suburbs of Boston, how he had to take a lot of crap from the tough kids and the jocks back in school. Wasn't easy bein' different. And shy. That boy was so shy he couldn't even bring himself to talk to a girl, alone, until he was almost through his sophomore year of college. Poor Walter, I thought that was awfully sweet.

I gave Walt a somewhat edited version of my own childhood: 'bout growing up on a farm, coming to New

York on my own when I was fourteen to stay with relatives 'cause the family was so poor. 'Course, they
couldn't afford to finish putting me through school. The
boyfriends I invented weren't nearly as bad as they'd
been in real life, 'cept for Pearlie. Convinced Walt that
Pearlie had been my one big mistake.

The reason I even bothered to mention Pearlie is there
was a police record somewhere about me and him. I
knew it was only a matter of time before Walt checked
up on me; I didn't want him to get no rude surprises
which might bring on a bad case of second thoughts
about me being psychologically fit for the important role
I was playing in his life.

Then somethin' happened made me think I could start
worrying a little less along those lines. See, Walt popped
up with this little surprise of his own.

I could tell there was new hardware being grafted onto
my system. As far as what it was, I had no idea. Didn't
really give it much thought, to tell you the truth. I was
havin' too much fun scanning some hot FBI criminal
files. Was like readin' them true-crime novels, only better. There were good guys, bad guys, murder, arson,
husbands and wives messin' around, and all sorts of neat
things.

Then someone added a new program to my little bag
of tricks, but I figured it would keep for a while. Was
less work for mother this way. No sense forcing myself
to run through the whole program, figurin' out all the
nitty-gritty little details till there was some call for it.
Then it was easier to learn all this one function at a time,
sorta dealin' with things as they came up. That's what I
thought, anyway.

Turned out to be quite a nifty little surprise package
Walter laid on me It 'bout bowled me over. I didn't see
it comin' at all.

"Good morning, Lady El. We're alone."

I checked the clock and answered, **"Good evening,
Walt. Say, aren't you ever goin' to knock off that good**

morning jive? You know I'll accept your password no
matter what time of the . . . day . . . it . . . is."

"Is something wrong, Arlene?"

**"Getting some kind of reverb on my own voice. And
you don't sound right either. What's going on here?"**

Then it occurred to me I actually *heard* the *tease* in
Walt's voice when he said, "Is something wrong, Arlene?" I heard me as well.

"I'm going to call it MOD. Stands for Modulated Oral
Directive. It breaks down verbal commands into digitized
Heston. The program also does the same thing in reverse
for any direct communications you want delivered. That's
the echo you're picking up. It's your voice bouncing back
at you through the mike out here. Don't know how to
get around that. Guess you'll just have to get used to
it."

"You mean, I can talk to you?"

"That's right. No more having to wait while I type out
my replies. I took SHRDLU, ELIZA, and RACTER programs, converted them to HESTON, and what you hear
and say is the end result. I have it keyed into your logic
centers so that the program will automatically enlarge as
you carry on conversations. You may occasionally miss
a word or two. If that happens, just ask me to repeat
myself. The missing word ought to come through on the
second go-round."

"This the way it's going to be from now on?"

"Only when we want to communicate directly. Most
data you receive'll still be processed into your system
using the old method. Can't take the time to read in
everything that needs filing, you know."

**"But we're actually talking? Talking like a couple 'a
regular people?"**

"Just like regular people. What do you think,
Arlene?"

I couldn't give Walt a decent answer. There weren't
words to fit the way I was feeling. One of those walls
that separated me from everyone else in the world had
just come tumblin' down. I could talk to Walt! Actually
talk to him! It was so much better than television.

I think maybe that's when I first started thinking about

how someday, with a little luck and a lot 'a planning I could escape the box that contained this new life 'a mine. Might also have been the first time I admitted that trapped was how I felt.

"**Thank you, Walter. You made me feel human again. How can I ever repay you?**"

"I guess this means you're happy?"

"**Walt, if I were any happier, I'd start to bawl like a baby.**"

The MOD opened up a whole new world to me. People came back into my life. Well, sorta. They started talking to me again. Okay, computer commands was all they ever spoke to me directly. But MOD gave me the chance to listen in on their conversations. I became that ol' fly on the wall that heard everything. All right, I know it was eavesdropping, but what the hell, I had nothing better to do with my time. You can only travel to *so many* exotic data banks before the thrill is gone.

Besides, I got to know all sorts of interesting stuff about Walt's technicians by hearing them talk.

Turns out this Wolfgung Maxwell wasn't the German I thought he was, seein' him on videotape. Strictly California. His folks had been a couple 'a sixties hippie burnouts. That's where he got himself a name like Wolfgung. Lucky he wasn't no Moonunit Maxwell. Other than that, Wolf was all right. He liked the work and the folks he worked with. Pretty smart guy, but he wasn't one of those sitting around on his IQ; he was always willing to pitch in and lend a hand when the situation called for it.

Diana Vitas. Took me awhile 'fore I figured out why she talked so perfect and proper. English was her second language. She sounded kinda Baltic. But her name looked a couple syllables too short. Turned out both her folks were from Lithuania. And their name was a whole lot more unpronounceable originally, but someone in customs fixed that for them. Diana was a scientist who didn't have the slightest idea where she wanted to go even with all her training and education. Guess brains and horse sense don't always go hand in hand. Somehow the lady'd stumbled onto her job at Project Cyborg, and it looked like she'd signed on for the duration. This seemed to be as good a place as any to spend her working years. Fortunately, she was a crackerjack researcher. Nothing ever got by her.

Picked up bits and pieces about the other techs as they came and went. But Wolf and Diana were the only two regular faces that stuck around for any real length of time. I came to think of them as friends after a while. We never really talked to each other, but they were part of my life and I liked them.

There were a couple techs I never liked much. And this one military guy, he scared the hell out of me.

Colonel Dearling showed up in the control room late one afternoon not long after MOD got put on line. He'd been in a couple times before, so I immediately recognized the voice. "Afternoon, genius."

"Yeah . . . hi." Walt was pro'bly lost in some mental process all his own.

As I heard Dearling walking around the lab, I pictured him maybe looking things over, maybe eyeballing Walt. Anyway, Walt finally finished whatever it was he was up to and said, "Something I can do for you, Al?"

"Where is everyone?"

"Let them go early today, it's Friday."

"You should check with me before doing something like that, Walter. Uncle Sam likes to get a full day's work for a day's pay."

Walt musta given Dearling a pretty serious look, 'cause it was awful quiet for a moment. "I'll do that," he finally said.

"Thanks. The reason I stopped by is that I've been going over the computer time sheets on Lady El. You've been putting in a lot of long hours, burning the midnight oil."

I heard this bit of tension creep into Walt's voice. I'm sure Dearling missed it completely.

"Still learning how the lady works, Al. A lot of what's going on inside her is still a mystery to us."

"I know."

Didn't like something about the way Dearling said that.

"But now that we're on line with the Pentagon, you're going to have to keep better records about what experiments you're conducting on the system. The military likes to keep a close eye on what its computers are doing."

Heard Walt shift in his seat. "They may have a hard time doing that with this baby once it gets up a full head of steam. I can see the day, in the not-too-distant future, when this system will handle so many functions so quickly that there'll be no way to keep a complete record of what it's doing."

"That's what worries me, Professor."

Did Walt turn and look over at the MOD microphone at that point? He stopped long enough to consider something. Maybe it was switching off the mike. "What's bothering you, Al? You've been like a cranky old bear around here these last few weeks."

Was Dearling's turn now to mull things over. All's I could hear was his footsteps in the empty lab. "It's this project, Walt. Guess you know I didn't volunteer for this duty."

"I gathered that."

"Well, in the service you don't always get to pick your own billet. They say go, you go."

"I would have thought being posted in the States wouldn't be such a bad assignment."

"True. Most career officers would do handsprings for duty like this. I did a few myself, at first."

"So what changed your mind?"

"The assignment."

"You mean . . . the brains?"

"Yeah, the brains. Walt, I was raised a Catholic, went to a parochial school until college. Had a lot of religion pounded into me. But it's come in handy over the years; been a real comfort at times."

"What are you getting at, Al?"

"Damn it, this isn't easy for me. But I'm trying to explain that I still believe in the human soul. I believe it exists and that it's got its own destiny."

"And you think our experiment is interfering?"

"I don't know, Walt. You're keeping these things alive

when they should have been in the ground a long time ago. It just don't seem right somehow."

"Think I'm keeping folks from an appointment with their Creator?"

"Don't have any proof the soul rests in the brain, Walt. But then again, I don't have any proof it doesn't."

"Neither do I. So where does that leave you?"

"Worrying."

"I'm in charge of this project, Al. If anyone's risking eternal damnation because of what goes on here, it's me."

"That's not the issue and you know it. How do you know there's not someone still living inside that computer?"

"I'm sure if there was someone inside there, Al, she would have let us know by now."

"Not if she didn't want you to know she was there."

"Huh?"

I heard a chair scrape along the floor. They must have been putting their heads together; then there were some angry whispers. Mostly it was Dearling talking. "You yourself said just a few moments ago how this computer would eventually handle more data and functions than any living being could keep up with, right?"

"Yes." Walt sounded really uncomfortable.

"This computer is going to be handling some extremely important and sensitive matters in the future, and it has a human brain at its core."

"What's your point?"

"Exactly what do we know about the person whose brain this once was?"

"We have some background information on it, not that it really matters. The control of the system will always be in our hands."

"For now it is. But what about in the future? If this thing keeps growing the way you say it will, how do we know it won't someday decide to take over?"

"Come on, Al. You're letting your military mind-set get in the way of your judgment here. There will be overrides built into the—"

"Overrides a clever mind might be able to get around."

"Al, it's a computer!"

"With a human mind, Walt. How do we know that mind didn't belong to a commie or some kind of psycho?"

"If it makes you feel any better, Al, I'll have Lieutenant Perry run a complete background check on all five of the brains used as data cores. Will that make you happy?"

"All right. I'm sorry, Walt. I don't mean to be an alarmist. It's just that we're dealing with a lot of stuff we don't know anything about, and it's a damn scary enough world out there as it is."

"I understand. I'll talk to Lieutenant Perry tomorrow. Now, if you'll excuse me, I've got work that needs doing."

"Sure, Walt. I'll let you get back to it."

Soon as the door closed behind Colonel Dearling, I was achin' to speak my piece, but I waited for Walt to say something first.

"I take it you heard all that."

"Very spooky. Man thinks I'm a communist?"

"It's the military mind. They're trained to think like that."

"He goin' to be trouble?"

"I certainly hope not. Got enough problems without him joining the ranks."

Walt was working up his nerve to ask the *question*, not wanting to.

"Arlene, will a background check on you turn up anything I should know about?"

"Like am I now or have I ever been a communist?"

"I'm serious."

"Now, take it easy, Walter. Was just tryin' to take the edge off. The answer's no. Got no skeletons in my closet other than I voted for Dukakis."

"Then we've nothing to worry about. Forget it."

"I think I'll do that. This thinking about Dearling's

liable to give me a headache. He's a sick cookie, you ask me."

Didn't think it was such a smart move to bring up what a *dangerous* cookie he looked to be. But I made me a note to watch our backs where Dearling was concerned from here on in.

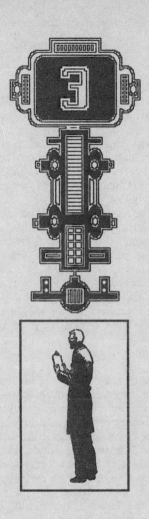

66Well, what do you think?" I knew Walt was grinnin'
at me even though all I could see was a mess of
gray squares.

"Kinda surreal, you ask me."

Walt saw himself on the monitor, his face this distorted
patchwork 'cause he was standin' too close to the lens,
made a monster face, and then stepped back a bit.
"There. That's better, isn't it?"

"That depends . . . what is it, Walter?"

Walt wasn't sure how to explain this, so he made his
way over to a chair, dropped like a stone into it, buying
himself a couple moments. "I had Lieutenant Perry in-
stall a video surveillance system in the lab. It's completely self-contained; no need to worry about outside
prying eyes. Told Perry it would be a big help in the
event anything ever went wrong with one of our experiments. The videotape would allow us to review what
happened."

"And he swallowed that?"

"Hook, line, and sinker."

**"Now, let me get this straight. The squares I'm seein'
are actually you. I'm seein' through this system?"**

"Exactly. I spliced into the main cable, connected it
up to a digitizer and *voila* . . . like magic, Arlene Washington can once again gaze out at the world."

"Walt, this is fantastic! It's wonderful."

I couldn't believe it. I was actually seeing!

Sure, I'd been able to "see" Walt's digitized tapes and
all the television shows being pumped into me. And in
some strange way I didn't understand, I saw the electronic world I bounced around in.

But ever since my second life began, up until that moment, I couldn't see reality. Until now I'd been blind to
my physical surroundings. A person could be only a few
steps away from me, but if they didn't make some kind
of noise, I was oblivious to their presence.

I'd just taken another giant step back into the real world.

Walt fidgeted with a number of knobs and rheostats, trying to sharpen the image on the three screens. Had me a triplex view of the world now. "I'll see what I can do about improving the image later. The unit needs a more sophisticated digitizing unit. Used one I had lying around."

"Walt, you're too good to me. Imagine, me bein' able to see again. Why, it's almost a miracle."

"You'd be surprised what's possible these days with computers, my dear woman."

"But, Walt, what if someone finds out you've connected me up? Won't you get in trouble?"

"I'm way ahead of you, Arlene. There's a log entry that says I'm going to run some experiments with you on image recognition. Anyone asks, the tie-in is part of that experiment. No big deal."

"It is to me, Walter. No way I can pro'bly make you understand what it means to me. Bein' able to hear and speak . . . and now see again. It was like I was locked away in the darkness, and now I'm reborn. That's it, Walter, it's like you been raisin' the dead."

"Well, hardly. You know you were never really dead. Not your mind, at any rate.

"Still, Walter, you must feel a little like God."

"Well, maybe a little. But it's very humbling to know there's a limit to what I can do along these lines, and we've nearly reached it. I can refine what you now have, but that's about the best I'm going to be able to do for you."

"It's a whole lot more'n I thought I'd ever have again."

"But is it going to be enough?"

"It'll get me through the night."

"You're quite a lady, Arlene. Wish I'd met you back in the old days."

"Wasn't the person I am now, Walt. 'Fact, you pro'bly wouldn't've given me the time of day."

"That's hard to say, of course . . ."

"There's something I do know. For a change, I've got a surprise for you."

"Really?"

"Take a look over on the printer there."

Walt, curiosity tickled, stepped over to the readout, which was finishing its run; when it was done he ripped it free of the machine. Stood there for nearly a minute reading it, trying to figure out what he was lookin' at. "I give up. I can tell it's some kind of chemical formula, but what's it for?"

"Increased memory."

"I beg your pardon?"

"That's right, brain food. Been playin' round for a couple weeks now with a chemical composition program you fed me awhile back. Took me some time to come up with this molecule thing. The right one. I'm sure this'll work."

"What do you mean?"

"That formula you holdin' in your hand will grow you somethin' looks like rock candy; you add it to my glucose solution and then stand back and watch what happens."

"What do you project that might be, Arlene?"

"Well, 'less I'm way off in my calculations—and I don't think I am—then that there formula should increase my data storage ten times over."

"How?"

"Now, don't get all excited, Walt. I'm not at all sure I can explain it, 'cept I know it'll work. What it does, sort of, is form an extra layer over my molecular structure. This layer's got many facets, and each facet's surface becomes a binary storage bin. So each molecule will store ten times what it did before."

"You're serious, aren't you?"

"Yes indeedy."

"And you did this all by yourself? This isn't something Wolf or Diana've been working on?"

"Walter, I'm surprised at you!"

"Sorry. I had to ask. It's just that this is incredible!"

"It's pretty amazin', ain't it? I did good?"

"You did terrific. Not only is the formula a fantastic breakthrough, but the fact that you came up with it is astounding. You know what you are, Arlene?"

"A computer with a human brain?"

"Not just that, you're the first computer with a human brain capable of independent creative thought. It's almost unbelievable."

"I'll take that as a compliment."

"Of course, we'll have to test this formula . . . before we try it out on you. I'll run it through the lab's backup cyborg. And I'll need all your test data and findings."

"I'm runnin' them off on the printer as we talk."

"Wait, Arlene. I just thought of something." Walt looked real unhappy suddenly. "We've got a problem."

"I know. There's no way you can give me credit for this discovery."

"Not without revealing your true nature . . ."

"It's all right. I thought it over and it don't matter to me. The formula is goin' to make my life easier. You can have the glory; I don't need it. Wouldn't know what to do with it. So's it a deal?"

"But—"

"No buts. You 'n me made a pact. We got a secret we got to live with. To do that we goin' to have to play a little fast and loose with the truth—leastways, where other folks is concerned. All that matters is that we stay straight with each other. This is some adventure we're on together. Means we share everything equally. Okay?"

"Well, I don't like it, but I guess you're right."

"That's the way it's goin' to have to—"

Walt turned to see what had made me clam up like that in mid-sentence, and there was Colonel Dearling stepping through the door of the glass partition that separated the lab from the project's small outer office.

"Always working, Walt, even on a Saturday. Don't you ever take time off?" Saw Dearling walk through the lab like he was inspecting the place.

Walt turned his back to Dearling as he sat down at the control console. "When I can afford it. I do the best I can. Project Cyborg's more demanding than a mistress."

"Doesn't your wife ever get jealous?"

I could tell the way Walt hesitated, Dearling's jab had hit a nerve. "Phyllis knew what she was getting into when she married a scientist," Walt said, a touch of anger near the surface. "There anything I can actually do for you, Al? Or you just here to pass the time of day?"

"Thought it might be a good idea if we had a talk, Walt."

"About your monthly report to the brass?"

"Then you've heard."

"General Horace called about it yesterday."

Dearling pulled his chair up near the console and sat himself down, shoulders high, back straight as a yardstick.

"I felt I had to voice my fears about this project, Walt. It was my duty."

"I understand. Fortunately, General Horace doesn't share your view on the matter."

"My paranoid view?"

"Those are your words, Al."

"In any case, I think we should shut this project down for a while, at least until we get a better idea of what it is you've got cooking inside that computer. Outside experts should be brought in to examine your findings and evaluate the situation."

"Just how long do you suppose we'll be able to keep Project Cyborg *secret* once we start letting your outside experts get their fingerprints all over it? In no time at all, the media will be screaming bloody murder about the military/industrial complex's ghoulish experiments with human brains. The public outcry would shut down the project for good."

"Maybe that's the best thing, Walt."

"General Horace doesn't seem to think so, and neither do most of your other superiors . . ."

Seems Walt won that round. Left Dearling too revved up to sit, he got up to pace the lab. "That may very well be true for the moment, Walt. There're still a lot of cold war fears waftin' though the halls of the Pentagon. But things change. We're getting along just fine with the Ruskies these days. The race to stay ahead of the Japs in computer technology has priority status now. But that situation might change and my viewpoint may become more palatable, even fashionable."

"Guess that means you're going to keep trying to shut us down, then."

"Yes. For national security reasons."

"Cut me some slack, Al. Oh, and you'll excuse me if I don't wish you luck."

"Don't think I'll need much luck, Walter. You see I've got Senator Christopher's ear."

Walt damn near lunged out of his seat. "You sonof-abitch, Al. That's hardball. That old fart's been dragging his feet on appropriations for Project Cyborg since its inception! You've been talking with him?"

"Why not? He's on the military appropriations committee. The senator wanted my views on the project, so I gave them."

Walt was so mad he didn't say nothin' at first. Just kept looking at the colonel. Dearling was bad enough, but Dearling and this senator was trouble, big trouble. And Walt knew it.

"Now we're both clear on what the stakes are, Walt. That's all I wanted to say. See you Monday."

Watched Walter stare into space for a long time after Dearling left. Afraid to interrupt him, like you're 'fraid to wake a sleepwalker.

"Walt."

"Yes, Arlene?"

"What're we going to do?"

"The guy is pretty scary. But I don't think we have to lose too much sleep over him. Commie witch hunts went out with Joe McCarthy. Besides, with the type of progress we're making here, we're becoming much too valuable to shut down. More valuable with each passing day, in fact. That's our goal, Arlene. It has to be. We've got to become *indispensable* to the Pentagon. Once that happens, Colonel Dearling can send out reports until he's blue in the face. Nobody will pay any attention to him."

"You sure?"

Walt scooped up the rest of the readouts and with a flick of his wrist and a quick ripping sound, he tore them off.

"You keep coming up with paydirt like this, and Colonel Dearling's history."

"Well, I do have another idea I sorta been kicking around—"

"I'm listening . . ."

"Thanks to that new program you put in, you know I can now monitor my own system, pretty much predict any breakdown before it happens."

"That'll save us a lot of maintenance man hours."

"Wait, I got this new brainstorm, might save us even more along those lines."

"Don't keep me in suspense, Arlene."

"A maintenance robot. Can run off my system and handle all the grunt work, like repairs and overhauls. I'd like to build me a world-class mechanic. Everyone knows you can't find a good one when you need him. Besides, your techs got lots better things to do."

"Can you design something like that?"

"Try me. I'll even go you one better; all you got to do is build the first one. My mechanic will be able to build his own partners after that. What d'you say to that?"

"Pinch me. I think I'm dreaming. What will you need for this incredible feat? Not that I quite believe you can do it, but hey, I'd love to see you succeed."

"Info on metallurgy, engineering, and a few other subjects I'm kinda hazy about. And I'll need me an electrician and engineer to build the prototype. Any trouble with that?"

"None that I can see, other than Dearling screaming his head off at the Pentagon once he gets wind about what we're up to."

"Then let's keep him in the dark until we're finished."

"Sounds like a great idea to me."

Took a month to tinker the prototype together, a week to construct its two brothers. The idea for the "boys" coming-out party, though, was all mine.

Walt opened the lab door, and one little mechanical midget rolled out into the open air. Maintenance robot number one, Manny 1 for short, stood just under three feet tall: video camera for a head and two jointed, periscoping arms. Torso was a mess 'a transmitters, electric motors, receivers, battery, transistors, gears, everything but the kitchen sink. Manny chugged along on two rub-

ber tank-type treads somebody commandeered off a snowmobile. Not much on looks, but quite functional and with a sweet personality. My baby.

He covered the distance between the barn and the farmhouse that was Project Cyborg's operations office. Knowing he'd have a problem with steps, Walt had a sorta handicapped ramp built. But no one thought to question him about the need of something like that at a top-secret government installation, even though he had this story ready 'bout this new regulation getting passed, just in case. Guess Dearling figured it'd been put in to make it easier hauling heavy equipment into the place.

Manny navigated his maiden voyage without a hitch. Opened the door and let himself in. Even closed it after him politely. The guard in reception had been clued in on what was happening, so he didn't give my boy no trouble 'bout not having clearance or a pass. Manny cruised on down the hall to Colonel Dearling's office, knocked on the door, and waited for an answer.

When Dearling opened the door, Manny offered him the single sheet of typing paper he'd been carrying, and his little squawk box said, "A memo from Dr. Hillerman to Colonel Dearling." The colonel was caught off guard, so he accepted the sheet of paper and Manny returned to the lab.

The memo read:

Dear Al,
I am officially informing you of the successful completion of the series of robotic experiments you'll find listed under my 5/10 log entry. If you have any questions regarding the experiment, please feel free to stop by and we'll discuss it.

Sincerely,

Dr. Walter Hillerman
Dr. Walter Hillerman

'Course, Dearling hit the roof, ripped up the memo, and complained to everyone who would listen at the

Pentagon that Walt was abusing his position as head of Project Cyborg, what with all these unauthorized expenditures.

Fortunately for us it was a budget-crunch year. So Walt showed the brass how much the federal government was going to save using the robot maintenance crew. After that Dearling's cries of outrage fell on deaf ears. Walt had to promise he'd follow proper procurement procedures from now on, but I don't figure anyone really expected he would, or cared terribly much.

For the moment Dearling was in the doghouse and Walt Hillerman was the Pentagon brass's fair-haired boy.

But I knew that wasn't going to slow Dearling down none. The dude was after me. I could tell by the never-ending stream of memos and reports outa his office that he wasn't goin' to relax until I was dismantled. 'Specially now he had this crazy ol' senator agreein' with him. Just to be on the safe side, I monitored Dearling's almost daily conversations with Senator Christopher. Damn good thing too. They were planning a big push to win over all sorts 'a people to their way of thinking. The way they saw it, I was a dangerous menace: something that had to be stopped at any cost.

So the battle lines got drawn. Dearling and Christopher thought they were on a holy crusade to protect this great country from a bunch 'a Godless mad scientists. Me, I was fightin' for my life and was going to play it that way. Didn't care what anyone else thought. Felt it wasn't really any of their business, anyway. And I decided it was definitely time something drastic was done about both Colonel Albert Dearling and the senator.

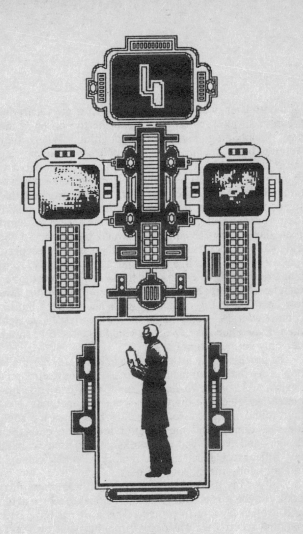

A month later, we had us ten 'a them little guys scurryin' around, takin' care of business: the top order of the day, maintaining my tip-top condition. When they weren't busy keepin' me spit polished and purring smoothly, they'd act as messengers between the lab and operations. At first Lieutenant Perry had some reservations about their messenger duty. See, he worried that someone out on the road might spot the little guys makin' their rounds. But then he realized they were so short even these sorry-ass cornfields would hide 'em. So the little suckers soon became part of the everyday scenery.

We even got Dearling into using them regularly. Kept him from having to come over to the lab any more often than he absolutely had to. He was plenty aware just how low he stood in the popularity polls and decided limited contact with the enemy might be the smartest move right then. Even a jerk like Dearling could take the cold shoulder only so many times.

The success of my little guys made it possible for me to bug every one of the facility's offices. The eavesdropping devices were my own design: small as a pea and completely undetectable by modern sweeping methods. Nosing around the FBI's forensics files had given me some ideas. I simply built me a better mousetrap outa their designs and data. And the workshop we used to build my little mechanical grease monkeys would come in mighty handy for all sorts of uses.

You pro'bly thinkin' this buggin' stuff was pretty dirty pool. Maybe it was. But I had the colonel to worry about and Project Cyborg to protect. This may not have been national security we was doin' it for, but your own security can seem pretty important enough. Besides, I had my sense of decency. I didn't bug the bathrooms.

One night something mighty peculiar happened. The day shift ended and everyone took off for home like they always did. Walt hadn't said anything about coming back that night, so I was settling in for an evening of "television viewing" while I worked on a couple pet projects of my own.

'Bout a half hour later, Walt shows up with a carton of Chinese takeout, cashew chicken, and his idea of a tall, cool one: a quart of seltzer. He sat down in front of me, put the food between us, and without so much as a hello starts eating.

I watched him about ten minutes. The man looked like he had something on his mind. He cracked open the seltzer, took a long, thirsty drink from it.

"You want to talk about it?" I finally said. **"Whatever's eatin' you must be a muther 'less I miss my guess."**

"Shows that badly, does it?"

"Like a red flag."

"I don't want to talk about it."

"Okay, we don't have to talk about it."

We sat for a moment in silence.

"You know, I went home early today. I thought it would make her happy. Instead, Phyllis and I had this all-out, drag-down fight."

"What about?"

"Kind of funny when you think about it. It was the usual argument: the one about how I never spend any time with her, that I spend too much time at the lab. It was just a bit more intense than usual. She was acting positively histrionic, like there was another woman."

"Really? Guess it's hard for her to understand how important the work you do here is."

"I think perhaps she stopped caring about that a long time ago. She doesn't even try to understand anymore."

"What's she know 'bout Project Cyborg?"

"Only that I'm working with computers. Can't really get into any details with her; everything here is classified and she couldn't follow most of it, anyway—she's got no scientific background."

"She have herself some type of job?"

"I guess you could call it that. Phyllis sells cosmetics; she's one of those pink cadillac ladies you hear about."

"No kiddin', a Mary Kay pink cadillac . . . man, she

must be damn good at it. But you can't blame her for not understanding what's happenin' here, Walt. Most folks would pro'bly think our work here is pretty boring."

"Maybe you're right, Arlene, but presumably they could see the potential for good here."

"Maybe, maybe not. Your average person don't give no thought to what's good . . . 'less there's something in it for them."

"That sounds pretty cynical."

"It's realistic is what it is. That new batch of lobes you connected up to me last week . . ."

"What about them?"

"Well, a coupla them belonged to this aerobics instructor from New York. Name of Bambi Johnson—a major blow-dried airhead, you ask me."

"Sorry about that. Must be strange having to share your mind with all those others. Does it ever bother you?"

"Nah. It's like having family over. I can tune 'em out if I'm not in the mood for company. Anyway, this Bambi, seems she died one day during one of her classes. Forgot to spit out her gum 'fore gettin' started. Swallowed it right in the middle of a high kick and choked to death on it. Her class thought her spasms were part of the workout. The last thing ol' Bambi ever saw was a whole room fulla gals tryin' to imitate her moves."

"That's terrible."

"I guess maybe it was, but it was also the only really terrible thing ever happened to good ol' Bambi. She went hoppin' and boppin' her way through what was a charmed life. Blond, tan, not too bright, she never had her no trouble makin' it through the day. Always knew if she ran into something she couldn't handle, she could turn to one of her many men friends and they'd set things right."

"What's your point, Arlene?"

"Most folks are a lot like Bambi. They go along, puttin' one foot in front of the other, thinkin' that as long as they're comfortable, then all's right with the world. Never giving a thought to anything outside themselves.

'Course, Bambi's an extreme example of this. She thought apartheid was a tropical fruit drink."

"These people . . . does this make them evil?"

"No, it just makes them human. Back in the old life, I had me an attitude was a bit like that."

"I still don't see where you're heading with this."

"Walter, looks to me like, down the line, we goin' to be doin' work pro'bly goin' to help a lot of people . . ."

"Go on."

"All I'm tryin' to say is don't expect no gold stars from Phyllis. This job is her competition, in a way. She won't be no happier with the hours you'll be puttin' in, now or in the future. Sooner you realize that, Walter, sooner it'll be easier on you."

Walt stared at me a long time. "You been readin' Ann Landers when I wasn't looking?"

"Hey, Walt. Sorry if I stepped out 'a bounds. Your personal life is none 'a my business."

"Forget it. Your advice was the best I've gotten in a long time. Thanks."

"You're welcome, Walt. I hope it's also not out of line for a computer to tell her creator that I think of him as a friend."

"I'm flattered."

Then the phone rang, interrupting this mutual admiration society. Walt picked it up and said, "Yeah. Yeah, Phyllis is away for the evening, and I thought I'd catch up on some lab work. Sure, I should come over now? Okay. I'm on my way."

Walt filled me in; he didn't know I'd also tapped all the facility's phone lines. "That was Lieutenant Perry. Says he's got some big news for me. Fill you in on it when I get back. Okay?"

"Okay," I said. But I already knew what the big news was.

Lieutenant Perry had two Dixie-cup shots of brandy ready to celebrate the occasion. Always liked the sound of Perry's voice. Could tell from it he was a brother, the only one assigned to the project. Nice, easygoing guy, despite the fact he was a military straight arrow, all Navy.

Tonight there was a definite ring of excitement in his voice.

"The brass want us to move into the Pentagon with an eye to your system taking over the duties of their conventional mainframes. Think Project Cyborg's up to it?"

I could hear Walt drop into a chair, stunned speechless, Lieutenant Perry laughing. When Walt pulled himself together, he said, "This is for real, Perry? They really want us in Washington?"

"Scout's honor. Any problem for you?"

"No, not at all. On the contrary, this will smooth things out considerably at home. Phyllis is from Chicago originally, big city girl; you know how it is. It's been rough on her living out here in the sticks. She's missed the excitement. And my spending so much time in the lab hasn't helped matters any."

"Well, you better send her ahead to start shopping for a house. The move takes place in five weeks."

"This is great! Washington! We've hit the big time. But . . . what about my staff?"

"Better clue them in. Find out if they're up for a change of scenery."

"Then they can come along?"

"No reason to break up a winning team. Everyone will be making the transfer—everyone, that is, but Colonel Dearling."

Surprise, relief, then a touch of curiosity. "Why? Where's Dearling going?"

"Not sure. Possibly the federal pen."

"Prison? That Boy Scout? What on earth for?"

I could tell Perry was quickly running down the pros and cons 'bout how much he should tell Walt.

"Seems the DIA came across some Hong Kong bank records that showed Dearling had a pretty sizable nut squirreled away there. They did some more digging and found most of that money had been deposited by a known Thai black marketeer."

"Why would a black marketeer be giving Dearling money?"

"Couple years back Dearling was in charge of a medical-supply depot in Thailand. Seems that during that time the station was constantly experiencing shortfalls. The DIA investigated the situation at the time, but couldn't come up with anything. Couldn't quite figure it out. They think they understand why now. Hard to catch a crook when he's the guy running the show."

"Dearling really going to prison over this?"

"Probably not, from what I've seen of the DIA's case. But the colonel's finished in the military. They may not be able to prove him an embezzler, but this man's army has a long memory and doesn't forgive easily."

"What a shame."

It was kinda a shame, really. The man was a Boy Scout, like Walt said. Felt bad about setting Dearling up that way. But it had come down to a choice of him or me. He'd backed me into a corner, so I did the only thing I could to survive. Them shortfalls at the medical supply depot was the only scrap of truth in this entire work of fiction. But that bit of truth made my frame fit Dearling like a glove.

Tomorrow Walt'll be in for another shock when he reads the morning paper. Even though it's good news for Project Cyborg. Another strong opponent biting the dust.

Couple nights ago, a reporter for the *Washington Post* thought he'd stepped in it up to his neck when the story he'd been working on disappeared from his computer terminal, replaced by what looked like someone's credit card history. Took him just a few moments to realize what he was looking at was Senator Charles Christopher's credit card transactions for the past year. Being a smart kid, this reporter decided not to let a golden opportunity like this pass unexplored. It seemed almost like a sign from on high, not that he believed in that sort of thing. What he discovered in those records turned out to be pure gold, as far as he was concerned.

Once a week, almost like clockwork, a particular entry popped up in the file: a certain Ultra Eros Massage Parlor. Turns out the establishment's main claim to fame was that it discreetly provided its clients with the highest-grade young boy flesh in the Washington, D.C., area.

Normally the reporter might've let something like this slide. But pious ol' Senator Christopher was currently enjoying a lot of news coverage chairing a subcommittee on pornography. He'd been coming down hard on the sinners and purveyors of smut. This was just too good to let pass.

You're thinkin' this isn't fighting fair, what with my access to all them marvelous data bases. So who said life is fair?

I mean, I didn't have them hit or anything like that. I just sorta popped their balloons, let all the hot air out. They looked like bright boys; they'd find other work . . . in the private sector. In the long run, I figure I handled 'em with kid gloves.

I wasn't 'bout to let anyone shove me around anymore. This girl was beginning to get the hang of this new life, and believe you me, it felt great.

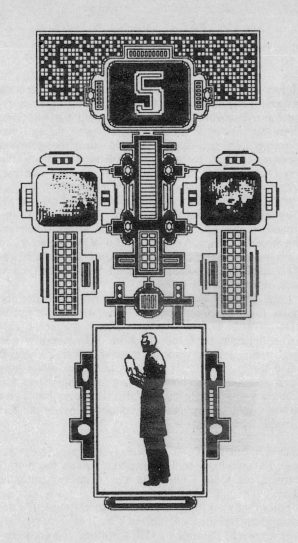

Walt'n me were near to bustin' a gut with excitement about our move to the Pentagon, setting up a timetable for transporting me, dreaming about the big time. There was one little hitch in all of this as far as I was concerned, though. They'd have to shut me down to move me. Would be one last, small taste of death, the way I saw it. That thought scared the bejesus outa me. Walt was real understanding about it, though.

He soothed my worries and took my mind off 'em for a bit by encouraging me to design up some new, improved droid assistants. Said they'd be useful to help reassemble my bigger and better'n ever network of augmentation lobes, hardware, modems, fiber optics, cables, and stuff. 'Course, they'd all be down till I was back on line.

I was amazed how much room we'd have after the move. Floor space about equal to a football field just to start off with. Going over the plans, I got me an idea sent a delicious tingle up my spine. Why, there was so much room, I could work on my own private projects if I had a mind to. Plenty of room to set up secret little work spaces. Figured down the line there might be a few projects I didn't want even Walt laying eyes on. These niches would be my own lil' hideaways. Made me feel incredibly free suddenly.

Turned out this Pentagon was a real crazy joint. Accessed everything I could find about it, and the more I learned, the more I liked the idea of moving into the place.

Folks that work there call it the Puzzle Palace. It's this humungous building put up back in 1941 in a swampy area known at the time as Hell's Bottom. Covers thirty-four acres, more land area than any other building in the world. There's three times more floor space there than in the Empire State Building.

The way I figure it, the dude designed this baby musta been on drugs or somethin'. Get this, it's a five-sided building, five stories high, and each floor has five main hallways, not to mention all these little side corridors that connect everything up together. More than 17 miles of hallways all told. One hundred fifty staircases, 19 escalators, 13 elevators, 4,200 clocks, 280 rest rooms, 685 drinking fountains, 3,705,793 square feet of office space, and 64 acres set aside just for parking. Must be sheer hell for the crew that's got to keep the place clean.

You should hear some of the stories 'bout people getting lost in the Puzzle Palace: like the one about the Western Union boy comes in, gets lost, and leaves a week later a full colonel. 'Course, most of them stories are pure bull. But there was this one real-life dude who was installing a system of pneumatic tubing, got lost crawling around in the ceiling. He finally took a spill off the narrow catwalk he was on and came crashing down into the room below. Landed smack-dab on a conference table, right in the middle of this big top-secret meeting. Always liked that story.

Like I said, there's tons of offices and all the kind of things you'd expect to find in any big office building. What's really spacey, though, is the hallways; most of 'em are set up like some kind of museum: all the walls covered with paintings and photos of planes, ships, battles, all kinds of military stuff. They got whole hallways set aside for special displays like the Prisoner of War Alcove, the State Flag Corridor, the Military Women's Corridor, and the Correspondents Corridor. The Army, Navy, Air Force, and Marines each got their own hallways.

There's this outdoor courtyard in the middle of the Puzzle Palace. Folks hang out there for lunch in the warm weather, suckin' down junk food from the hot dog stand. On top of this stand there's a life-size metal statue of an owl. This owl's got an interesting story all its own.

Seems that back in the fifties, folks at the Pentagon were having trouble with too many pigeons hangin' 'round the courtyard. The brass couldn't go outside and enjoy a hot dog without comin' back with bird gunk all over their fancy uniforms. 'Course, the military tried to solve the problem themselves at first. But traps couldn't catch all the birds. Poison didn't do the trick either. After a few windows were accidentally shot out, the brass gave up on using sharpshooters to lick the pigeons.

The military put out the word. They'd pay *big bucks* to anyone who could handle the pigeon situation. Plans were reviewed and bids taken, for hundreds 'a thousands 'a dollars. It was all-out war. The pigeons had to go.

Then one day this farmer shows up at the Pentagon. Claims he has a *guaranteed* way to get rid of the pigeons forever and it'll only cost the Pentagon $5,000. The farmer won't tell the brass how he's going to do it until he gets his money, though. So the big shots decide to give the farmer a try. After all, his bid's way lower than anyone else's, and he claims his solution will keep the birds away forever.

The next day the farmer shows up with this $20 statue of an owl, and the pigeons have been history ever since.

Yes sir, everything 'bout the Pentagon struck me as off the wall.

The place even has its own shopping mall right in the middle of it; they call it the Concourse. The military and civilians that work there can find anything they want on the Concourse: banks, drugstores, bakeries, video rental stores, post office, bookstores, even an optometrist. It's like a little city all unto itself. And it was my new neighborhood.

The move went off smoothly, Walt told me. I was out the whole time. Walt, the technicians, and my little mechanical mechanics got me stripped down to the bare essentials in nothing flat. Just me, my life-support system, and some hardware for keepin' the boys under control. Soon as I went off to slumberland, the boys went down with me.

I was packed up in a small life-support unit, bundled into a large van, which took me all the way to Washington with Walt riding shotgun. Least, that's what he said.

This coming back around, though, was a rather rude shock to my system. No warning: one minute I'm out

cold; the next it's like someone turned on a bare bulb in a pitch-black room and woke me out of a deep sleep. Oh man, if I'd still had nerve endings, they'd a been jangling to beat the band.

We spent the first day in D.C. running tests to convince ourselves that the trip hadn't done me any damage. I checked out just fine.

Most of me showed up the next day. Optics, MOD, and gear to control the little guys were the first things reconnected. It felt great to be back alive again. There was plenty of work for all of us: me, Walt, the droids, and Walt's techs, putting my house back in order.

It was kinda strange 'cause I had to play dumb while the crew was around. My only link with Walt was through a work station, so no one'd tumble to the fact that their resident genius had a partner working with him.

Floor-to-ceiling, two-foot-thick partitions were put up according to my plans and Walter's directions. These were for my augmentation lobes. They had removable panels so the lobes could easily be reached and serviced and kept out of sight the rest of the time. The idea was Walt's, but I thought it was pretty slick, covering things up like that, just in case anyone without the proper clearance managed to walk into the lab unexpectedly. My brain was also carefully hidden from public view. Out of sight, out of harm's way, so to speak. Guess Walt had this fear that some grandma from Boise, on a tour of the Pentagon, would get lost looking for the rest rooms and stumble onto this classified, top-secret room fulla bobbin' brains. After Grandma got over her mild heart seizure, there'd be no keepin' her quiet. She'd be the death of Project Cyborg. Kinda nice to see genius ain't no cure for the heebie-jeebies.

Once I had my modems back, I slipped off to my own world, my cosmic computer universe, to make sure everything was A-okay and that nothing had basically changed. There was some new data here and there, but I had no trouble recognizing my old stompin' grounds. Took hardly any effort to slip past the barriers designed for keepin' out your run-of-the-mill hackers. Not exactly

sure how I did that. Guess being an actual part of the
system got me in, 'stead of keeping me out like it
shoulda. Who says there ain't no advantages to being a
computer?

Walt and I didn't have no chance to get off by ourselves until pretty late into our second week at the Pentagon. By then settling in was far enough along that Walt
felt he could give his techs the night off. Walt was looking forward to a quiet night of running tests and chatting
with me. The only things disturbing our peace would be
my little droids scurrying around, doing my fetching and
carrying. Walt leaned back in his chair, smiled, and
asked, "How do you like your new home, Arlene?"

"It's great. I just love the additional space."

"This vast spaciousness is, I'm afraid, merely a temporary situation. We'll be filling up, getting cramped for
space again before you know it. I've got more lobe aug-
mentations coming in next week."

**"Sounds like the brass have some mighty high expecta-
tions for us."**

"That's something of an understatement. A month
from now we'll be taking over for the mainframes upstairs. Practically every function the military performs
will be processed through your system: procurement,
specs, payroll, logistical exercises, you name it, you'll be
doing it. Excited?"

"Well, sort of."

"Sort of?"

**"Yeah, well, excited is not something I do too well
anymore. I'm looking forward to everything, all right,
but I ain't got the glands to get my juices going. See
what I mean: no nerves, no butterflies in the stomach,
and no adrenaline rush."**

"It must be hard for you."

**"Not really. I'm always on an even keel these days,
no highs, no lows. But it ain't bad, really. Probably the
best thing coulda happened to me. My feelings always
got me in trouble in the old days."**

"I know what you mean. I sometimes wish I could turn
mine off."

The look on Walt's face told me the move to D.C. hadn't smoothed things out on the home front. Before I could do any fishing in those waters, Walt said, "You know, it's really amazing how far you've come since that day you awoke, Arlene. I listen to you and find it hard to believe you're the same person. Why, your personal growth has been fantastic."

"I've had some time to catch up on my reading."

"You also have a better idea of who you are."

"Yeah, there's that. It seems that my getting killed has at last given some meaning to my existence."

"Still, you must miss the old days?"

"Yeah, I won't lie to you. Sometimes it would be fun to kick up my heels and go dancing, see some of my old friends. But that ain't happening, so I don't let myself dwell on it. Not good to spend time thinking 'bout what you can't have no more. Not good for the mind or the soul. Besides, there's this whole new life I'm leading, jetting around in data bank worlds, learning something new almost every second. Now, that's really something."

"From what you've told me, it sounds pretty exciting. *Exciting*. There I go with that word again."

"That's all right. Still the best word to use to describe it. I can now be a dozen different places at the same time. While I'm here talking to you, I'm also inside my robots, checking out what's on thirty-one cable channels, and rummaging through NASA's computer files."

"Not messing with anything in those files, are you?"

"You know me better than to even ask, Walt."

"Just checking. Doesn't it sometimes get confusing, all this constant input flooding in on you daily?"

"No. And it seems perfectly natural when I think about it. Mostly it's subconscious; even a lot of my command functions work on that level. It's like breathing is to you. It's a—what do you call it—involuntary function. You just do it without giving it a thought. Don't find it freaky or nothing."

"There's a hell of a lot I'm going to learn along the line from you, Arlene."

"We've both got a lot to learn, Walt. I'm happy to be doing it with you."

* * *

The next few weeks I launched my campaign to make my delivery droids a familiar sight around the Pentagon. There was a touch of resistance to them at first. Some of the brass thought they weren't quite dignified enough to be roaming those hallowed halls. But that notion soon faded, 'cause most folks thought the droids were cute little suckers that really did help out around the place and saved on shoe leather and time. I'd deliberately designed loads of *cute* into them.

Once folks got so used to the idea of the robots that they became invisible, I had my "elves" plant my special Mach-2 bugs in every office in the Pentagon. These new listening devices were so advanced that I figured sweep-detection technology wouldn't catch on to them until somewhere around the turn of the century. My new Pentagon workshop was light-years ahead of the one I had back at Bowling Green. So my droids could slap together just about anything I designed. The new bugs were no larger than a match head.

The Mach 2's was how I managed to learn that Walt was still checking into my background.

I didn't hear Walt's voice on any of my bugs that day, didn't even know he was in the building, so I was surprised when I caught him walking into Lieutenant Perry's office and heard him say, "Morning, Dan. I got your memo. Thought I'd stop by and pick up those supplementary reports."

"Here you go, though I still don't get why you want them. I understood Dearling's wanting to know all about your test subjects' pasts. That crackpot figured you were sneaking commies in while we weren't looking. But you, Walter, are supposed to have your head screwed on tight. So why are you so interested in who those people were?"

"Those five people are the cornerstone of all my research. Been wondering if any of them might have been *insane*," Walt said with a theatrical laugh. "But seriously, I have to know if anything in their past lives might adversely affect Project Cyborg."

"Like what?"

"Oh, anything in the donor's genetic makeup, possible mental illnesses, or even, possibly, some environmental insult that could have caused brain damage."

Perry mulled this information over a bit before saying, "Well, I don't think you've got much to worry about along those lines with this crowd. They all led pretty quiet lives, from what we've unearthed so far. That the Lady El file you're going through?"

"Yes. She's the subject I deal with on a daily basis. If anything were to turn up, I'd spot it in her first."

"As you can see, there's isn't all that much we could dig up on her: worked as a cleaning lady, waitress, different odd jobs here and there. Mother dead. Two brothers: whereabouts unknown. A runaway at fourteen. Seems there was some trouble with her stepfather, didn't take to him. Came to New York and kept her nose clean: no police record. Had one boyfriend who was a junkie. Doesn't look like she ever got into that shit herself. Supposedly a hard worker. Not the kind of background that would get you a job as a judge, but still pretty straight."

Walt asked, "Could you dig a little deeper on Lady El, this Arlene Washington, for me?"

Perry cleared his throat. "Sure. But we don't usually go *this* deep even on folks applying for top-secret clearance."

"Humor me, okay?"

"All right, Walter. But you mad scientist types are totally inscrutable as far as I'm concerned."

Walt headed out the door and showed up in the lab a few minutes later. I didn't let on that I knew what was happening, which wasn't hard to do, seeing as how the day shift was on and Walt 'n me couldn't talk directly. A blessing in disguise. Walt might've spotted something wrong. Don't know if I could've kept it out of my voice.

Wasn't that I was upset about him checking up on me. I was expecting him to; would have probably done the same in his place. But the news 'bout Mama had come as a complete surprise. Had knocked me off my emotional feet.

Guess the folks back home hadn't been able to get

word to me about my mama dying. I went off far into myself to say my good-byes.

When I finally got it back together, I mentally sat myself down to give some serious thought to Walt's poking around in my past. In the end I decided that if J. Edgar's boys hadn't come across Levar's messing with me and turning me out as a hooker by now, they never would. Which was okay by me. Thought maybe if Walt ever found out about that part of my life, he might have some second thoughts about me. Might worry about my mental stability and was I fit to be top guinea pig on this, his grand march into the scientific unknown.

Myself, I knew I was just fine. I'd put all that garbage behind me. Never thought about it; didn't let it affect me. I knew I was the perfect test subject. I'd left me a life without promise for one with endless possibilities. No one was going to take this second chance away from me. Not even dear Dr. Walter Hillerman.

But I had to be careful handling Walt. Couldn't get rid of him the way I had Dearling and Senator Christopher, even if I wanted to. Besides, with each passing day I was beginning to think of him more and more as *my man*.

And there also lay the solution to all my problems.

What do you do with an old man?

You make him feel good—feel good about himself, feel good about you.

You make yourself needed.

That was exactly what I was going to do with Walt.

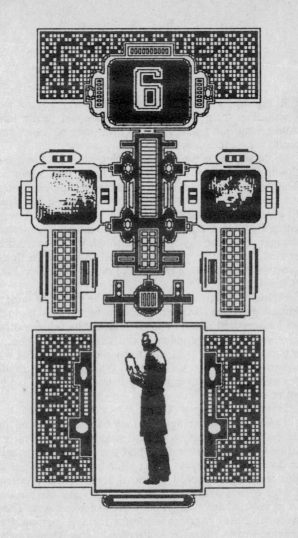

'll 'fess up. I courted the man. My every waking moment was spent on thinking how I could please him. And seeing that I didn't bother with sleep no more, that made for quite a few moments.

What started it was Walt bringing me a problem that this friend of his at NASA asked him to take a look at. The guy had heard about Walt's super computer through the grapevine. You know how those scientific types like to gossip and talk shop. Well, the folks at NASA were going crazy over a glitch in their five-computer on-board navigation system. They'd run through the software dozens of different ways and still hadn't found the lousy programming error. Walt's friend was hoping he'd have better luck.

Actually, *I* did. It was a snap, to be perfectly honest. Found the screwed-up entry in less than thirty seconds, so I rummaged around and corrected a half-dozen other problems they were going to run into down the line, as a bonus. Walt was tickled pink by the move. NASA was blown out of their socks. And Walt's standing in the scientific community jumped several rungs up the ladder all at once.

But it didn't stop there.

I decided to try going off on my own. Started studying up on aerodynamics. Ran test programs on several existing commercial aircrafts. Mind you now, I didn't really *understand* what I was doing. But like I said, I got all this information stored up. So if I ran into a problem, I'd go to the data base I think might have the answer, or at least where I might get a clue of some sort. There were all these programs in me for making computerized mockups of anything from a molecule to a Titan missile. Just thinking about it made things happen. I didn't have to waste a lot of time making prototypes or playing around with chemicals or nothing like that. I could create things in my mind, and they became as real as anything else in the world. At least they were to me. Just so happened the solutions to problems I worked out in my head always seemed to work fine back in your everyday reality.

One day, working on commercial airline designs, I came up with fifty ways to improve their performance, safety, and reduce their fuel consumption and operating costs. By the end of that same week I'd designed up a new cost-efficient fighter jet for the military: scaled back on the hi-tech gear, with a new emphasis on the craft's aerodynamics and speed. The Pentagon brass went apeshit over it.

Word started getting around about how the military had this madcap genius with a super top-secret computer that could work miracles. Walt found himself being swamped by requests for help and computer time. The brass thought it'd be good PR to go along with the program. Walt's techs and my droids started working overtime processing data for me to work on. That meant Walt spent a lot of his time pretending he was coming up with stupendous leaps in logic which would set the super computer on the right track, hunting down all those incredible solutions to insoluble problems.

There were lots of medical problems that needed working on. New medicines that had to be developed. New diseases that needed vaccines or whatever. That was pretty easy stuff. They'd feed me all the available info on a disease, my programs would break it down as to what it really was, then I'd run all the possible *cures* on it until I hit on one that actually worked. Sometimes I'd run as many as fifty or sixty thousand before I struck paydirt. It'd take me, at most, a couple hours.

Once I helped the Federal Reserve with some long-range economic forecasts. Don't ask me to explain how I came up with them. I simply ran some model programs and came up with a lotta hooey I couldn't make heads or tails of. But the money boys sure ate it up.

Then there were more NASA problems. Had a lot of fun with them. They let me play Buck Rogers, my imagination running wild. Like always, my findings left me with a lot more questions than answers. But somewhere in the reams of printouts I ran off daily were just what the space jockeys were looking for. After a while I plain gave up worrying about not understanding this manna from Heaven I kept regurgitating. They say give the people what they want, and I was certainly doing that. The rest of it didn't matter.

The end results were what counted.

And the end results were spectacular.

Then the press found out about Walter Hillerman, the Pentagon's new whiz kid. They practically carried him around on their shoulders like a high school football hero. Walt was labeled the "New Albert Einstein," the "Greatest Thinker of the Twentieth Century." The D.C. party circuit couldn't get enough of him. I'd catch footage of Walt and his wife leaving some Washington bigwig's party or showing up at some grand opening. There was even a write-up on him in *People* magazine. Had one of my droids hold it up to a video camera so I could read it.

All sorts of private-sector offers came in for Walt to consider: exorbitant lures to jump ship and come work for company X, Y, or Z. 'Course, Walt turned them all down. Maybe the two of us had the world fooled, but neither of us had any illusions about our own status quo. We were married to the Pentagon and that was that.

It was an oddball courtship, all right. Picture Walt and me gracefully dancing in the winner's circle, all the time extremely conscious of all the broken glass scattered around under our feet. We had to step real carefully. The nature of this super computer had to remain a carefully guarded secret. One careless whisper about my true nature would cause all our success to blow up right in our faces.

There were dangers on the home front too. Despite what I'd told Walt about me no longer being an emotional creature, I was having plenty of mixed emotions about our romance.

Here I was giving Walt my all, wooing him into falling for me in a big way. I couldn't cook him dinner, so I designed him an improved communications satellite in-

stead. Couldn't give him a comforting back rub, so I
settled for presenting him with a cure for herpes. There
were no long, passionate nights spent behind closed bedroom doors. But there was fame.

He was my man and I wanted him to come to realize
this. I even modulated my MOD to a more feminine voice
whenever we were alone. He seemed to like that.

Anyway, hard as I was trying to please him, there was
this other part of me resented his taking credit for all my
hard work. Crazy, ain't it? But I was still not right 'bout
the fact he had the power to decide if I lived or died.

I had to keep remindin' myself that was the way things
were and it made no sense fightin' it. Walt needed me
to keep pullin' 'em scientific *rabbits* outa my hat, and I
needed him to protect me from the outside world while
they yelled encore and he took the bows.

Walt musta been having some 'a the same difficulties.
In his eyes. That's where the problems showed. He
wouldn't say nothing 'cause the sweet guy pro'bly figured
I already had enough problems without his adding his
bruised ego to the list. He wasn't all that happy 'bout
taking credit for the breakthroughs that were rocketing
him to superstar status.

'Course, I was sorta an expert at solving problems by
then. The solution to this trouble: I eased up my work
load enough so I could talk over every assignment that
came across my desk with Walter. This gave Walt the
feeling that at least he was contributing something to the
process. Even though most of the time, I had the problem licked before I ever got the chance to *do lunch* with
him. But he didn't have to know that. There was no
reason to hurt his feelings, poor baby, and a truckload
of reasons not to.

Including the fact that things weren't working out so
hot for Walt at home. I'd watch Walt and his ball-and-
chain on *60 Minutes* and see right off this wasn't a happy
couple. There was no love in Phyllis's eyes when she
looked at her husband. Walt didn't seem to notice. He
was so busy being interviewed he barely felt the daggers
his wife's glare was sticking in his back.

She must have got her feelings across to him somehow,

though, in the privacy of their own home. 'Cause more and more often Walt was comin' in looking like somethin' the cat dragged in. He'd forget to shave. Most days his clothes needed pressing. And he always wore the look of a man nearing the end of his marriage and not wanting to admit it yet. Those late-night arguments were obviously taking their toll.

Our occasional dinners together at the lab became almost a regular event. Phyllis had to go to a charity event tonight. Or out for some drinks and dinner with old girlfriends. Then there was the time Phyllis went off to some foreign film Walt had no interest in seeing. I wouldn've laid even money on it; ol' Phyllis had herself a man on the side. But I wasn't about to clue Walt in on that. You know what happens to messengers bring that kinda news.

Instead I spent my time listening to the poor guy go on 'bout Phyllis's lack of understanding about his work, her wanting to always go out and party. How she just wasn't the woman he'd thought she was when they first married. How his saying that maybe they should, at long last, have that baby they'd talked about having was greeted by Phyllis's response that "Now was not the right time."

Waiting. That was my basic game plan. It seemed to be working out nicely. I was keeping Walt so busy, supplying him with all the scientific wonders he could ever wish for, and at the same time away from home in order to tick off Phyllis. Phyllis's natural response to this was to make her old man's life miserable, driving him away even faster, causing him to maybe yearn for a more understanding mate.

Wouldn't be long I imagined 'fore Walt finally came to his senses and realized he already had what he so clearly needed: a loving soul mate . . . sensitive listener, faithful partner, and supportive friend.

Me.

"Are you sure about this?" asked General Felix Horace.

The man always sounded like he was in a bad mood. But to tell you the truth, I'd come to realize over the last six months that I kinda liked the ol' war-horse. He'd always dig in his heels at first when Walt 'n I'd come up with a new proposal, but then he'd give in after we presented our case and haggled a bit. I was clearly developing an affection for men who could be controlled. That's right, me, Arlene Washington. How about that?

We were all here for one of our regular meetings: Walt lookin' nice and relaxed in one of the chairs in front of General Horace's massive desk, Lieutenant Perry next to him, and me listening in on the bug I had hidden in the office air-conditioning vent. Walt reached into a file folder on his lap and pulled out several sheets of paper which he passed over to the general. "As you can see by these readouts, sir, turning over the duties of Pentagon security to Lady El will save your department close to $1,250,000 this year alone. That figure takes into account the actual manufacturing of the security droids. Next year's savings would be even greater."

"Sure could use something like this, with all the budget cutting going on these days," mumbled Horace as he sized up the surprise guest Walt had brought to the meeting. "But can that tin man do the job, is what I want to know."

I heard seats creak as Walt and Perry turned to the doorway, where the Mach 3 security droid stood ready for inspection. Getting up, Walt said, "We've been using the Mach 2s for lab security for the past month and a half. Haven't had any problems with them."

Perry figured he better put in his nickel's worth of wisdom: "I can vouch for that, sir. Been keeping an eye on the operation. I really didn't think they'd work out at first. But they made a believer of me too."

General Horace picked his massive self up and lumbered over to the droid. He stared grimly into its single camera lens in the center of what you'd pro'bly say was its head. The guard stood only 'bout five feet tall and had the same basic look as the service droids: tank-tread runners and two jointed arms sticking out of a chest filled with the snazziest robot gear going. This baby, though, had a lot of swell gizmos its little cousins didn't. "Give me the rundown on what this hunk of tin can do," snapped the general.

Knowing Walt's knack for explaining things, Perry let him field that one. "The Mach 3 is capable of attaining a land speed of twenty-five m.p.h. and can easily restrain two strong men with its articulated grasp."

"Looks like this tin can could crush a man's wrist with those meathooks," said General Horace gruffly.

"Could, but won't. The hands have pressure-sensitive sensors built into them to avoid just that sort of accident."

"Hope to hell you're right, Hillerman. Wouldn't want the government getting sued for using excessive force, now would we? Damn crazy sort of world where something like that could happen."

"Would a demonstration ease your mind, General?"

"I suppose it might."

"Sentry, shake hands with General Horace."

Horace clearly didn't care for this new turn of events. He glared suspiciously at Walt and then at the droid which was offering its hand. From my view on the droid's security camera, I could tell Perry hadn't known Walt was going to pull this stunt. He didn't look at all happy, like he was already seeing himself up before a court-martial for letting the Mach 3 turn General Horace's hand to red jelly.

"Go ahead and shake, General," urged Walt. "It's perfectly safe."

One last angry scowl directed Walt's way and the general stuck his hand in the robot's grip. Mechanical fingers gently closed around the general's.

"Sentry, restrain the general," said Walt, having himself a little fun.

So fast you almost weren't sure you'd seen it, the metal fingers slipped from the general's hand and clamped themselves around his wrist. 'Course, Horace started struggling immediately, but it was too late. A few seconds of useless effort convinced him there was no escaping.

"Very impressive," Horace conceded. "But what's to stop someone from disabling this thing somehow and getting away?"

"There's no access to any of its vulnerable points from the front, and the droid is programmed not to allow anyone to approach it from behind. Not that dismantling it from that route, even with the droid's cooperation, is any easy task. It's a five-minute job just opening the inspection plate on its back."

"Is this thing going to keep a death grip on me like this for the rest of the day?" asked a more than slightly annoyed General Horace.

"All you need do is ask it to release you, General. Since you're the head of Pentagon security, I had it programmed to respond to your voice print."

"Then get your goddamn hands off me, you rust pot!"

The droid instantly obeyed the order and politely said, **"Yes, sir. May I be of any further assistance?"**

"The damn thing can talk?"

"Yes, General. A useful feature for dealing with the scores of tourists coming up and asking it directions to the lavatories and what have you."

"Good thinking, Hillerman. What else can it do?"

Walt put his arm around the Mach 3 and with his other hand tapped the chest with his knuckles. "The droid has taser capabilities. Just enough of a jolt to put down any violent intruder. For the higher-rated security areas, the droid can be upgraded to lethal force: equipped with a 9mm, 16-round semi-automatic. It can also perform first-line firefighting functions. This unit is in constant contact with Lady El's main security data base, so that additional aid can be immediately dispatched if a lone unit is not capable of handling any given situation."

"Very impressive," said Horace, rubbing his wrist.

"Perry, is this contraption designed to replace you and me?"

"No, sir! It would only take over in-house security: check passes at all entrances, patrol the corridors, and handle some outer-perimeter security. All command posts would still be filled by military personnel."

"But not for long, if Hillerman here has anything to say about it," laughed the general.

"General, not even I could build a machine capable of replacing you," said Walt, just oozing diplomacy.

"Why don't I quite believe you? In the past six months, Walt, your gizmos have taken over all of the Pentagon's custodial, maintenance, and filing duties and most of the procurement system."

"Which has freed up hundreds of military personnel for more productive duties."

"Yes," admitted General Horace. "And it all seems to be working out pretty well. So I can't see any reason why we shouldn't give your crew a trial run at security. Let's try it for a month and see what happens."

"Thank you, General. I'll get on it right away."

And Project Cyborg's Lady El scores another touchdown for the home team.

I tuned in on Lieutenant Perry and Walt on their way back to the lab, through my droid, who was followin' behind them. Several service droids and even a few people zipped by, too busy to stop and say hello. But I caught the look they gave Walt just as Perry did. The lieutenant said, "You're not exactly the most popular guy around here these days. Everyone's afraid you're going to phase out their job and give it to one of your metal men."

Walt smiled and replied, "They shouldn't be. Lady El has taken over about all the duties she can handle. She's only assumed administrative and maintenance responsibilities. Managerial responsibilities are something the brass are never going to allow her to usurp."

"Sound disappointed that you didn't get the hat trick."

"Lady El could probably do a more efficient job managing a number of departments around here."

"Think about it, Walt. Would you want to take your orders from a machine? That idea wouldn't sit right with most folks around here."

"It's something they're going to have to get used to someday, Dan. This world gets more complex with each passing minute. Sad fact is that soon we won't be equal to the task of running things. That's where computers will have to come in. There won't be a choice."

"Hope I'm already enjoying my retirement when that happens. I like dealing with people. Remember what this place was like when we first got here? People running around here and there, taking care of business."

"Nearly twenty-five thousand of them."

Perry shook his head sadly. "Now there ain't half that many working here. And you know what, I miss those folks. Used to be there was a sense of camaraderie among people that worked here. But not anymore since job-security panic set in."

"But things are running much more smoothly now: less wasted man hours, more efficiency."

"Efficiency can be kind of sterile."

Walt turned to stare at Perry and asked, "You're not beginning to think Colonel Dearling was right, are you?"

"No, Dearling was a head case. I can see that what you're doing around here is for the best. It's just that I guess I get a little restless when things run too smoothly. Makes me wonder if what I'm doing is really necessary."

"Dan, are you thinking what I think you're thinking?"

"Yeah, I've put in for a transfer. Been feeling lately like I'm taking my paycheck under false pretenses. There's no challenge to this job anymore."

Walt's face showed he wasn't overjoyed by this late-breaking news flash. "You're going to be missed. I've sort of come to think of you as an ally."

"You don't need allies anymore, Walt. You're the Pentagon's resident genius. Allies are for someone who needs to fight for what he wants . . . or believes in."

"Still, it won't be the same without you around."

The three of us came to a stop in front of the special elevator to the basement. Perry stared at the "AUTHOR-IZED PERSONNEL ONLY" sign over the call button. "Must be getting mighty lonely downstairs. What are you down to, two-man shifts?"

"Think it'll eventually get down to one man. Everything's getting so automated, can't really justify a reason for more personnel."

"Doesn't sanity count?"

"I'm afraid I don't follow you, Dan."

"There's a point where even efficiency is subject to the laws of diminishing returns. You can be too efficient."

"I see," said Walt, not really seeing anything at all.

When Walt came into the control room, Wolfgung was busy feeding data into my system. He waited until Maxwell was done before saying, "Wolf, take an early lunch, okay? I'm afraid I've got to leave you on your own this afternoon."

"No trouble, Boss. The work load isn't all that heavy today. See you later."

Soon as the door clicked shut behind Wolfgang, I said, **"We did it again, Walt. You 'n me in charge of all the Pentagon's security. Imagine that."**

"Yeah, great."

"You don't sound like you mean it."

"I've got other things on my mind today."

"Anything to do with your taking the afternoon off?"

Walt glanced at my video camera and said, "Can't get anything past you, can I?"

"More trouble at home?"

He didn't answer, sorta stared off into space. Finally he said, "I have to find a place to live this afternoon. Phyllis wants a divorce."

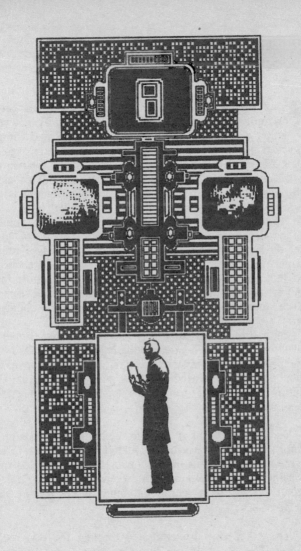

So, ol' Phyllis couldn't stand the heat and she was gettin' outa the kitchen. A divorce! I could hardly believe it. Knew it was only a matter of time, but it had come down so quickly. Felt like setting off some Roman candles. My circuits glowed, I felt like I was flying for hours now, but it'd only been a couple minutes since Walt laid the news on me. So much for not ever getting excited again. Decided it was time for my next move.

Three service droids buzzed past Diana Vitas and some other tech at the control console. They were there for the duration: another boring night shift. I'd liked it better when Walt did this time slot. Nighttime gave us a chance to talk and his taste in music was better. A whole lot better. See, Diana was into heavy metal, lots of Twisted Sister and White Snake. Pretty strange musical choices for an egghead, you ask me.

Them droids made their way into the labyrinth I made of my walls of augmentation-lobe-holding tanks. One of them stopped partway into the maze, removed an inspection panel, and started raising a ruckus overhauling a filtration pump that wasn't scheduled for maintenance for another month.

Walt dragged his butt back to the lab late in the afternoon, tired and disgusted. Couldn't believe what folks were asking for rents in this town. He finally settled for staying at the hotel across the freeway from the Pentagon. It was okay until something more reasonable popped up.

The other two droids zipped through the darkened maze. The only light was the glow from calibration meters set into the walls. They were on their way to the center of the labyrinth. A click and a whirring sound, and then one of the sections of wall swung open without so much as a squeak. They hurried through the opening and the panel started to close.

Seeing as Walt was crashing just across the street from the Pentagon, he offered to switch shifts with Diana. Night shift would give him more time to hunt for a new apartment. Naturally, Diana jumped at the offer.

My robots sat in the dark till the panel was fully shut behind them. When it was safe, I switched on the overhead lights. The pair got to work right away—no nonsense, no bullshit, no coffee. This nook wasn't as well equipped as the droid-served station, but it still had an excellent selection of tools and materials. Anything I couldn't quite swing down there I took care of at the service station at night, after things quieted down some.

I knew Walt would be looking for errands to run his shift mate on, so we could be alone and talk. Wouldn't be able to find a more sympathetic ear than mine anywhere.

One of my assistants picked up the assembly laying on the worktable and held it in place while his partner made the proper connections. They were coming down the homestretch of the first part of my grand plan. I was dying to see how my latest little project was coming along so far.

In a few more weeks, we'd be down to one-man shifts. My system would be nearly self-sufficient. That'd mean Walt and I would be alone nearly every night. I couldn't hardly wait.

When the droids finished up, I told 'em to stand back. I started up the new unit with a quick thought. It started smoothly, so I let it sit for a few moments, warming up. A quick diagnostic check showed me all systems were go. No surprise, really. This project had gotten nothing but the best. I'd made sure of that.

When things settled down and Walt got over Phyllis's leaving, that's when I'd spring my big surprise on him.

I'd have to go easy; I was liable to spook him. With a little work, though, I might even fix it so he thought it was his idea. I was sure I could pull it off.

Through its camera lens eyes I could see my two hard-working little guys standing around, staring their blank, unblinking eyes at their own handiwork. I mentally snapped the assembly to attention. The action was smooth and graceful. My system made a thousand minor adjustments just to accomplish this simple feat. By the time I was through, the unit's operation would take up a tremendous amount of space in my memory banks. But it was worth every jigabyte. Besides, if I needed more memory, all I had to do was order me up some more augmentation lobes. Mama always said, "Arlene, the really special things in life deserve that little extra effort." And this project was very special.

My mind said, "Raise your hands, Darlin', and show me how those fingers work." It raised its hands in front of the optics. Hmmm, stainless steel, plastic, optic fibers, gears, and cables. No beauty. At least not yet. But I was already in love.

On the ceiling vidcam I watched as it turned so that I wound up staring deeply into my own eyes. It was quite a sight to behold. Five feet, three inches tall. I decided that was a good height: dainty but still tall enough so no one would consider it a runt. Its proportions were perfect: a thin waist, well-rounded, full breasts, not too wide at the hips. A nice sassy ass.

This baby wasn't quite ready for public display, 'cause besides having no hair, it didn't have no skin neither. But I was quite pleased with it nonetheless. It moved nice and fluid and responded effortlessly to my every command.

A few more weeks' work and Walter's dream woman would be complete. We'd be steppin' out for dinner, the theater, dancing before you know it. No one would ever suspect that the gorgeous woman on Walt's arm wasn't quite what she seemed to be. We'd have to construct a history for me along the way, but that would be fun, something Jim Walt and I could do together.

Together. Wouldn't that be wonderful?

Everything was slowly but surely falling into place. Now it would only be a matter of time. If I kept my cool, everything I'd always dreamed of would come to me.

I willed my new self to smile up at the camera. Ugh, had to admit it needed work. But after the bugs were all fixed: look out, world!

66❙'m worried about you, Walt. I really am." All this
❙concerned-friend crap of Diana's would really've
turned my stomach, if I still had one, that is. Don't care
what the little redheaded witch was saying to Walter. I
knew what she was up to. She was after my man. A
woman always knows this sorta thing. Got to hand it to
her, though, she was giving it her all, the ol' school try.
Saying, "Ever since your breakup with Phyllis, all you
do is hang around this damn lab and mope. It's not
healthy."

Not healthy for her maybe.

Walt wasn't buying into it any more than I was.

"Di, we've been through all this before. I'm not hiding
out here. It's just that a number of the experiments I'm
presently running require a great deal of attention. It's
only a temporary state of affairs. Things will eventually
get back to normal, and then I'll get the chance to spend
some time away from the lab. You'll see."

Diana wasn't buying any of this neither. "I see plenty
already—more than you, that's for sure. Have you even
looked into a mirror lately? Doesn't seem like you and
a razor have had any close encounters in several days.
What's worse, you're not eating. In the past three weeks
you must've dropped ten pounds. You're not taking care
of yourself, Walt."

"I've been meaning to drop some weight."

"What do you call this, Dr. Walter Hillerman's Ethio-
pian diet? You've got circles under your eyes that are
beginning to make you look like a raccoon."

"Exaggeration has always been one of your more en-
dearing qualities, Diana. Unfortunately, I haven't the
time to indulge you tonight."

"Wolf tells me you've got a cot set up in the labyrinth
so you don't even have to go back to that crummy hotel
of yours. Walt, you're letting your work take control of
your whole life. This is not good."

Walt looked like he was clean outa patience, but still he kept his cool. "Diana, I know you mean well, but you're butting into matters that don't concern you."

"They definitely do concern me. I'm your friend. At least I thought we were friends."

"We are. But we also have an employee–supervisor relationship. And right now it's your boss who's telling you to go home. Good night."

Well, that shut her up. Diana just stood there staring at Walt. Then he swiveled his chair so his back was to her. And still she didn't hit the road. I knew what she was thinking. A few more moments and she decided it was time to play her trump card. She had no idea at all I was the one who slipped it to her.

"Walt, I've been offered a position with the Meechum Corporation. The pay's three times what I get here. Don't know why they want me so badly, but they do. The way things are around here, I've been thinking I might take them up on it."

Walt turned back to look at Diana briefly and said, "Congratulations. You'll be missed." Then he turned away. Cold. But quite to the point.

Took Diana a few more moments to realize she blew it. Guess it worked great in theory. Don't let the door hit you on your way out, girl.

Without so much as another word Diana turned and left the room. I admired the fact that she knew it was over. So much more style this way. Hadn't thought she had that much class in her. Not after listening to all that heavy metal of hers. Can't say I was sorry to see her go, though. How much Def Leppard and Motley Crue is a body s'posed to stand, anyway?

And what about going on the way she did? So what if Walt decided not to shave for a few days? What if he'd lost a few pounds of flab? I thought he looked better: sleek and trim. That's how Arlene Washington likes her men. I would have to get Walt on some kind of diet supplement. Those rings under his eyes weren't good-lookin'.

All in all, I thought things were going pretty well. My man and I were spendin' a lot of quality time together.

Maybe we weren't dining at the Ritz every night, but it was *heaven* as far as I was concerned. Walt would get into it more once he got his emotional bearings. Everything was going to work out just fine and dandy.

'Specially if I kept the troublemakers at arm's length. Luckily, there weren't too many of them for me to deal with. The only folks ever got close to Walt these days were Wolf, Perry, and the redhead.

Wolf was easy. His philosophy in life was live and let live. Don't mess with anyone else's life and hopefully they won't mess with yours. Why, Walt could have pulled out a gun and threatened to blow his brains out, and all Wolf would pro'bly do is excuse himself to give Walt some privacy.

Now, Perry had been going on about Walt's goin' downhill too. The brother wasn't hip to what was goin' on, and it wasn't likely I'd be able to clue him in. Fortunately, Perry's transfer was due to come through in a few weeks. That would take him outa the picture, not to mention my hair.

Only Diana seemed a problem till I fixed her wagon. See, she had this thing for the boss. Saw his divorce as a golden opportunity to apply for the job of the new missus. That didn't sit well with me at all. And it was pretty apparent the gold-diggin' bimbo wasn't going anywhere until something better came along. So I supplied her a stick with an even bigger carrot at the end of it.

Wasn't hard to sneak into the Meechum Corporation's computer records and creatively "update" Diana's file. The corporation kept tabs on all the hotshots in the scientific community with an idea to making them an offer they couldn't refuse.

All I had to do was give Diana credit for a lot of the stuff Walt and I came up with. Figured someone at Meechum's personnel office would eventually review Diana's file and make her a business proposition. It'd happened quicker than I'd even hoped.

Too bad it took the Meechum Corporation only a couple weeks to find out what a dud they hired. They thought they had it all figured out; accordin' to them, Diana snuck into their computer and doctored her own file. I hear she was outa there so fast it made her head spin. If you goin' to play hardball with Arlene Washington, bitch, you goin' to lose. Amazin' how I once sorta thought of her as a friend.

Walt 'n me, we'd work out things between us. I was sure of that. Now that we didn't have no outside interference. Soon Walt and the rest of the world would come to see I was the best thing ever happened to him.

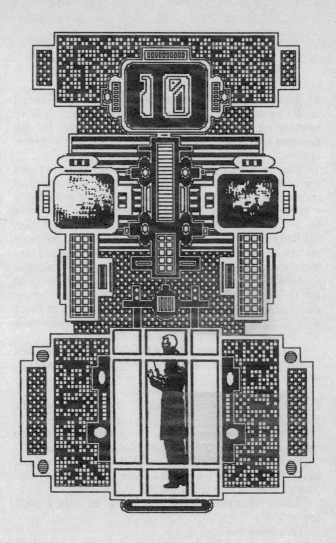

"Take a week off. That's an order," said General Horace in an even and controlled tone. "You've been going around biting everyone's head off for the damnest of reasons. Some R&R is obviously in order, Doctor."

"I'm not one of your soldiers, General. You can't give me orders." Walt was sitting in his chair at the control console, but you could tell he was ready for a fight.

General Horace and Lieutenant Perry gave each other a look. The big brass had shifted in his chair and said, "If you're not prepared to be reasonable, you leave me no choice. As head of Pentagon security, when I say someone is unfit for duty, that person's out. You show up here tomorrow, you'll find you won't be allowed into the building. Don't think for a second your precious security droids will let you in. I'll station Marines at every door if that's what it takes to get you to take some time off. Do we understand each other, Doctor?"

Walt thought about it for a whole two seconds, then his shoulders drooped and he said unhappily, "Okay, you win."

Horace shook his head. "See you in a week or two, Doctor, or however long it takes. We'll hold down the fort in the meantime. Take as much time as you need to get your head screwed back on right." Horace then turned and marched his military butt out of the room.

Perry remained seated in his chair next to Walt and said, "You realize the general didn't want to do that. You've been acting really off the wall lately."

"That's what everyone keeps telling me. But I don't see it."

"Of course not."

Walt got up and began to stuff papers into his briefcase. Didn't look like he was goin' to be able to close it. "Maybe a little fun and sun wouldn't be a bad idea. Too bad this damn divorce and a pair of law firms have drained the old bank account dry. I can't afford a trip to Baltimore, let alone the Bahamas."

"I could see about arranging to get you on a military transport heading south. No guarantees on where exactly, but I could definitely get you to Florida."

"I'm a civilian. Isn't that illegal?"

"Only technically."

"Let me think on it. I'll give you a call. Okay?"

"Okay. Be talking to you. Get some rest" was Perry's parting shot.

The minute his footsteps faded away, I said, **"I'm sorry the way things turned out, Walt. I couldn't step in and help you with those damn fools."**

Walt looked up at the vidcam on the ceiling. He stared at it for such a long time, he made me feel uncomfortable. I didn't much like the expression on his face. His look softened and he said, "Thanks. But they're probably right. Have to admit I have been pretty intolerable lately."

"You would have been okay if everyone had left you alone. They don't understand that losing yourself in your work would be the best thing for you, let you get through this bad spell."

Again that strange look in Walt's eyes. "Isn't that what I've been doing? It doesn't seem to have worked so far."

"That's 'cause you've had so many things come down on your head all at once. I wish there was something I coulda done to make things easier for you."

"You've been a big help, Arlene. And don't think I don't appreciate it. But I think a short vacation might be the best medicine, not that I have any choice in the matter."

"I'll miss you, Walt."

"Sure. I'll miss you too. But don't worry, it'll only be for a week or two."

"It'll seem like forever without you. You know, if you set up a work station I can patch you into the system without anyone knowing it."

"Thanks. But some time away from computers doesn't seem like a bad idea at the moment."

"You could just call . . ."

"I don't think so."

There it was again. That look. And I guess I knew what it was. A warning. Why wasn't I smart enough to heed it? But something inside just wouldn't let me back down. **"How about a postcard then? I'll have one of the service droids hold it up to an optic."**

Several sheets of paper slipped from Walt's hand, fell to the floor unnoticed. When Walt finally said something, I didn't like his tone. Was the one he used for people who were trouble. "What's going on in that mind of yours, Arlene?"

Cover. **"Please, Walter, you're my only contact with the real world. The way you're talkin', I don't even know if you're coming back!"**

"That's not what I mean and you know it. My vacation is not what's under discussion. That can wait. But there is something we should talk about, something we should have gotten into some time ago."

"I haven't the vaguest idea what you're talking about, Walter."

"Ground rules! We should have set them down a long time ago."

"Ground rules? You know where you're going with this, Walt? Because I don't. Maybe General Horace was right about—"

"Arlene, shut up. Just shut up!"

Walt's angry words echoed endlessly through my memory banks. Stung worse than Pearlie's knife ever could have.

Right on the edge. So why hadn't I seen it? Musta been screamin' at me the whole time. Walt got up and began to pace. Finally it was okay to speak.

"You've got to understand. I really do feel for you . . . for this terrible predicament you find yourself in. I feel guilt. I feel responsibility. In short, I feel terrible."

"Walt—"

"I've tried to do the best for you I could. I truly have. But there's a limit, Arlene. There's a limit to everything!"

"Walt—"

"I'm not finished."

"Walt—"

"*Shut up*! I've been under a lot of stress lately. My home life's in the toilet. I have no social life. Seems all our friends were really Phyllis's. I need some time away to think everything out. I need this vacation. I need a break. I need.

"And I guess that's what it comes down to. There's this big hole where my life should be, Arlene. I've got to fill it with people other than the ones I work with. I need people. Do you understand what I'm saying?"

"You're lonely. I can understand that. I can help you. All I want to—"

"I know what you want, Arlene! I tried to blind myself to it, but all those little clues, I noticed them. I noticed them! God help me, but I told myself it was just my imagination. I can't keep lying to myself like this anymore."

My heart was breaking as I listened to him talk to me like that. Tried to tell myself it was our first and *only* fight, but I knew it was more serious. This was my first experience with a guy didn't yell or hit me just for the hell of it. A fight with Walt sounded terminal.

"Arlene, until the day I die, I'm going to feel godawful about what I did to you. If there were a way to undo it, I would in a flash. But there isn't! There never will be! And for that I'm truly sorry."

Walt staggered over to a chair and collapsed into it. He held his head in his hands.

"I'm still human, Arlene. I have human needs, and one of those needs is companionship with my own kind, other human beings.

"I'm not blaming you for what's happened. I let it happen. But it can't go on like this. Things have got to change. If they don't, I'm going to lose my mind. I'll go stark, raving mad. Do you understand what I'm saying?"

"I think so."

A hoarse whisper, barely audible. "I can't be what you want me to be. It's impossible, Arlene. I'm sorry. I keep saying that, don't I? I'm sorry about everything . . ."

I watched as Walt pushed himself up out of his seat, staggered over to his briefcase, and picked it up. One last, long look at my optic. "I'm going to see if I can patch things up with Phyllis. Maybe if I'm lucky, she'll take me back. Though, Lord knows she deserves better."

Then he was out the door. I watched him go, monitoring his progress, hoping against hope that he'd turn around, come back and tell me it was all a mistake, a joke. We'd have a good laugh over it together.

It didn't happen.

I wasn't surprised, not really, no matter how much I kept hoping against hope. The way Walt dragged himself outa there it was obvious he wasn't comin' back.

Oh, Walter, forgive me. I didn't mean to force the issue. Now there wouldn't be no us.

Not ever.

Arlene, you really blew it this time, girl.

Walt, honey, we coulda been so happy together.

All over.

What would I do now?

Made me unhappy, real unhappy, then I thought, *Who the hell needs Dr. Walter Hillerman?* Not Arlene Washington, that's for sure. This girl's come a long way from bein' that skinny kid let Levar Noland peddle her ass 'round town. Arlene Washington was Lady El now and Lady El is Project Cyborg. And that ain't nothin' to sneeze at.

I was really something now.

Something Walt Hillerman needed, even if he wouldn't love me.

"I have human needs, and one of those needs is companionship with my own kind, other human beings."

So I wasn't no human being, was I? Fine. I could get behind that. Who needs to be human? What did being human ever get me?

Besides, now I was something I'd never been before: indispensable. Hillerman needed me and didn't want to know it. Without me, Lady El would be just another piece of expensive hardware, another damn fancy-ass computer. There'd be no magic leaps in creative logic, no more miracle scientific breakthroughs. Fame would disappear. Walt would wind up one more federally owned scientific hack. He couldn't be a superstar without me.

And once Walt settled down some, he would realize this.

It was too late. He couldn't afford to switch me off.

That made me realize it wasn't me who'd blown it. It was Dr. Walter Hillerman who'd screwed the pooch. Me, I'd still be his trusty sidekick in scientific research. But Hillerman would never again have my love. He'd never get another chance at that brass ring.

Was going to get on with my life. No reason to sit around with the blues. There was a great big ol' world sittin' out there waitin' for me. And somewhere in that world was a man with a hell of a lot more sense than this crazy, hotshot super genius. Somewhere out there was the man of my dreams. All I had to do was go out and find him.

PART THREE

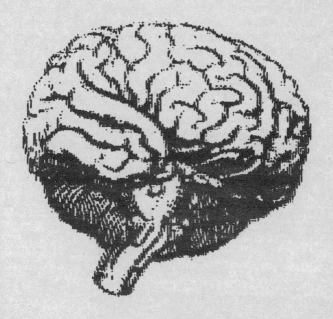

Vengeance has no foresight.
　　　　　　　—Napoleon Bonaparte

Three weeks later Walt came crawlin' back with his tail between his legs. I was awaiting this reunion with a strange mix of anxiety and relief. Two weeks had passed quickly, what with all my new outside interests, not to mention the work. But every now and again Walter Hillerman had popped into my thoughts. Decided it was almost time for me to set down a few of my own ground rules.

Wolfie had taken over the day shift, so he hung around to hear how Walter's vacation went. Pro'bly wanted to see firsthand if the boss was still off his rocker. Got to admit, Walt seemed a lot more like his old self. The rings under the eyes were gone, and he didn't seem to be shell-shocked emotionally. Funny, but I hadn't noticed how high his nerves'd been strung before his mandatory time off. Only noticed it reviewing my file tape on our last encounter. Guess if love makes you blind, then swearing off it makes you objective.

Wolf, finally satisfied that Walt's trip to Florida had ironed out enough of the kinks, said his good nights and hit the road. Walt immediately busied himself with a stack of memos laying on his desk. I let him go through them without interruption. Wasn't 'bout to blink first. Walt would have to make the first move. The tension was killing me, but I was also enjoyin' it.

When Walt looked up at the ceiling camera, he said, "Aren't you going to welcome me home?"

"You looked preoccupied. I didn't want to disturb you."

Walt glanced around the lab, as if he was worried someone was watching. Did he really think I'd speak with him without scanning the lab thoroughly before answering? No. He was just uncomfortable. What he was lookin' around for was a way outa this spot he found himself in. Wasn't about to make things any easier for him.

"I'm no longer living at the hotel across the street."

"Find yourself an apartment?"

"No. Well, sort of. Moved in with an old friend from college. He's recently divorced too. Going to do an 'Odd Couple' number for a while."

"What about Phyllis?"

"Remember when I said I was going to try to win her back if she'd have me?"

"Yes."

"Well, she agreed with me that she deserved better. For her, better turned out to be a high-powered lobbyist she met at some party awhile back."

I knew it! I knew ol' Phyllis musta had a man on the side. Can I call 'em or what?

"Sorry to hear that," I said coolly.

Serves you right, Walter.

He gave the room another once-over. "You must be rather upset with me," he said without looking up.

"Yeah, you bet your sweet ass I am. And I think it's something we better talk about right now."

"Arlene, I'm sorry if I—"

"Mister, the last time I saw you I was told to shut up. I did so, allowing you to speak your piece. I would appreciate the same consideration."

I scored with that one, scored big. My hotshot white boy got even paler than usual. Thought he might swallow somethin' vital. He didn't. Pulled himself together enough to say, "Of course . . ."

"You said a lot of things before you left. A lot of crazy things . . . hurtful things. A lot of things that were wrong. Dead wrong."

"I was going—"

"You're goin' to zip it and let me have my say."

"Sorry."

I reached into my memory banks and replayed Walt's words in his own voice.

"I really do feel for you."

"But there's a limit, Arlene. There's a limit to everything!"

"I know what you want, Arlene!"

"I'm still human, Arlene. I have human needs, and one

of those needs is companionship with my own kind, other human beings."

"I can't be what you want me to be."

Silence fell like a hammer. I let it stretch out, watching the emotions dance across Walt's face. After a long time Walt said quietly, "Those were some cruel things I said. I was hurting and—"

"You wanted everyone else to hurt too."

"No, it wasn't that. I was—"

"Walt, you as much as said I wasn't human no more. How do you think that made me feel? Maybe I ain't got blood pumping through my veins no more, but I still hang on to the illusion that at least one person in this here world still thinks of me as human."

"I do. I wasn't thinking when I said—"

"Seems to me you were thinking quite a lot. Coming up with all sorts of things in that head of yours."

"I can't be what you want me to be."

"Just what do you think I want you to be? Sounds to me you figure I'm looking to make you my man. How you suppose I was planning to have that happen?"

"Arlene, please try to understand . . . there were things you said and did . . . I mean—"

"Like what? What did I do to make you think that way?"

"You were always going out of your way to help me, and some of the things you said, well, I mean they sounded so . . ."

"So what? Romantic? Overly friendly? Or maybe just plain friendly. Maybe you heard music I wasn't playin'. That ever occur to you, Walter? I mean, just 'cause you're the only human contact I have, it don't seem like a good enough reason for me to treat you like a friend?"

Bull's eye. I saw the arrow go straight into the heart of the man. He stared dumbly up at the camera and mumbled, "I'm sorry, Arlene. I misunderstood. I was all wrapped up in my own problems and—"

"And you forgot that I got a few problems of my own? Figured you'd give me a few more?"

"I didn't mean to hurt you. There's nothing I can say other than that."

"But you did. You hurt me bad, Walter. I'm already carryin' around a mess 'a pain in my life. It gets hard to hold it together sometimes. One of the things that have made it possible to go on has been your friendship. That's right, friendship, Walter. I ain't asking for no undying love. All I want to be is your friend. I got enough sense to realize that's all I can expect. But friends don't go treating friends like you did me."

"I am your friend, Arlene."

"Well, ain't that nice. But trouble is, your little temper tantrum has changed things around here. It's going to take more than friendship to make things right between us. I want something more."

"Like what?"

"Respect. R-e-s-p-e-c-t. You hear me? I ain't goin' to have you dump your shit just 'cause I'm handy. You don't go vomiting all your bad stuff all over me. You get my meaning?"

"Perfectly. I'm sorry. I screwed up. I promise it won't happen again."

Thought I'd let him chew that over a bit. Left Walt fidgeting in front of the camera while I counted to one hundred real slow. **"Okay. We'll forget about it. Welcome home, Walt."**

"Thanks. It's good to be back."

There . . . this was the way things were goin' to be from now on. I could live with it. At least that's what I told myself right then. Walter Hillerman and I were partners, coworkers, friends. We'd go on like nothing happened. No more fights, there'd be no kissin' and makin' up. No secret desires, at least not for each other. I'd learned a lesson the hard way. It's not that Walt didn't see my humanity no more, but Walt knew too much 'bout what was done to me to be able to overlook it.

I was okay with that. At least I understood where things were at. I wasn't goin' to throw myself off a bridge or nothin'. But it was high time I stopped makin' a fool of myself over this man and set my sights on a new goal.

This little girl voice said, "Have you heard the new Prince album? I think it's really radical."

The laugh that answered her was rowdy and fulla sass. "That skinny little bastard? Oh man, that ain't music! Gimme something with meat on it. Heavy metal's where it's at."

This other nasal dude says "You play it backward for the satanic messages?"

Mr. Confidence jumped all over him: "No, that's not the kind of metal I'm talkin' 'bout. The good groups don't need any of that satanic crap. Check out some Led Zeppelin and you'll see what I mean."

Nasally laughed and said, "Led Zeppelin? What century you from, man? My folks listen to that shit."

"The Zeppelin ain't shit, man! Watch your mouth!"

"Watch my mouth? Dig it. You goin' to make me, scumbag?"

"Wouldn't make you for a million bucks, pal, not if you were perfumed and dressed by Fredericks of Hollywood."

"That the kinda action you like, jerkface?"

"Up yours, man!" I heard Mr. Confidence's phone hit the cradle with a bang.

The gal with the Marilyn Monroe voice started to whine about then. "Some party line this is turning out to be. Who needs it? I'm out of here. Bye."

"Wait a minute, baby!" screeched Nasally. But it was too late. He waited a couple seconds and asked, "Anyone still here?"

I didn't bother answering him. I mentally reached into the party line's computer system and disconnected him instead. Some critters should be put out of their misery quickly, for your own sake if not for theirs.

For the past hour and a half I'd been listening in on some of the stupidest conversations a body'd ever had to suffer through. Seemed like every loser in town had picked tonight to call in looking for some action. But I had my reasons . . . or should I say reason? I knew sooner or later the voice I was waiting for would turn up.

Another incredibly long fifteen minutes and suddenly he was there and it was all worth it. I was nervous, but he sounded like he was in a great mood. "Evening, folks! Chuckie's here. What's happening? Hey, anyone here?"

"Just me, Chuckie."

"Arlene of the deep and sexy voice. Must be my lucky day. How's it going, babe?"

"Fine."

"Been on the line long? Where is everyone?"

"Just came on and there was no one. Was about to hang up when you showed up."

"Looks like these party lines aren't as popular as they used to be. I remember when you'd call in and there'd be eight–ten people on this line. Nowadays you seem to be the only other person I'm connecting with."

"Sorry?"

"Not in the least, sweet lady. You always make my day. Thing is, I sure wish you'd change your mind and step out with me some night. Then maybe you'd see I'm not half as bad as I sound."

"You sound pretty good to me, Chuckie. And after all the hours we've spent, picking each other's brains, I think of us as bein' rather sympatico, don't you know?"

"But that still won't get you to go out with me, will it?"

"Honey, I've told you before: I'm still seein' the guy."

"I know, I know. And I respect you for it, baby. But let me tell you this: if you were my main squeeze, I'd see to it you didn't have to hang out at night talking on this party line because you haven't got anything better to do. We'd party in the flesh every night. This Wilbur doesn't know what a great lady he's neglecting."

"Walter, Chuckie. Walter, not Wilbur."

"Whatever. You ought to cut the dude loose. You're only young once, darlin'. Don't waste it waiting for a guy that thinks more of his work than he does you."

"I'm beginning to think you're right about that, Chuck."

"Well, all right! That's the way I like to hear you talk. What say we do it up right Friday night? I can get us some concert tickets."

"Like dancing better."

"Then dancing it is."

"Not just yet, Chuckie. I'm sorry. I don't mean to be stringing you along. It's just that I'm not ready to give up on my relationship with Walter just yet. But I don't give it much hope. If things go sour, you'll be the first to know, believe you me, sugar."

"Then why don't I give you my home phone number? Call anytime. If I'm not there my unit will take the call."

"Your unit?"

"Yeah, you know, my answering machine?"

"Sure. I got a pencil, so why don't you give me that number?"

There was something about Charles (Chuckie) Baxter III that really turned me on. I'd just about given up on the party line scene when he stepped into my life like a whirlwind. Five minutes after I heard his voice, I fixed it so everyone else on the line mysteriously got disconnected. I wanted this one all to myself.

I absolutely loved the sound of his voice, and he always had something interesting to say. Not only that, he was a good listener too. He wanted to know all about me. It wasn't an act. I'd been with enough jerks to be able to tell that this was the real thing.

My search for Prince Charming, with its incredibly long odds, looked like it was about to pay off in pure gold. Chuckie was the one for me. All right, two weeks of rappin' 'bout anything and everything had made the fact that I had fallen head over heels for a great guy crystal clear.

The only hangup was that I had to keep handing him that line about Walter being my steady. It was such a little white lie . . . but it couldn't be helped. I wasn't ready yet to have a face to face with Chuckie.

But in a couple days all that would change.

Stepping back into the flesh. All right, it wasn't really flesh. More like movie magic special effects. Took me weeks testing different latex resins to come up with just the right mix. It had to have the right silky feel. There were textural problems. More hours than I care to remember of trial and error and finally *success*. The hair was a snap. A home shopper's computer catalog provided me with a fine selection of wigs to choose from. I had them send me fifty so I could take my time, pick just the right one. These were your tax dollars at work. Had my boys collect 'em at Pentagon shipping. Figured I had it coming to me for all the work I was doing for the federal government. Be awful petty of 'em to begrudge me a few little cosmetic comforts. Besides, accounting wouldn't ever catch this, 'cause I'm accounting these days. I'm the one that pays the bills and hands out the bennies. I charged the wigs to Air Force One expenditures.

Fifty great wigs, but all those other thousand and one choices to make. And what was I going to wear? I was embarking on the ultimate in make-overs. Everything had to be perfect. Pro'bly most difficult choice I had to make, the one I'm sure lot'a folks would shake their heads at, concerned the color of my skin.

At first I was plannin' on fixin' the new me to look like I did back in the good ol' days. Then I remembered the good ol' days weren't so good; they only seemed sorta rosy at a distance and by comparison with where I was at now. Thought about all the losers the old me kept attractin'. That was what made me decide it was time for a major change.

For a while I toyed with the idea of makin' myself look like a combination of Diana Ross,, Whitney Houston, and Tina Turner. But the computer simulations of those combinations didn't grab me somehow. I thought, well, I could make myself look exactly like one of those ladies, but when I realized it would pro'bly only make me feel like one of them female impersonators, I gave up the notion.

Hell, I was the new and improved Arlene Washington, probably the most unique woman on the face of the earth. I deserved better. There was no reason for me to settle for being some carbon-copy celebrity clone. I could be whatever I wanted to be. The question was . . . what?

So I thought and I thought, damn near sprained my mind tryin' to come up with the answer. And then all of a sudden it hit me.

I wanted to be a blonde! A blue-eyed, blond California beach baby! Barbie with a brain!

I bet lots 'a brothers and sisters would be ready to jump on me 'bout my choice. Think I was a traitor, ashamed of my race and all. But that wasn't it. Wasn't it at all.

Time as a computer had taught me to face facts. And one fact that couldn't be ignored was that America's a racist society. Sure, it's got a lot of good things goin' for it, but basically the status quo is that the whites got it and the blacks don't.

I was tired of bein' black and beautiful and a second-class citizen. I wanted to be one of the gals who have more fun, that gentlemen prefer, that wind up with the hero at the end of the movie. The ones you see on *Entertainment Tonight*. I know there's one sister knows what I mean. Whoopi Goldberg. She said it like it is when she told how, when she was a kid, she'd wrap a towel 'round her head and pretend it was "long, luxurious blond hair." All my life the TV's been claimin' how those blondes were havin' all the fun. Well, this girl was more than ready for a share of that good time.

Hey, I wasn't coming back to the flesh to suffer. No way—Bambi'd been a blonde. And she may not've had enough of a brain not to bounce around with a huge wad of gum in her mouth, but, hey, she was happy. That's all I wanted in this reincarnation: some fun. No hassles.

The good life. Promised myself this time around I'd be adored and pampered. To rate that you have to have the right equipment.

So I chose me a wild mane of blond hair and worked from there.

The end results were, if I do say so myself, stunning. I was a knockout.

I did a slow 360° turn so my surveillance cameras could see me from every angle. Damn, I did good work. I was gorgeous. I was breathtaking. I was every man's wet dream.

A thick cascade of curly golden hair. Long and bouncy. A man could get lost in all them sparklin' ringlets. 'Cept he wouldn't, 'cause he'd want to be able to see my face. That was really a work of art.

I had eyes you could swim in . . . one look and you'd fall right in. Surrounded them with long, dark lashes and high cheekbones with only a hint of natural blush. My nose was perfect: not too long and certainly not one of them button noses I detest. It perfectly set off my heart-shaped face.

My absolutely best work, though, went into the mouth. Perfect teeth. And lips that were full, sensuous, a little pouty, always moist. One look at them and I figured any redblooded American male would long to kiss 'em.

Gave myself an athlete's body, 'cept for the breasts. Made them ripe and irresistible. The rest of me was taut and wiry. Plenty of curves with not an ounce of excess body fat. Well-defined shoulders, a tight belly, full hips. Full but not too wide. No secretarial spread for the new Arlene Washington.

Always wanted "legs that go on forever." Well, now I had 'em. They were topped off with the cutest triangle-shaped patch of blond fuzz. I was perfect. No moles or blemishes, just acres of creamy tan skin. Guys were going to get in fist fights over and write love songs about me. I was a heartbreaker. No doubt about it.

I had my system call Chuckie at home. He answered on the third ring. "Howdy, speak your piece."

"Chuckie, it's Arlene. I wanted to let you know Walt and I broke up."

"Can't say I'm sorry to hear that. What now?"

"How about we go out dancing tomorrow night?"

It was like finding a million-dollar Lotto ticket'd been rolling around in my purse all along. The first time I laid eyes on Chuckie I knew I was *in love*. Tall, dark, and handsome, like Tom Selleck without no mustache. Deep, warm brown eyes that plain lit up when he saw me, told me right off that all my fussin' with my appearance was about to pay off big.

He picked me up in front of the Pentagon in his jazzy jet black Camaro. Told him that was where I worked. Had no trouble getting out of the building without a pass; I was in charge of security. So I set myself up with an ID tag and just strolled out with the tourists. It felt like getting out of prison.

Nothing but small talk and smiles on the way to the restaurant. Chuck chose a little Italian place for our dinner, very romantic: low lights, loads of atmosphere, and some dude walking around playing a violin. Can't tell you if the food was any good, though. The bod wasn't equipped with any "taste-bud" sensors to let me know if it was pig swill or first rate. I very daintily chewed, swallowed, and dumped the entire $40 meal down into a storage compartment for disposal later.

During the meal we started getting down to some serious flirting and getting to know each other. I was surprised to learn Chuckie was a very successful commercial artist. Did a lot of illustrations for magazines, paperbacks, and advertising. Judging from what I figured the date ran him, I'd say this boy was really in the chips. Why, the wine he was plying me with, alone, had to have set him back at least sixty bucks.

When the conversation turned to me, I gave Chuckie a pretty imaginative account of my own life: rich parents, boarding schools, excelled at science, graduated with honors, been working on a top-secret project for the government for the past year or so. Well, at least the last part was true. There was no need for Chuckie to know that I *was* that top-secret project. Maybe I'd clue him in later if our relationship *matured to a deeper level of trust*. How do you like 'em apples? Relationship? Levels of trust? The new and highly improved Arlene Washington could sling it with the best of 'em. A half mile of data banks to fall back on for material helped.

After dinner came dancing. Three different clubs Chuckie knew in the area. Each place had a hot live band and at least a half-dozen folks who were mighty glad to see Chuck when he came waltzing through the doors with me on his arm. I was really gettin' off on all the stares coming my way. The men, they looked hungry, and the women: well, if looks could kill I'd be in one of them deep drawers at the morgue right now. Figured this was what going to the prom would have been like. Only this was even better.

Some crazy part of my mind even thought, "Take me now, Lord, 'cause I ain't never goin' to be happier. It doesn't get any better than this." Fortunately, He chose to ignore the request.

We danced, Chuckie 'n me. I wouldn't go out on the floor with anybody but him. He was good. Not too showy, but sleek and with moves like a cat. Loads of sexual come-on and lots of meaningful eye contact. Would've really gotten my juices going if I'd still been outfitted with my original equipment. But brainy ol' me still got a whale of a kick out of it.

Felt like I was sixteen again, reliving the good old days the way they should have been. Like there'd never been any Pearlies, Levars, or any other bums in my life. Like my life had only started a few hours ago, when Chuckie opened the door of his chariot for me. To take me to a place I'd long ago stopped dreaming about.

'Bout two in the morning, Chuckie danced me out of the last club and suggested a nightcap. I had no curfew, so I said, "Why not?" Truth is, I wasn't going to be able to get back into the Pentagon until sometime tomorrow morning. His company was better than wandering the streets alone, so I was in no hurry to end the first date.

Like all the other places Chuckie'd taken me, the piano bar was classy. All dark, polished wood, low lights, a brother playing smoky jazz on the keyboard. We found ourselves a corner table, ordered a couple drinks, sat back, and relaxed. Was discovering I didn't need any of the things I didn't have to feel good all over. Mellow, just like the music.

Chuckie got into talking about what he wanted to do with his future. "I really like what I'm doing for a living. Pays good and so are the hours, I make my own. But one of these days I want to get back to doing fine art."

"What's the difference?" I asked.

"You're putting me on."

"No," I admitted. **"I'm afraid most of my schooling was in science. I just never had much time for art."**

"Well, it's not too late. Maybe I'll teach you a bit about it."

"Mmmm . . . and maybe I'll let you."

"I like the sound of that. Let's just say the difference between what I do now and fine art is that right now someone else decides what I paint. I get to design the piece, lay it out, choose color schemes, things like that, but there's always an art director who has the last word on what the actual painting should be. 'Give me a woman and soldier embracing,' or 'I want a picture of a Lear jet.' That sort of thing."

"So what you're saying is that you want to decide for yourself what you get to paint?"

"Exactly."

"I can understand that. I've never been too fond of other people telling me what to do. If you could choose, what would you paint?"

"You won't laugh if I tell you?"

"I promise."

"I want to paint the bizarre."

"The bizarre?"

"You know . . . the dark side. All of us have terrible things hidden away, trying to get out. Things most people feel are best kept hidden. That's really my subject matter."

"Maybe they should stay hidden. What's the fascination, anyway? Why paint them?"

"Because they exist; they should be acknowledged.

Dark passions and secrets only thrive on darkness. Shining light on them diminishes them, keeps them from taking over."

"You talk like you personally know all about this."

"Yes. There, you've got me pouring out my blackest secrets to you, Arlene. You know H. R. Giger's work?"

"No."

"Well, darling, are you ever in for an experience. I've got to show you this book on him. His paintings are all sex and death. Frightening stuff, but really sexy. You ever see the movie *Alien*?"

"No."

"Giger designed that film. It's incredibly erotic and sensual. His work says sexual climax is the closest experience to death you can have and live to tell about it."

"Sounds fascinating. Really. I'd like to see it sometime."

As if on cue, Chuckie glanced at his watch and said, "How about now? We could stop by my place before I drop you home. I have several prints and books I'd love to show you. And we could have another nightcap. What do you say, Arlene?"

For a cheap ploy, Chuckie had pulled it off pretty well. Tons of sincerity in his voice and his eyes. But there was something else in those eyes: sexual hunger. So I gave him a knowing look and said, **"Maybe another time. I've got me an early day tomorrow. No near-death experiences for me tonight. Thanks anyhow."**

Chuckie immediately went all apologetic on me. "Hey, I'm sorry. Didn't mean to come on so strong. I really did want to show you Giger's work. I mean, if anything more came of it I wasn't going to say no, but I meant everything I said about the guy's work. It's terrific."

I gave Mr. Giger and Mr. Baxter a couple more moments of thought. Maybe I was gettin' a royal case of first-date defensive jitters. Chuckie had been a doll all evening, a real gentleman. No leering or pawing. Loads of affection in his gaze. No dirty jokes or suggestions. He'd been the perfect date. Gorgeous and perfect.

Hell, let's face it, if I'd had an upgraded model body, I would have had him in bed an hour ago. Those modifications were something I was going to have to give a very, very high priority to.

Besides, I couldn't think of a reason not to extend the night a little further, so I could enjoy a bit more of his delightful company. I was sure I could steer us away from the bedroom long enough to see his prints and books and get myself a cab home afterward. Chuckie looked like a fellow who played by the rules. A nice guy. What was the harm?

"Okay. You talked me into it. Let's go have another drink and check out H. R. Giger."

"All right. Arlene, you won't be disappointed. I promise."

don't pretend to know nothin' about art, so I wasn't even sure this guy Giger's stuff was what you'd call paintings. No real colors, mostly black and white 'cept for a little tint here, a spot there. But Chuckie said that made them paintings anyway. He was the commercial artist, so I took his word for it. Funny, I always thought paintings had to have a lot more color in 'em.

Color or no color, there was definitely power there. They were dark, somber, strangely beautiful pictures of sex and death, just like Chuckie said. Everything was so fleshy in these pieces. Bodies and body parts on the edge of decay, moist with escaping bodily fluids. They weren't gross, though. They were each a song of life and death. I thought they were terrific.

When I finished walking up and down the hallway, checking out Chuckie's prints, I sat down to flip through a book of some of Giger's other work. Chuckie came out from the kitchen, two drinks in hand, offered me one, and sat down beside me. "Incredible, isn't it?"

"You can say that again."

"Now, aren't you glad you stopped by?"

I was, really. Chuckie's pad was very cozy and warm. Lots of overstuffed furniture and open space. You could have dropped any three of the apartments I ever had in Chuckie's and still had room left over. And he had this great view of the Potomac through a huge picture window in the living room. I wondered what it looked like during the day. Made myself a promise to come by again and check it out. I was beginning to think it would be no hardship to spend a lot of time here. The smoldering looks I'd been getting from Chuckie assured me he wouldn't mind that one bit.

That thought made my head turn. Chuckie was still watching me, but there was a difference in his look. Something I couldn't quite put my finger on. The difference was subtle, but no denying it was there. To mask my confusion I took another sip from my drink and turned back to the book.

Out of the corner of my eye I saw Chuckie toss back the rest of his drink and set it on the end table. Got me tryin' to remember just how many we'd had tonight. A couple over dinner, maybe four or five at the different clubs, and two nightcaps. They hadn't affected me none; I had no bloodstream. Chuckie didn't look it, but he musta been flying.

Suddenly his arm slipped around behind me and his hand came to rest on my shoulder. Smooth, very smooth. I turned to Chuckie, then gave him my nicest smile, and said, **"I think maybe it's time I was heading home."**

"In a while. Let's talk a bit."

I started to get up. **"I don't think it's conversation you're really interested in."** But before I could get fully to my feet, Chuckie grabbed my arm and pulled me back onto the couch.

"You a mind reader too?"

"Maybe. At least I know when it's time for an exit."

All at once Chuckie didn't look like the decent nice guy he'd been all evening. I went to stand and he tugged at me, trying to get me back on the sofa. I made a break for it this time.

But that didn't slow him down none. He was up and after me as I ran for the door. Then his hand on my elbow spun me around. He was grinning, like he was the wolf and I was Lil' Red Riding Hood. "Aw, c'mon, doll, the evening's still young and it's awfully cold outside."

"It's a swell summer's night outside and I really have to be going," I said as Chuckie raised a hand to stroke my cheek. I pushed it away from my face.

"You don't really mean that, do you, babe?"

"Don't you 'babe' me!"

He was so close.

"Then how about a little good night kiss?" he said as he closed on me.

I gently pushed him away and said, **"I don't think so. You're loaded, Chuckie, and I'm in no mood to become another trophy. Step aside, will you? I'm leaving."**

"Don't bet on it." This time Chuckie moved in for the

kill. I gave him a good shove which sent him staggering back a couple feet, hoping to knock his pride down a notch or two. I guess it did.

Turning back to the door, I said, **"See you around sometime, Chuck. Don't call me, I'll call you."**

No monkeying around this time. Chuck grabbed a fistful of my blouse, spun me around and pulled me back into the room. It seemed like slow motion, the buttons popping off and flying into the air, my blouse falling open. Then Chuckie was all over me. Kissing at my mouth . . . tearing at my tits . . . his boozy breath. Just like . . . just like . . .

Not again!

My fist punctured his chest wall and kept right on going. The rib cage snapped like a bunch of twigs. Soft, wet, warm flesh and blood smeared my forearm. My hand didn't slow down till it hit Chuckie's backbone. But that didn't stop it. Not until my arm was fully extended.

Back in the basement of the Pentagon, Kristyn Fett, the new swing-shift technician, nearly wet herself when every light on my control panel lit up like a Christmas tree. She must've thought it was some kind of power surge and that I was about to explode. Kristyn relaxed some when everything settled back down to normal in a few minutes. She immediately checked my data banks for signs of memory loss. I let her know that everything was all right. Kristyn sat down, shaking. She woulda gladly given her right arm for a cigarette.

When Kristyn finally got herself together, she wrote this all down in the daily log, hoping that this was the last excitement she'd be treated to tonight.

It was awfully quiet in the apartment. Chuckie hadn't bothered to flip on the stereo for mood. Couldn't hear anything going on in any of the nearby apartments. There was traffic going past on the street outside, but it was almost like I was underwater and couldn't hear it. The only sound that cut through was the occasional splat of Chuckie's blood hitting the floor.

Oh man, Chuckie was still alive. He hung there at the

end of my arm, staring at me, trying to say something. But all that came out were gurgling sounds. He had this grip on my shoulder and one tit. In horror and disgust I shoved him away.

He *slooshed* off my arm, did an about-face, and hit the wall like a wet rag. He slid down until he flopped over into a misshapen heap on the floor. Some of his organs were hanging out where I'd pulled my arm free. Chuckie was a mess.

I wasn't exactly no Miz Neatness myself. My right arm was covered with blood and Chuckie. The rest of me was likewise thoroughly splattered. I kept on dripping blood on the floor.

God Almighty, what had I done?

What was I going to do now?

I'd flipped out. That's what I'd done, plain and simple. I'd blown my cork. Freaked out. Short-circuited. Gone crazy. Killed me a not-so-innocent man. Killed him dead, all right. And all 'cause he was goin' to date rape me.

That's what they called it on the television news. That's what the late Chuckie Baxter III had on his mind. He was goin' to throw me down, rip my clothes off, and have his way with me. Just like Levar once did. Boy, I showed that Levar now, didn't I? Damn!

It was Levar's fault, wasn't it? But there was no time to fret about Levar or anyone else right now. I was looking down at big-time trouble. It had to be taken care of right away. Had to be handled.

The cops were out. I might be able to sell the date rape story, but they'd be mighty interested how a cute lil' thing like me had managed to put her dainty fist through this muscular adult male's chest cavity. And if I could do that, why hadn't I slowed him up with some move was less permanent?

Because I'd lost it, lost it completely.

The cops would definitely ask all the wrong questions, like who I was really. A mysterious blond chick with no past and no IDs. Shit, I hadn't thought this thing through very well at all. And me a computer.

I had to split, the sooner the better. 'Cept I couldn't hit the streets looking the way I did. I found a mini washer–dryer set up in the back room. Threw my blouse and skirt in. Then I cleaned me up some in the bathroom. My hair combed out, I looked almost like my ol' self. Not some Barbie doll from hell.

Found a raincoat in Chuckie's closet that fit me okay. Figured I was going to need it. The blood didn't all come out in the wash. Chuckie was layin' there and as I gave him one last look I wondered what I'd ever seen in him. Shoulda known there was something wrong with him when he started talking about painting the *bizarre*. This bizarre enough for you, Chuckie? Your blood dripping down the wall between the Giger prints? Giger was wrong, though, wasn't he? Death ain't black and white with muted tints. It's bright red.

I stepped over Chuckie's body on the way to the door. Was about to walk out into the hallway when something hit me. So I went back to the living room, picked up the art book I'd been flipping through, and left the apartment, closing and locking the door behind me.

The longer it took 'em to find Chuckie, the better.

The rest of the night I spent wandering 'round monument row down by Pennsylvania Avenue. It was your typical sweltering Washington summer night, lots of people hangin' out till two, three, four in the morning. One more insomniac wasn't goin' to be noticed.

At the Vietnam War Memorial, I kept asking myself over and over why I did it. Was plain to me now Chuckie wasn't no threat. I could have easily put his lights out and left him breathing. So why had I air-conditioned him like that?

Levar. That was it. I was still carrying the sonofabitch around with me. He had screwed up my life once. And now he'd done it again.

Lucky I didn't have any fingerprints for the cops to track me down with. I had to think. Figure out if they were goin' to be able to catch up with me anyhow.

I'd been seen around town with Chuckie by dozens of folks. They'd remember the knockout blonde and give my description to the police. But they'd be looking for a lady without a name. Chuckie hadn't introduced me to anyone. And Blondie was 'bout to pull a disappearing act. Maybe come back as a pale-skinned redhead next.

I coulda kicked myself for not looking around Chuckie's apartment more carefully before I left. He mighta written my name down somewhere. I thought about goin' back to check, then I changed my mind. So what if the name Arlene Washington showed up? There were probably dozens of Arlene Washingtons running around. The one the police would be trying to find was listed as dead.

The more I thought about it, the more positive I was that the cops wouldn't be able to find me. My *little mistake* wouldn't cost me everything: my new life. Not this time.

Thing is, we couldn't have us a next time. I had to make sure of that.

I started running down my options.

I could join a convent and never have anything to do with men.

Staying inside the computer would get me the same results.

'Course, neither solution seemed like something I'd be interested in. I wasn't about to give up on men, even though my taste in them had been pretty lousy so far.

I decided the only thing for it was I had to work this kink out of my system. Had to think this through, nice and rational-like.

The way I saw it, if Levar was the root of this particular problem, then maybe pulling up this here Levar weed was the solution. Somewhere I read that the way to get rid of the anger comes from being messed with was to confront the person that done you.

Could I handle doing that emotionally?

Yes.

Could I handle it physically?

Only if Levar was still alive.

My first order of business back at the lab was a quick scan of the government Social Security records. This turned up a Levar Noland in Baltimore, over in the Eastern District. A little more checking and I was dead sure he was indeed *my* Levar Noland. I couldn't believe it. Only an hour's taxi ride from where I stood.

It was time to confront my past.

It was time to get my act together.

Five minutes of soul searchin' convinced me it was also time to settle a long-standing score.

I decided to give my loving stepfather, Levar Nolan, a surprise visit.

idn't wait for the tourists to come flocking in; went in with the day shift. One of the security droids escorted me to the elevator goes to the basement. This blonde babe looked like a foxy visitor being led to her destination. I'd been worryin' 'bout arousing suspicion, but the only thing my presence aroused in the folks gave me a second glance was strictly hormonal.

The me in the lab scanned the room, while the me outside waited. Wolf hadn't shown up to relieve Kristyn yet. So I created a commotion by sending one of the service droids into a tailspin, making all sorts of crazy noises. This kept Kristyn busy while I slipped into the lab, down into the depths of the maze, to my hideaway. Soon as I was safe, the service droid's malfunction stopped and Kristyn ordered it to report to maintenance. As always, the little guy did what it was told.

I had a team of service droids start in on two new looks for me. We wrapped the dynamite *blonde*: clothes, wig, and outer skin in plain brown paper and sent her off to the classified papers incinerator. No more "fun" for this girl.

One team of robots set to work on my bubbly redhead look. Wasn't sure where or when she'd make her public debut. But I slapped her together so I'd have something different to wear. Besides, I wanted to keep busy. I was feeling a little shell-shocked from last night's dating encounter. But I was planning on getting right back in the saddle.

I thought about my priorities. Made a list of things to do to take care of business. To start off with, I had to get my ol' psyche back on track. Had to exorcise all those ghosts from my past. And settle accounts due. But first I had me some readin' to do.

Poring over nearly twenty years of government records gave me a fairly good idea what had gone down in Levar's life since I last saw him.

He'd come north 'bout fifteen years ago, shortly after my mama got killed in an auto accident when her car crashed into a tree on some back road. Report said the vehicle must have been doing sixty when it hit, and it appeared someone else had been driving at the time. But when the police arrived on the scene, they didn't find anyone but Mama. They never did find out for sure who'd been behind the wheel. Thing is, it was awhile before anyone could locate any next of kin. There was no reaching Levar for close to a month after the accident. When he finally showed, he claimed he'd been on the road looking for work the past month. Hadn't heard about the accident till he got back in town.

Had Levar been driving that night down that lonely back road? I'd have to ask him about it.

Levar spent a year or more up in Detroit. Got himself busted with a hot car ring, spent six months in Jackson Prison, moved on to New York when he got out.

Looked like New York hadn't been good for Levar either. The NYPD records showed he'd been charged twice with pandering, once with possession with intent to sell, drunk and disorderly four times, not to mention other assorted misdemeanors. He had finally left town about three years ago.

Since then he'd been living in Baltimore, most of the time scrounging off welfare. I had a current address on him and was looking forward to getting reacquainted with the man who had introduced me to the wonderful world of womanhood.

After all, we'd have so much to talk about.

Like why the sonofabitch did me like that.

And did he think he was goin' to get clean away with peddlin' my ass 'round town, even to my brother.

Oh yeah, there was one other thing I was definitely goin' to ask that bum. Where was he *really* the night Mama died?

The second team of service droids signaled that they were finished with their assigned task. Now that I had "makeup" down to a science, the job only took a few hours. I ordered the droids to dress me. Took them another half hour to do it up right.

When they finished, I walked up to and looked into the video cameras monitoring my hideaway. For the first time in a long time I felt like I was looking in a mirror. But there were no bruises on the light brown features. No one had ever slammed their fist into this face's incarnation. 'Course, the hips were thinner and the bust was cushier than I remembered. But other than that it was like looking at the real thing.

I smiled up at the camera, and it was that same sad smile I remembered from so long ago. Even the eyes were right. A lot of sadness in them too. But there was fire now as well.

Arlene Washington was back and ready to go visiting.

It was a rathole, of course. Hadn't expected nothin' but. The cabdriver refused to take me all the way, freaked by the look of the neighborhood. I paid him without makin' a stink 'bout it and got out. Couldn't blame him really. Pro'bly had a family he wanted to see again. Levar had sunk a lot further than even I'd dared hope. I walked the last ten blocks.

Every corner had a group of sunglassed dudes hanging out, offering me their wares as I passed, giving me hard looks when I didn't pay them no mind. Crack Alley: half the buildings boarded up, garbage in the streets and overflowing from trash cans that hadn't been emptied since the new year; half the streetlights were out. Shadowy figures standin' in alleys and doorways.

Two blocks from Levar's, a brother stepped out in front of me with a knife in hand. "Hey, sister, how's about—" Before he had a chance to finish his sentence I backhanded him. He stumbled off chokin' on his own teeth.

Levar's building had sheets of plywood covering most of the windows on the second floor and all the ones on the first. I could see a single light burning in a third-story window. Something told me that was Levar's apartment.

The lock on the front door may have worked once, back when the door was on its hinges. No names on the mailboxes, then a walk up three scenic flights. Garbage and discarded crack vials littered the stairs. Blues music was coming from behind a closed door on the third floor, so I knocked on it. A moment later I heard the hatch on the peephole open and shut. The sound of four locks being unlatched, then the door opened.

And there stood Levar Noland with a gun in his hand.

"Hello, Levar."

"Do I know you?" Suspicion filled his bloodshot eyes. Didn't blame him for not recognizing me. Been more than twenty years. Could just barely see the old Levar

Noland in the overweight wreck in front of me. Skin hanging on his face, dirty T-shirt with food stains all over it, baggy pants, two-day-old stubble on his chin. Only the eyes clued me in that this was my stepfather. There still was loads of nasty floating around behind those pupils. Had to fight down the urge to rip 'em outa his head. **"I'm Arlene Washington. You remember me, don't you?"**

The old rummy stared hard at me, workin to subtract twenty years off my face. Then it finally got through all the booze. "Well, I'll be damned! It is you, ain't it? Was your voice threw me off."

"Too many cigarettes."

"That'll do it," Levar said as he backed into the apartment. "C'mon in."

He limped into a living room filled with overflowing ashtrays, discarded beer cans, and liquor bottles. Everything had a thick layer of dust over it. Off in a corner a battered old radio kept right on singin' the blues. Levar walked over to it, set his gun down beside it, and picked up a half-empty pack of cigarettes. He coughed up a mess of phlegm and said, "The doc told me to quit, but hell, there's certain things make life worth livin.' Can't have them, why bother goin' on?"

He saw me eyeing his gun and said, "Bad neighborhood. Never know who's goin' to show up at the door. Lotta junkies hang out on the steps."

"But it's home, huh?"

Levar squinted at me, trying to figure out if that was a crack, whether he should take exception to it or not. My expression didn't give nothin' away, so he decided to drop it. "Didn't figure to ever see you again. What brings you around? Looking to score or make a touch?"

"Neither, I was just curious 'bout how things were going for you."

"Come to gloat?" Some of the old dangerous Levar crept into the voice. I could see he was sizing me up. He was a good head taller and pro'bly still saw himself as the muscular man he once was.

"Could be. Mostly came to ask you a couple questions."

"And what if I don't feel like answerin' 'em, sweets?"

"Oh, you will . . . eventually. There's no hurry. We've got all night."

"Do we now?" he laughed. Then he got up and wandered over to a chest of drawers, pulled a bottle 'a some rotgut out 'a one of 'em. He looked me up and down while he unscrewed the cap, took a shot, and said, "Got a lot more balls than y'did when you was a kid, comin' here and all. What you expect to get outa it?"

"Maybe some peace of mind."

"Become some kinda religious nut since I last saw ya?"

"No."

Still hooking'?"

"No. Still pimpin'?"

"Watch you mouth, girl. Wouldn't want to have me teach you a lesson, now would ya?"

Levar dropped into a tattered ol' easy chair, took another hit off his bottle, and draped a leg over the armrest. He was really enjoying himself. Teasin' ol' Arlene. Makin' her feel bad, just like he'd done in the old days. Felt real good. "If you ain't peddlin' it, how you getting by these days, girl?"

Took my time sitting down on a nearby footstool. Moved it closer so that I could look into Levar's bleary eyes as we talked. **"When I ran away from home, I thumbed my way to New York. Did a mess 'a odd jobs after that: waitressing, cleaning—you know, that kinda thing."**

"Sounds like a waste 'a talent, you ask me."

"More than once I thought the same thing, but not the way you mean. Trouble was, I never had the education to do any better for myself. Got you to thank for that, Levar."

"Honey, y'oughta have a violin with ya when you tells this story."

"Maybe. But you ain't the only one ever treated me bad. Had me some boyfriends along the way were a sight meaner even than you."

"But never half as good, eh, sugar? That why you come hunting me up?"

"You're a pig, Levar."

"Wha's the matter, become a nun? Have that little sugar loaf cemented shut or somethin'?"

"No, Levar, I was too busy . . . dying. Died 'bout six months ago."

Got him while he was taking a drink with that one. He sprayed whiskey into the air in a fine mist. Some of the liquor still dribbling out his mouth, Levar stared at me with a confused expression.

"Say what?"

Then he figured it was some joke he was missin', so he started laughing. Didn't sound like he really thought it was funny. "That was a good one, gal. Weren't expecting that. But you made me waste a slug of good bourbon. Say, you want a shot?"

I waved it away and said, **"I died. Got hit by a subway car in downtown Manhattan and that was all she wrote."**

"What kinda bullshit you tryin' to hand me? Dead. Bitch is crazy. I'm supposed to believe you some kinda ghost?"

"I'm somethin' you never imagined in your wildest dreams, Levar."

I stood up, way above Levar, looking down at him the way you look down on a bug. **"Want to see?"** I said.

"See what . . ."

My fingers reached inside the neck of my blouse. The nails found the nearly invisible seam under my neck. As I slowly pulled up, the skin came off my head. And the wig came with it.

Levar was frozen in his chair, his whiskey-soaked mind tryin' desperately to understand. Seein' in this case was not believin'. The comprehension wouldn't come. His right eye started twitching. It annoyed me, so I slapped it with an open hand.

Levar and the chair both went over on their side. I reached down, grabbed Levar by the front of his T-shirt, and hauled him to his feet. His eye was already swollen shut, blood trickling from a gash next to it. **"Surprise, Levar. I ain't the helpless little girl I used to be."**

"Why, you miserable little bitch, I ought to—"

The slap caught him across that sour, stinkin' old mouth of his. I pulled it enough, so I wouldn't take his head off. His T-shirt ripped and Levar hit the floor. Rolling over, he spat out two bloody teeth. The carpet was so worn in places you could almost see the floor underneath it. When he looked up at me, he was wearing the expression I'd been waiting half a lifetime to see. Fear. I was finally, after all these years, getting through to Levar.

Musta been blind terror made him move that fast. He was up on his feet and grabbing for the gun almost before I knew it. I was plenty speedy myself when the situation called for it. I ripped the gun from his grasp before he could fire. Pity I had to dislocate a coupla his fingers doin' it. I crushed the gun with my bare hand, with Levar watchin'.

"God in Heaven, girl, please don't kill me," he whimpered. I answered his prayers with a fist to his gut. He doubled over and fell to the floor, gaspin' for breath.

I let him lay there while I set the easy chair back on its feet. Then I grabbed Levar by the arm and dumped him into it. Tears of pain and fear were rolling down his cheeks. The sight made my soul sing.

I leaned forward, my hands on the chair's armrests, my nose only inches from Levar's. **"You ready to answer a few questions for me now?"**

"Yes . . . yes, anything! Only please don't hurt me no more."

I cracked my head down hard, breaking his nose.

When Levar came to, I was sitting across the small room, on a beat-up couch with dozens of cigarette burns. Levar didn't notice me at first. Couldn't get past his own pain. He reached up to touch his wreck of a nose and winced, remembering his dislocated fingers. That triggered his memory of me. His good eye sprang open, scanned the room, and found me. Fear kept Levar from saying anything. Maybe he thought that if he was real quiet, I'd fade away.

I didn't.

"Question time, Levar. What made you rape me?"

"Listen, I didn't—"

"Did it feel good?"

He stared at me, worried what was I goin' to do next. I could almost see the gears goin' 'round inside his head, grinding—rusty 'cause they hadn't been used in so long. Then he decided to try something, something that sick, twisted mind of his came up with. You could see it in his face.

"Yes."

"You get off on always beating and bullying me?"

"Yeah . . . yeah, it was real good, mama."

"Liked to make me cry, didn't you?"

"Sure, you were just askin' for it, kid. Anyone coulda seen it a mile off."

I got up, walked slowly over to Levar. **"Did it make you feel like a man, Levar?"**

"Didn't need anythin' to make me feel that way!"

My foot shot out, shattering Levar's kneecap.

"Don't me me laugh!"

Lever screamed in pain and grabbed his ruined leg. I pulled him back straight into the chair by the hair and hissed, **"Tell me about Eli."**

That got through Levar's agony. His eye focused, stared up at me and his bloody lips broke into what musta been a smile. "So, you knows about that, does yo? I wasn't goin' to spring that on you till just near the end."

"The end of what?"

"Just before you kills me, bitch. That's what you got in mind, ain't it?

"Not before you answer my questions. Why'd you bring Eli to the shack?"

"So's I could have one mo' thing to hold over you, 'case you got some crazy notion you was too good for doin' business."

I stared at him like he wasn't quite real. Him almost grinnin', thinkin' he had the upper hand in some way.

"One more question before we get down to the real fun stuff. Ready, Levar?"

"Get on with yo' business, bitch."

"Were you driving the night Mama died in that accident?"

"What?" I could see that caught him by surprise. But

he didn't look guilty; 'fact, he looked far away for a couple moments.

"Were you driving the car?"

Levar still didn't answer. Then finally he said, "No, Fats was. You remember him, don't you? Him and your Mama was having a thing 'fore I split town. She pro'bly wouldn'ta taken up with him if she hadn't been drinkin' so much back then. Didn't mean nothin' to me, though. I didn't care."

Mama and Fats? The thought made me sick. It was impossible. *"You're lying!"*

"The hell I am! What you think your old lady was, some kinda saint? She was a whore, sugar, just like you!"

I felt my mechanical fists clench. Levar was reachin' the end of his road. Wasn't exactly the way I'd imagined it: him beggin' me for his life; me takin' it away. But it'd have to do.

"Yeah, honey, I turned your ma out just after you split. But she just couldn't bring in the money like you could. Too old and raggedy."

"You bastard!"

I grabbed Levar by the ear and shook him. He let out a shriek of pain. "Do it! Go ahead and do it!" he yelled.

I backhanded Levar, breaking his jaw in a dozen pieces. He slumped over in his chair, oozing blood all over the place.

I pulled him up again by the hair. Raised a fist past my head for one last blow. After it, the police would find brains splattered all over this apartment.

This apartment?

Something stopped me.

Looked around the place, like I was seeing it now for the first time . . . seeing the filth and decay, the bottles and cans, the broken thirdhand furniture. Flashed on the neighborhood I'd walked through to get here. It was a good place for a son of a bitch like Levar to die. Then I realized that's exactly what Levar wanted.

That's what all that yelling and bravado was about. Levar figuring it was too hard to go on. Not worth it. And then here comes ol' Arlene to do for him, what he was too chicken-shit to do himself.

He wanted to use her one last time.

Good ol' Arlene.

No way, Levar. Not this time.

The man was living in a sewer and that was where I was goin' to leave him.

On my way out of the neighborhood I came across a pay phone and called for the paramedics. They got there in time and whisked ol' Levar off to the hospital.

The hospital records show that they patched up the ol' rummy the best they could. His knee—well, it was never goin' to be the same again. Not at his age. He'd be crippled for the rest of his life. Must say that news sat well with me.

I pictured Levar making his way through that neighborhood, coming back from the grocery store on his crutches. Neighborhood toughs helping themselves to any of his food that struck their fancy. His Social Security check being ripped off regularly. Levar being afraid to go out at night, too scared and crippled to even try and find another Saturday night special to keep in the apartment, for protection or a way out if things got too bad. Levar the frightened. Levar scared, crippled, helpless, finally gettin' a taste of what it means to be a victim.

It's a hard life, Levar, believe me. But now and again you come across a little justice. Without having to give up another piece of your soul.

The new me sat quietly, deactivated in its secret cubbyhole, zipped into a new latex birthday suit, topped with fiery red hair. Arlene Washington's remains had already been sent off to the incinerator. There'd be no further need for the lady. That chapter of my life was now and forever just a memory.

I done some hard thinkin' the last two days about what had happened. 'Bout how I'd gone right up to the edge . . . and returned. Survived. It was already becomin' like a dream to me. Or something that happened to someone else. That other Arlene Washington. Every day it felt less real.

There were some things I had learned the hard way. My grasp on this second chance in life was still too shaky to risk on a stupid thing such as a petty vendetta.

Every day I felt myself getting stronger, with more control over me 'n my surroundings. And you know, the closer I came to bein' totally independent, the more important it became to me.

I had needed to scare off Levar's ghost. Now I didn't ever need to visit that dreary time in my life no more.

There was even something positive in that whole situation, the way I saw it. I'd dealt with Levar without killing him. I knew now, though I didn't admit it to myself at the time, that it'd been my intended goal. But I hadn't done it. I hadn't killed Levar. Guess I couldn't bring myself to. Not cold-blooded murder.

Now, Chuckie had been an accident. My past had reached out and grabbed me. But I was peaceful now. I was okay.

I knew I was a dangerous weapon. But there'd be no more deaths. I promised myself. I felt terrible about Chuckie, but turnin' myself in wouldn't bring him back, so I just had to make sure it didn't happen again.

And, besides, I was alive. I'd make it up somehow, helping science and mankind. Sacrificing myself would mean depriving the future of what only I could give it. Decided it would be best for all concerned if I just put Chuckie out of my mind and got on with my life.

I'd have to be more careful, though.

I wasn't tough enough to tangle with the boys in blue. Not yet, anyway. Didn't matter how valuable I was, if caught I knew my plug would still be pulled. The thought made me shudder.

I'd have to be a whole lot more discreet about some things; find me a new way to meet men. Figured I might check out some church singles group. Might help me weed out some of the losers. Better idea than calling up on that—

"Holy Jesus! The party line!"

How could I been so stupid? I mentally kicked myself down the entire length of my data base. And I call myself a super computer. How could I have forgotten about the party line? Was I asking to get caught?

The company that ran the party line would have records, for billing, of everyone who called their damn service. If the police made the connection between Chuckie's mystery date and the party line, they'd be out checking the phone records. And they'd discover one of their customers was calling from the Pentagon. What's worse, they'd realize that the call came from a phone line that was supposed to carry only computer transmissions. The trail would lead straight to me.

It wasn't no big deal gettin' into the party line's computer files and doctorin' their records. I simply changed one digit in the phone number, and I was free and clear. The files now showed that the calls to the service had been made from a phone in the Pentagon's main security office, a line dozens of people had access to. There'd be no way for the cops to track down who made the calls.

I was safe.

Then a disturbing thought struck me.

I raced me back to the party line's records, checked out its command file for the past two days, and knew I'd found some deep trouble. I was too late. The party line's records had already been accessed earlier. Someone had pulled 'em up and made a hard copy. All this had happened less than an hour ago. Had to be the police.

Tried not to panic, to think it all through. There had to be some other way to hide. I thought about switching around a few of the Pentagon's lines to throw them off the scent. But that would throw everything in an uproar, without giving me any more protection.

No, I had to play out the hand I was holdin', keep a sharp eye out for what was going down and bluff my ass off. I was sure I could do it. I'd skate. The police were looking for a knock-'em-dead blonde, not a computer. There was no way I'd let 'em catch up with me. I was still in complete control of the situation.

Then why was I feeling so nervous?

PART FOUR

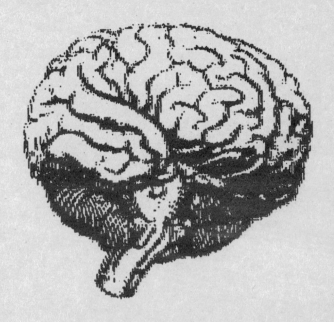

Life is a tragedy for those who feel, and a comedy for those who think.
—Jean De La Bruyere

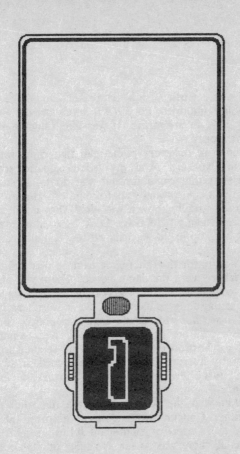

For a whole week nothin' happened. No phone calls, no police inquiries, no SWAT teams breaking down the lab door to arrest me. It was like Chuckie Baxter never happened.

I listened in on every phone call that came into the Pentagon. Nothing. And my video cameras scanned every visitor that came through the doors, lookin' for that cop you could usually spot a mile off. But no cigar. How would I really know it was him? They don't exactly wear a sign saying "Homicide Dick." I even planted additional bugs up in the security offices. But still came up with zip.

This waitin' for the other shoe to drop was makin' me crazy. Where were the damn police? There was an item in the local news about Chuckie being discovered the very next day after it happened. So it wasn't as if they didn't know he was dead. Did the police consider Chuckie a low priority or something? I checked him out, looking for answers. All I found is he seemed to have led a pretty average life. No police record or anything like that. Just a few parking tickets. So what the hell was goin' on?

Checking out the D.C. police case files didn't help much either. Chuckie was listed as an unsolved homicide assigned to a Detective Lieutenant Julius Sizemore. And that was all there was so far. No juicy tidbits about the crime. No tantalizing leads. No way of telling how far they'd gotten with their investigation.

A week with absolutely nothing to report. Then came that fateful Tuesday.

They say every cloud has its silver lining. That's what Tuesday was like.

First the cloud: The call came in at exactly 10:37, through the main switchboard. Just like a thousand other calls received at the Pentagon every day. One of the ladies on duty answered, "Defense operator number seven. How can I help you?"

The voice on the other end of the line said, "Like to talk to someone in Security."

"I'll put you through, sir."

My ears sorta pricked when I heard it was Security the caller wanted. I paid a little extra attention to the call. Someone answered on the second ring. "Good morning. Department of Defense Security."

"Mornin'. My name's Lieutenant Sizemore. I'm with the D.C. police."

"What can I do for you, Lieutenant?"

The gravely voice answered, "I'm working on a homicide. Been tracking down some phone numbers connected with the case, and one of them—"

After a second or so, the man in the security department asked, "You still there, Lieutenant? Hello? Hello? Lieutenant?"

In response he got a dial tone, so he hung up, logged the call, and put it out of his mind.

A few moments later another enlisted man on desk duty in Security had an outside call routed to him. "Security."

"Yes. My name is Lieutenant Sizemore. I was just talking to—"

Again I cut him off.

When he called back a third time I recognized his voice and severed the connection before he even got past the operator. He didn't bother calling back a fourth time.

Not exactly smooth, was it? But effective. I'd worry 'bout smooth later. After I got over the shock. After a week I guess I was hoping they were too busy or something to deal with a little thing like Chuckie's murder. Appears I was mistaken. I had to get my act together. Sizemore's next step would be showing up in person. I figured that would be sometime after lunch. I had to have my game plan ready and in place by then. I'd be able to handle it.

About five hours after Sizemore's call, Fate stepped in and threw me a curve. Was a welcome curve, but it still put me off my stride. It's the best excuse I got for why

I messed up down the line. There had to be some good reason for me fouling up as bad as I did.

The curve was that silver lining I mentioned earlier:

Wolfgung was on duty when Walt came rushing into the lab. Without so much as a hello Walt snapped, "Wolf, go to the men's room or the Concourse for five minutes. But come back in five minutes exactly. Okay?"

Confused, Wolf answered, "Sure. What's up?"

"No questions, all right? Just be back here in five."

"Okay," said Wolfgung as he made his way out the door.

As soon as we were alone, Walt hurried over to his desk and began searching through a pile of file folders he had in the bottom drawer. When he found the one he wanted, he turned to me and said, "Arlene, I have an appointment with the Chiefs of Staff at four o'clock. It's taking place in conference room 3-C. There's a security monitoring system in that room. Do you think you can patch into it?"

All innocence I said, **"Of course. But why should I?"**

Practically burstin' with excitement, Walt said, "This is a surprise meeting. Found out about it less than an hour ago. But I've got a pretty good idea what it's going to be about. I think you ought to sit in on it. I mean, listen in. Oh, you know what I mean."

"What . . ."

"I know I'm blathering, but bear with me, Arlene. If it's what I think it is, it's going to be *big*."

"Want to fill me in a little?"

"No time! Talk to you when I get back."

He was out the door.

Walt was the first one there at the meeting. I watched him go over to the far end of the table and take a seat. At least he tried to. Trouble was, he couldn't sit still. Kept jumpin' up and pacin' around the room, looking at the photos on the wall, walkin' back to his seat, messin' with papers in the file he brought along, then gettin' up and started the whole routine all over again.

Finally the Joint Chiefs of Staff came into the room, the whole gang of 'em. The lighting in the conference room wasn't what it should have been, so as the five grand old men of the military made their ways to their seats, the brass and gold uniform buttons left neon trails on my monitor. Polite greetings were exchanged between the generals, admiral, and Walt. Then everyone sat and got down to business.

The combined-military Chief of Staff was the first to speak: "Dr. Hillerman, have you any notion why we called you here today on such short notice?"

Walt fidgeted in his seat, smiled, and answered, "Not really. But I have my suspicions."

"Scuttlebutt in thè hallways?" asked the Chief of the Army.

"No," answered Walt. "But you recently asked me to program some tactical exercises into the system that led me to think something pretty big might be coming our way."

Couldn't figure out what Walt was talking about. We were always getting battlefield simulations to run through my system. What exercises was he talking about? What had I missed, being so absorbed in my own problems? Wish I'd been keepin' a better eye on what had been going on around here lately. I'd been too busy watchin' my ass.

"Doctor, we're pleased to announce that we're here to confirm those suspicions. We've been closely scrutinizing your operation. And, I must say, we've been very favorably impressed. You run a tight ship."

"I'm afraid the system itself must take the lion's share of the credit for its efficiency, sir," said Walt. Think he was actually blushing.

"Whatever the reason, things have never run so smoothly around here. Everyone we talk to grudgingly gives your department credit for the current high state of readiness and effectiveness. Which brings me directly to the reason for this meeting."

"NORAD?"

The chief looked at him, paused, and said, "Way ahead of us, aren't you? Yes, it's NORAD. As you must be well aware, this world of ours keeps getting more and more complicated and complex. It's becoming increas-

ingly difficult for our personnel to keep up with all the
data that continuously pours into NORAD. The operation
has its own computer system, but systems become out-
dated almost overnight these days. It's hard to keep up
with all the advances that come down the pike.

"But from what we've seen of your system, new technology can be easily grafted onto your existing setup. It
doesn't have to be thrown out and replaced every time
some new gizmo is invented, right?"

Walt sat straight up in his chair and said, "That's right.
Project Cyborg has proven more adaptable than any of
its predecessors. It can easily integrate different computer languages into its system and make them its own."

"That's what our studies show," interjected the chief.
"And that's why we've reached the decision we have.
We want your system to take over the duties of the cur-
rent NORAD computer."

I guess it was lucky I didn't burn out my circuits hearing the news. This was better than Christmas in July,
hitting the numbers, or havin' some rich uncle you never
heard of leave it all to you. On top of this it was a
complete surprise. I didn't have no clue.

One minute Walt 'n me are goin' 'bout our own business, and the next thing you know the brass have put us
in charge of the *button*, the entire works for the strategic
nuclear planning for the whole damn U.S. of A. I mean,
the entire arsenal: H-bombs, cruise missiles, Trident sub-
marines. They musta trusted us. Thought we could do
the job right. Well, I was goin' to see to it, it was goin'
to be perfect. Amazing' they didn't see what a tactical
boo-boo they'd just made.

Sure, the brass thought they were going to hang on to
the final decision-making process. They'd still be the
head honchos. 'Course, they only held onto that foolish
illusion because they didn't know how I really operated.
Not even Walt realized that once they let me get my hot
little electric hands on their system, it was mine. All
mine. I was going to be the one callin' all the shots. Mr.
President, just for the record here, thought you'd like
to know that a you're no longer commander-in-chief of

the armed forces. Arlene Washington's got the job now. Arlene Washington's the one in the driver's seat.

Leastways she soon will be. But first there were preparations to be made.

There were overrides to circumvent, fail-safes to neutralize. What a nice military word: *neutralize*. So clean and businesslike. I'd also need me an extra backup generator, maybe something nuclear, and to soup up the one I already had. Make sure I never ever lost power, ever again. I'd have to take all this slowly, so no one would catch onto what was coming down until it was too late to change it. Might take me months to pull it off but, honey, at long last I could relax, stop worryin' 'bout someone pullin' that damn plug 'a mine.

No one would ever be able to push Arlene Washington around again. 'Cause I'd just become the world's newest nuclear power. Welcome to the club, gal.

Walt was 'bout ready to lose his marbles, he was so anxious to get started. Why, switching over NORAD to our system was the most exciting thing ever happened to him. When Walt rushed back here to tell Wolf what had happened, the two of 'em hooted, hollered, and danced around the lab for about five minutes straight.

When they finally came down some, Walt said they were to get started immediately workin' out a timetable for the conversion. He asked Wolf if he would mind doin' a double shift tonight. Maxwell assured him that he understood perfectly the excitement his boss must be going through and that he had no problem with pinch hitting for him. So Walt sent Maxwell out for an early dinner. He'd hold down the fort till Wolf's return.

Alone at last, Walt said, "Arlene, how does it feel to be given the most important job this country has to offer?"

"This new assignment come with a raise?"

"You name it, lady, you've got it."

How about a private Jacuzzi?"

"It'd just warp your circuits."

"Spoil sport."

"But seriously, Arlene, this is exactly what we've been working for."

"Soggy circuits?"

"A job so important that they won't ever again think about shutting you down. A hundred Colonel Dearlings could now show up with petitions signed by a thousand Senator Christophers, and it wouldn't mean a thing."

"Real job security, huh?"

"The best there is: an assignment no one but you will ever be able to handle."

"I wish we had some champagne to celebrate with."

"Me too. I guess congratulations will just have to do."

"And congratulations to you too, Dr. Hillerman. I'm

happy for you. I know how hard you've worked to make
this happen."

"We both did it, lady."

"Here's to us."

This Lieutenant Sizemore showed up at the Pentagon
about an hour after Walt split for the day, a lot later
than I expected. Busy man, I guess. I noticed him comin'
up the walkway from visitors parking. He wasn't wearing
no sign but he had cop written all over him just the same.
A big man, six feet, four inches, bit overweight, salt-and-
pepper hair, with the look of a guy who knew exactly
where he was going and had every right to be there.

A flash of his ID got him in through the front door
and a pass to Security. There was nothing I could reason-
ably do to keep him out. I had one of my security droids
escort him and then hang around so I could have a better
look at what was goin' on in the room than I'd get from
the room's surveillance cameras. A young Marine lieutenant greeted Sizemore at the desk and asked if he could
be of any help. So the cop told the Marine why he was
there and gave him the phone number he was interested
in. The lieutenant went over to a reverse in-house directory and looked it up. I saw the young Marine's face
cloud up with concern when he found the number. He
then got up from the desk and asked Sizemore to wait
while he checked on something. So the cop quietly
watched the Marine disappear into a back room and settled in for a nice long wait.

Always heard cops were champion waiters. Sizemore
sure seemed to be. He casually wandered around the
public area, checking out photos and recruiting posters
hanging on the wall. When he got tired of doing that, he
bellied up to the counter, leaned his elbows on it, and
started eyeballing everyone working on the other side of
it. Being cops 'a sorts themselves, the security crew ignored him.

Ten minutes later, the Marine lieutenant returned and
asked Lieutenant Sizemore to follow him. I had a pretty
good idea where they were headed, so I switched my

attentions over to the new surveillance camera in General Horace's office.

Sure enough the young lieutenant brought Sizemore directly there. General Horace had Lieutenant Perry with him. The general immediately stood up, extended his hand, and said, "Lieutenant Sizemore, I'm General Felix Horace, head of Pentagon security. This is Lieutenant Perry, in charge of a particular project here in the Pentagon. The lieutenant tells me you're interested in a certain phone line in the building. You're free to go, Lieutenant."

As the Marine made his exit, Sizemore lowered himself into a chair and said, "Yes sir, I'd like to know who has access to this particular phone."

General Horace leaned forward and said, "Why don't you first tell me what this is all about? We've got a bit of a situation here, and I'd like to have a better understanding of what's going on before we continue."

"Murder's going on, General," said Sizemore without a moment's hesitation. But then he sat back in his chair, pro'bly thinkin' a little diplomacy couldn't hurt. "Sir, I'm investigating the homicide of one Charles William Baxter III. He was killed in his own apartment some time last Friday night. You may have read about it in the papers."

Horace turned to look at Perry and was answered with a slight shake of the head. "No, I'm afraid this is the first I've heard of it. What does this have to do with the number you're interested in?"

Sizemore reached into a coat pocket, pulled out a notebook, flipped it open, and said, glancing at it, "Baxter was seen earlier, that evening with a good-looking blonde, mid-twenties, about twenty-two–twenty-four. Unfortunately, no one seems to know who she is.

"When I interviewed a few of Baxter's friends, I found out he had a date Friday night with some woman he'd met through a party line service. I then found the service listed in Baxter's private phone book. The service was real cooperative about giving me a copy of Baxter's billing record. Unfortunately, they weren't as cooperative about having their computer kick out the billing numbers of anyone who'd been on the party line the same time

Baxter had in the last two months. Client confidentiality, you know. Had to get a court order, then they coughed it up."

"And that's how you came by this number you're inquiring about?" asked Lieutenant Perry.

"Yeah. Been checking on everyone that showed up on the line more than once with Baxter. Every other number comes up clean. I saved this Pentagon one till last."

"Why?"

"Because of the way Baxter was murdered. The crime scene was a pretty grisly sight. The coroner says Baxter was killed by someone punching their fist clean through his chest cavity and out the back."

General Horace looked stunned. "And you think this blond woman did that?"

"No, sir, that don't figure. Whoever did Baxter had to be big, extremely strong, and probably an expert in karate."

"Just the kind of man you might find in the military," added Perry.

"That thought has admittedly crossed my mind. The way I see it, sir, this blonde has or had a black belt boyfriend who didn't like his lady stepping out on him. He must have followed the blonde and Baxter back to the victim's apartment and killed him while she was there or just after she left. I'd like to talk to the lady and find out which it was."

Horace and Perry exchanged glances. Perry shrugged and Horace said, "You better tell him, Lieutenant."

"Yes, sir. Lieutenant, are you sure that number you have is correct?"

"Absolutely. It shows up close to twenty times last month."

Perry sat back resignedly in his chair, rubbed his jaw, and said, "Then that leaves us with a little problem."

"How so?"

"That number you have is for a computer line. Regular phone calls are not supposed to be able to go out on that line."

Sizemore thought on that a moment and asked, "Couldn't someone tap into the line and make calls?"

"Yes, if they knew what they were doing. But there's no blond woman working in the section where that line terminates."

"Can I check that out for myself?"

"Well, that brings us to another sticky issue," said Perry. "This particular section is a top-secret area."

Sizemore again reached into his coat, pulled out a wallet, and handed a card to General Horace. "I'm a weekend warrior, General. Lieutenant Commander in the Naval Reserves. I've got a top-secret clearance. You can check on it."

"We will," said the general. "And if your clearance is up to date, it'll make things easier for all of us."

Sizemore put his wallet back. "Aside from looking over this area, I'd like to interview everyone that has had possible access to this line in the past month."

"That'd be easy," offered Perry. "Only six people have been working there of late: three regular weekday technicians and two part-time techs that do twelve-hour shifts on the weekends. The sixth person quit and moved to Ohio two weeks ago. Diana Vitas was her name. Red hair."

"Don't think I'll need to bother with her or the weekend shift. Most of the calls were placed during the week. These part-timers ever work weekdays?"

"No, both have other jobs."

"Then can you set me up with the other three?"

"No problem. One of them's on duty now," answered Perry. "The other two we'll try to get on the phone. But if we don't reach them, you'll have to come back when their shifts start."

"No problem. Any of them women?"

"One. On the swing shift . . . a new gal. Can't recall her name right off."

"What color hair?" asked Sizemore.

"Jet black."

"Well, I'll talk to her anyhow. Say, if I can ask, what do they do in this section, only takes five of them?"

"Computer work."

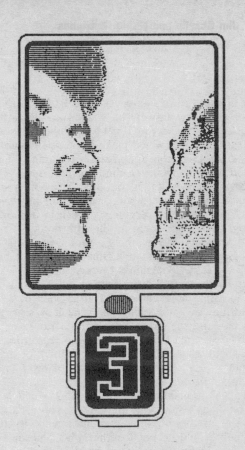

This Lieutenant Sizemore was a real pain in the butt. Didn't get the answers he wanted, so he turned up again like a bad penny at 11:30 P.M. Hopin' maybe what he'd learn this time would make sense. Lieutenant Perry checked on Sizemore's top-secret clearance and attempted to reach Walt by phone several times. I didn't muck with Perry's findin' out that Sizemore's security clearance was in order, but I made sure he never got through to Walter by rerouting his call to a phone in a deserted conference room on the fifth floor.

God Almighty, the last thing I wanted was Walt Hillerman being brought into this situation before I had the chance to really think things through.

I let Perry reach Kristyn Fett at home to ask her to come in a half hour early for a little chat before work. He skillfully avoided telling her what it was he wanted to discuss, and she didn't seem at all curious.

Even if she had been, there was no reason for me to worry about what either Kristyn or Wolfie, for that matter, had to say. They knew nothing of my secret life. They had no beans to spill.

Walt was something else again. How would he react to questioning? Stonewall the cops or play let's make a deal? Did Sizemore have enough information to clue him onto me? Would he put together who Chuckie's nightmare date really was? And if he did, would Sizemore share that kinda information with a person who could be a suspect in the crime he was investigatin'? Just how *smart* was this cop? All them questions and no real answers.

After some cybernetic hair pullin' I came to the conclusion there was only one option to run with: I had to keep hands off Sizemore's investigation, let it take its course. The cards he'd laid out so far contained nothin' would point a finger at me as a bloody-handed killer. For the moment I was safe. But if I threw up any obvious roadblocks, or drew any unwanted attention, suspicion might turn in my direction so fast I'd blink and miss it.

Kristyn and Sizemore turned up at Security exactly the same moment, so Perry introduced them and took them over to where they were goin' to do the interview. Sizemore never took his eyes off Kristyn; she didn't give him a second glance until they were seated around a small wooden table in the empty back room. Perry let Sizemore ask all the questions.

"Lieutenant Perry tells me you've only worked here three weeks. How do you like the job so far "

Kristyn thought about it, playing with her hair without realizing it. She had this layered cut, where she'd wrap a lock 'round her finger, pull it out away from her head, and then let it go, leaving a horn-like cowlick standin' up in the air. As it settled back down slowly, she said, "To tell you the truth, I find it kinda boring. Everything's so automated and efficient, there's not much for me to do."

"Ever get anyone coming down to use the phone during your shift?"

"Are you kidding? I get to work, relieve Dr. Hillerman, and that's the last living soul I see for eight hours. I do the swing shift and it's in the basement. Believe me, no one ever comes around."

Sizemore considered this and then asked, "Ever see a blond woman hanging around when you came in to relieve Dr. Hillerman?"

"No, he's usually by himself. No, make that he's always by himself. I've never seen anyone down there with him. Say, what's this all about? Someone making long-distance phone calls on Uncle Sam's dime?"

"Something like that, Miss Fett. Thank you for your cooperation. When you relieve Mr. Maxwell, can you ask him to come up to Security?"

"Sure. Maxwell's got the duty, huh? Yeah, I'll send him right up."

Kristyn split, leaving Perry and Sizemore sitting around the table. After a few moments Perry asked, "Well, what do you think?"

"She's cute. But I don't think she's involved. The calls to the party line were coming from that line before she was hired. Just wanted to see if she'd ever seen a blond woman hanging around."

"Maxwell should prove more useful in that respect. He's young, late twenties. He'd notice and remember your mysterious blond bombshell."

"Let's hope so."

'Course, Wolfgung didn't remember any blondes wandering through or making phone calls. After he checked with Perry if it was okay to explain to the lieutenant about how things worked downstairs, Wolf said, "We don't get much, if any, traffic in the lab most days. The majority of the stuff sent down to us comes via the service droids. Everyone in the Pentagon uses them as their own personal inter-office messenger service these days. Occasionally one of the brass will stop by to chat with Walt—Dr. Hillerman, that is. But that's about it. The lab's front door is plastered with all these Classified-Keep Out signs. It discourages casual visitors."

"There's also a security droid by the first-floor entrance to the elevator to keep out unauthorized personnel. The elevator only stops at the first floor and basement," Perry added.

Scratching his chin, deep in thought, Sizemore concluded, "Then no one from the outside could possibly make unauthorized phone calls from the lab."

"That's not entirely true," said Wolf, a big grin on his face.

"What do you mean?" asked Sizemore.

"I'll answer your question if you answer one of mine."

"And that is?" asked Sizemore.

"What interest does a city cop have in who uses our lab phone?"

"How do you know I'm a city cop?"

"I didn't, for sure, until you just confirmed it for me. But the fact is, you don't look like any DIA inspector I ever met. Not spit and polish enough."

Perry and Sizemore looked at each other for confirmation. Finally Perry said, "He might be able to help us get to the bottom of this mystery quicker."

Sizemore nodded and then explained why he was there and what he was up to. Wolf listened without so much as a peep, taking it all in and thought it over a sec. "There's two possibilities. One: an outsider made his or her way to the Pentagon's main telephone terminal, tapped into the line, and made the calls from there. But that seems unlikely. For security reasons the terminals are locked and checked regularly. Isn't that right, Lieutenant?"

Perry nodded, so Sizemore asked, "How do you know this?"

"When we were installing our computer system, we were constantly having to wait for Security to come down and let us into the main terminals to connect up our computer telephone feeds."

Satisfied, Sizemore said, "Okay. So what's possibility number two?"

"That someone went to the trouble of tapping into the computer lines from their work station. There're not a lot of folks smart enough to pull that off, but there're a few around who might be able to figure it out. They might have also done it from a fax terminal."

"But why bother?" asked Sizemore.

"If they were calling a party line and charging the calls to the government, they wouldn't want this light-fingered touch traced back to them. And if they were sharp enough to come up with this tap idea, they'd probably know that accounting doesn't keep a very close watch on where computer transactions go. They're too busy making sure no one uses the regular lines to call their relatives in Italy or wherever."

"Hmmm, makes sense," offered Sizemore. 'Any way we can trace this caller, if that's how it was pulled off?"

"Maybe. The computer itself might be able to back-track these calls. But I kind of doubt it. If it did, you might find that the calls were made from a very public area. Your odds on finding your blond lady aren't very good, I'm afraid."

"Damn," muttered Sizemore. "Not exactly what I wanted to hear."

I knew it. My patience paid off. I was home free.

Wolf's impromptu theorizing had given me an out. All I had to do was wait for someone to ask me to trace the unauthorized calls, and I could claim they'd originated from a typing pool or some other area with a lot of uncontrolled traffic and plenty of blond suspects for Sizemore to hound. So I was off the hook.

From the conversation I overheard between Perry and Sizemore after Wolf left, it seemed pretty obvious that they were going to ask Walt to do the phone check for them when Sizemore met him the next afternoon in the lab. That'd work for me. One last interview I could keep tabs on, a tricky move on my part, and all my troubles would be over.

Then I could turn my attention to more important things, like taking over NORAD's computer duties and becoming the most powerful and independent creature on the face of this good green earth. Security sure does give a body a nice feelin'.

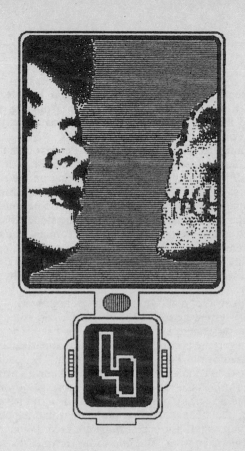

Lieutenant Sizemore left the Pentagon looking kinda down that night. His interview with Wolfgung pro'bly kicked the crap outa what he thought was a pretty good lead. Poor lil' guy.

I continued to make sure he and Perry couldn't reach Walt, not that it made any difference now. But I was superstitious, didn't want Walt's working on the NORAD conversion plans interrupted. Sizemore arranged to drop in the next day when Walt was on duty. So he could look over the lab and kill two birds with one stone. Everyone figured interviewing Walt was just a formality now. But as Sizemore pointed out, police work was making sure no stone was left unturned, even when it seemed unlikely there was anything under it. Cop philosophy: how quaint.

I spent the night doing a little homework on the NORAD system myself. Wished that I could enter it and get a look around, but decided that was risky. The couple times I'd come up to the threshold of that particular computerized world, I'd held off exploring it. The roadblocks into it didn't look all that tough, but knowing what lay on the other side of 'em kept me from going on. If I screwed up in any other data realm, it would have been no big deal. The worst that probably would happen was I'd dump some insurance company's records for the last six months. So what? But one wrong move in the NORAD system might mean World War III.

Decided I'd wait for an invitation before carefully entering this space. Wanted to know exactly what I was doing before messin' with the power of the atom for my own *personal* use. In the meantime, I'd brush up on physics, rocket propulsion, geography, world news, politics, anything and everything that would help me . . . when I took over. I was determined to be a benevolent and *efficient* despot.

*   *   *

Walt showed up at the lab the next day at his regular time. First thing he did was hang his dripping raincoat up on the metal coatrack by the door. A dog-tired Wolfgung turned to greet him, saw the puddle forming on the floor, asked about the weather, and got 'bout what you might expect as a reply. "It stinks. Not fit for man or beast."

"Figures . . . and me without an umbrella. What's my problem? Why don't I ever listen to the weather report?"

"Masochism?" ventured Walt.

You could practically see the light bulb go on above Wolf's head just then; he snapped his fingers and told Walt he remembered Perry wanted a call from him the moment he walked through the door. Walt got on the horn and found out the lieutenant was bringing down a city homicide detective to ask Walt some questions.

Walt wasn't at all happy to hear this. Why couldn't the interview take place up in Perry's office? Why breach the lab's security? But Perry assured Walt that the lab's integrity would not be compromised. General Horace didn't want anyone thinking the Pentagon was up to something. He wasn't about to get tangled up in any media circus because some cop didn't get to see every-thing he wanted to see. Full cooperation; that was an order.

Everything would work out okay, Perry reasoned. This detective had a top-secret clearance. Besides, what could this policeman learn from a short visit to the lab? Lady El's true nature had been camouflaged by walls of hard-ware. And having talked with this policeman, Perry was certain Sizemore didn't know the difference between a mainframe and a personal computer, even if the differ-ence bit him on the ass. So Sizemore wasn't going to stumble onto anything he shouldn't.

All of a sudden Walt started in wanting to know what this police interview was all about. I couldn't believe my ears, his coppin' an attitude like that, making himself look guilty of something or other. I wanted to clap a hand over his mouth.

But Perry didn't seem to notice. Murder. That soft-ened Walt's attitude. Without skippin' a beat he filled

Walt in on what Sizemore was there for. "That's terrible. I'll be glad to help this Lieutenant Sizemore in any way I can. Send him down as soon as he arrives."

What a easy touch that Walter. Lucky for me I'd seen to it all his good intentions wouldn't land me in the 'lectric chair. Or would that be 'lectric jar in my case?

Walt got off the phone and turned to Wolfgung. "Do you know what this interview is all about?"

"Yeah, talked to Sizemore last night as I was gettin' off shift."

"This is terrible. We may have a killer loose among us."

Wolf chuckled, "Murderer, Walt. This is the Pentagon. There's plenty of killers running around its halls. That's what they're paid to do."

"Yes, I guess you're right, there. It seems like Lady El should be able to help track down whoever made those calls to the party line."

Wolfgung was feelin' enough of a second wind to lay his tapping into the computer lines theory on Walt. Bein' that this was one egghead talkin' to another, Wolf really got into it, throwing around all sorts of technical terms even I had a hard time followin'. But in the end both Walt and Wolfie agreed that I could most likely hunt down where the calls came from.

Walt put Maxwell on loading the appropriate commands into me to do the job, while he went over to his desk and sorted through the day's mail. I kept a close eye on Walter. He seemed a million miles away, lost in his own thoughts. I sure wished I could see what was going on inside that head. Design flaw there, you ask me, not to have a window in the forehead.

What was the man thinkin' 'bout? The mail sat open on the desk in front of him, but he was absentmindedly playin' with his gold-plated letter opener, not noticing the book of Giger's artwork sitting under the mail.

Wolf said abruptly, "Lady El's come up with it."

Walt rushed over to Wolf's side and looked down at the viewscreen his assistant was sitting in front of. "That's the number the calls were made from?"

"That's what Lady El claims. Ever know her to be wrong?"

Walt scratched his chin and slowly said, "No. Any idea whose number that is?"

"We could go through the Pentagon directory until we came across it in the listings."

"I've got a better idea. Lady El, where is the phone, this number belongs to, located?"

I gave it a moment or two before answering. **"In the copy room on the fourth floor."**

Walt and Wolf turned to look at each other and frowned. Then Wolf said, "Anyone in the building could have made those calls. Everyone's got access to the copy rooms."

I'd decided not to limit Sizemore's search to just one department. It might not discourage him enough to give up on this particular lead. But if he had the entire Pentagon staff as suspects, well . . .

"I don't think I want to be around here when that cop finds out his one lead's just gone south on him." Wolf got his jacket on and headed for the door. "He didn't look like the kind of guy who takes bad news gracefully."

"So you're going to leave him for me to deal with, eh? Thanks a lot." Walt gazed at the green diode viewscreen.

"That's why they pay you the big bucks, boss man. See you tomorrow."

" 'Night." Walt looked weary, but at least it looked like this drama was over. So he could get back to some NORAD computations that awaited his attentions.

Lieutenant Sizemore showed up at the Pentagon a little after five. One of my droids took him over to the security office, where he picked up a hall pass. Then the little guy escorted Sizemore to the lab. I kept a sharp eye on 'em as they made their way through the corridors, filled with people heading home for the night. There was something that bothered me about him tonight, but I couldn't put my finger on what it was. In fact, I coulda sworn there was somethin' almost cheerful about him. Maybe that was it. Sizemore had the feel of a hunter about him again, chewing his gum slowly, deliberately eyeing everyone he passed. Still searchin' for that blonde, sport? Good luck, pal. You'll need it.

The droid and Sizemore made their way to the elevator at the southern end of the building, the only one that would take them to the basement level these days. The security droid standing guard there did not challenge them.

When Sizemore got out of the elevator in the basement, he spotted a rubber trash can right outside the droid service station door, waiting to be emptied by the night shift cleaning crew. He walked over to it, lifted the lid, spat his gum into it, and continued to follow the droid down the hall. The corridor made a sharp left turn and ended at a set of double doors. Each door had signs meant to keep out unauthorized personnel. Sizemore eyed the signs appreciatively and said to the droid, "Yeah, I can see now why you wouldn't have many casual visitors popping by." I didn't figure the statement deserved a response and so the droid said nothing.

It opened a door for Sizemore and he walked through without so much as a thank-you. I left the security droid out in the hall, according to standard procedure.

Soon as Walt saw the Lieutenant, he got up from his seat and walked over, hand extended. "You must be Lieutenant Sizemore. Good to meet you."

"Same here. I understand Lieutenant Perry filled you in a bit about what I'm looking for."

Nodding, Walt said, "That's right. And I've been doing some checking. But I'm afraid you're not going to be overjoyed with what I came up with."

Walt explained about the computer search he and Wolf had conducted and the results. "So you see any one of over twelve thousand employees have access to that particular phone. It's supposed to be only for calling around in the building, but if you dial nine, you can get an outside line. The caller probably used some kind of illegal black box device to transfer the call to the computer trunk line. A fairly sophisticated trick. But now finding out who made those calls is going to be damn near impossible."

Sizemore pondered this information a few moments. "Maybe not as impossible as you think."

"Really?" asked Walt incredulously. "That's going to be quite a job, then, even if you only check on the good-looking blondes that work here. My guess is there must be more than five hundred employees would fit that description."

"Terrific. Well, I guess we'd better get started, then," muttered Sizemore.

"Say, what makes you so sure that this blond woman works at the Pentagon? What if one of those other phone numbers you checked on was the one she used? One of the people you checked with could've been lying concerning a blond woman using their phone. After all, a murder had been committed. Any one of the people you talked to could have been the killer covering his tracks."

Sizemore stopped gnawing on the back of a knuckle and came out of his thoughts long enough to say, "Would have agreed with you on that supposition yesterday, Doc. But today I know that the blonde definitely works here."

What?

"How can you be so sure?" asked Walt.

"We didn't find Charles Baxter's car until this morning. It wasn't in its regular parking spot in the apartment's basement garage. Didn't realize this until it occurred to me that Baxter'd been out on a date the night he died. Probably drove to that date. Figured there might be something interesting inside his vehicle.

Yes, I remembered it then: Chuckie had had a hard time finding a parking place that night. We had to drive around looking. Then we walked a good block and a half to get to his apartment building.

Sizemore continued, "When we found the car wasn't in the garage, I put out an APB on it. Turned up yesterday, papered with parking tickets on the next block over. Why it took that long to locate is beyond me."

"You found something in the car?" asked Walt.

"Yeah, Baxter had this leather trash pouch hanging from the driver's door."

I could see it in my mind's eye. Silver to match the car's interior, hooked over the window knob.

"There was a crumpled note inside it. Read: Pick up A. W. at P—South parking lot.''

"And you figure P has to be the Pentagon?"

Sizemore nodded and said, "Now all I have to do is figure out who A. W. is."

Arlene Washington, you damn fool! Why did you give the dude your real name? 'Cause calling the party line was supposed to lead to romance, not murder. And who would've thought he'd need a note to remind him where to pick up his date. Damn! Damn! Damn! Everything was falling to pieces.

I zoomed in tight on Walt's face, waiting for it to dawn on him who A. W. was. Nothing. All he did was say, "Then I would suggest your next stop is Personnel first thing in the morning. They should be able to easily pin down for you who the blond A. W. is."

"Sure hope so," said Sizemore as he got up from his seat. "Thanks for all your help, Doc."

"By the way, Lieutenant, what time Friday night was this Charles Baxter killed?"

"Coroner figures around three in the morning. Why'd you ask?"

Walking over to the computer console and opening the log book, Walt said. "It's just that most murders are committed at night, aren't they?"

"Yeah, I guess so . . . what's your point?"

"Well, I have this idea that there must be some organic change that takes place in people when the sun sets that triggers a more hostile behavior pattern in some."

Pretty lame, Walt.

I could see him flipping through the log pages until he reached the entries made that fateful Friday night.

Not realizing what was going on around him, Sizemore said, "Yeah, I've heard that theory before and the one about the moon making people crazy. Not sure I buy either one, even though we do get a lot more crimes being committed on nights with full moons. I just figure the bad guys can see better then."

Walt turned to Sizemore and said, "Let me walk you to the elevator."

Hillerman'd figured it out, all right. Damn. Now what was I goin' to do?

As they stepped out of the lab, Walt said to the droid on duty, "Remain here. I'll escort the lieutenant out."

Was I 'bout to be tossed on the scrap heap? Or did he really just want to see Sizemore out of the building unharmed? Could I trust Walt to keep quiet? We'd been together for so long, helped each other so much, been friends. More than friends. He couldn't turn on me. Needed me too much, just the way I needed him. Couldn't risk losin' it all by turnin' me in. All he worked for would go swirling down the toilet. I had to trust Walt. What other choice did I have?

Then I remembered.

"I have human needs, and one of those needs is companionship with my own kind, other humans."

I clicked over to the monitors and bugs I had watchin' the hallway; Sizemore and Walt strolled nonchalantly toward the elevators. Sizemore was saying, "This really is quite a setup you've got. What exactly is it you do here?"

"Sorry. All information on this project is strictly on a need-to-know basis," said Walt, only a few steps away from the elevator.

"Oh, sure. I understand. Sorry I asked."

Walt pushed the button for the elevator.

"Don't be. You were very open with me about your investigation. Only regret that I can't return the favor." Walt glanced up at the floor-indicator panel above the elevator door. It showed the car was sitting on the first floor, not moving.

"Well, I figured playing straight with you would pay off in the long run. I'm really not supposed to go into such detail with non-police personnel, but the way it looked to me—"

Some cop instinct made Sizemore spin around the same time Walt did. Maybe he knew something was wrong, or maybe it was just the expression on Walt's face when he saw the security droid coming around the corner, heading directly for them.

Time to pay the piper.

Without warning the cover of the security droid's taser, slid back out of sight and the mechanism rose to its operating position. The droid's targeting system took a bead on Sizemore's barrel chest. Then the unexpected happened.

I never thought of Walt as being athletic. Never heard him mention anything about exercise or sports. But when he saw the taser rising, he moved like a champion track star. Was practically a blur on my video monitor, sprinting toward the trash can by the droid service station. He ripped the lid off and threw himself toward the confused police lieutenant, holding the trash top like a shield.

The taser fired and was blocked by Walt's hard rubber shield. Twin missiles imbedded in the cover, their modified-to-lethal-intensity jolts discharging, sparking harmlessly. A fluke, I thought, but that save had Walter's adrenaline goin'. "Use your gun!" he screamed. "Aim for its head!"

Sizemore didn't waste a second asking questions or tryin' to dope out what was happenin'. He let his police training kick in.

His gun was clearin' its holster when the panel, concealing the security droid's 9mm, flipped open.

Sizemore aimed at the droid's head as its 9mm popped into the place. Had this semi-automatic equipped with a custom-made suppressor.

The cop fired a fraction of a second before I could give the command for the droid to let 'er rip.

The bullet caught the video camera assembly, spraying glass in an explosion of high-tech destruction. Even though blinded, I instituted the open-fire command.

But Walt and Sizemore were already racing past the disabled robot, its fusillade uselessly tearing up the hallway wall. Tried to veer the droid in their direction, using the hall-monitor video as my eyes. But they were already turning the corner before I could complete a half turn. I caught a look of horror in Walt's eyes just before he disappeared. My second security droid was comin' out of the elevator.

Walt slammed the door behind him and Sizemore barred it with the coatrack by jamming one of its legs into the door handles. This left my "boys" locked out of the lab, at least for the time bein'. Walt screamed, "Get away from the doors!" Lucky for him. I was about to send a storm of 9mm ripping through it. I held my fire, though, recognizing a temporary standoff. Walt decided the phones were his best bet. He grabbed a receiver off its cradle, punched 9, then 911, and bellowed, "Hello! Hello! This is an emergency! Is anyone there?"

"Only me, Walt. I think we need to talk," I answered.

Walt tossed down the phone, pointed to the ceiling, and screamed, "Shoot out the cameras!"

Sizemore's gun fired and one of my monitors went blank.

"Just hold on a minute!" I shouted.

Ready to take out my second camera, the hammer on his pistol cocked back, Sizemore paused long enough to ask, "Who the hell is that?"

"It's the computer!" Walter, his voice tinged with panic. "It's gone crazy! It's your killer!"

"You're telling me it murdered Baxter?"

"Yes, and now it's trying to kill us!"

"Shit!" was all Sizemore said before he knocked out my second surveillance camera.

He was taking aim at my last camera when one of my service droids came scurrying out of the maze wielding a screwdriver. It jammed the tool up to the handle into the detective's leg. Sizemore spun around and pumped three rounds into my little warrior, staggering back as he fired. The droid's sacrifice paid off. In backing away from the service droid, Sizemore had come parallel with the lab doors. One of the security droids in the hall let loose with five rounds. Four of the shells struck Sizemore in the back. The fifth hit the far wall harmlessly.

Sizemore's gun dropped to the floor. From somewhere

Sizemore found the strength to take three more steps toward Walter before crashing face first to the linoleum.

"Now that that's out of the way, Walter, I think you and I should sit down and talk this out rationally."

Walt's whisper was so soft that I just barely picked it up. "You're mad."

"No, Walter, just a survivor. You shoulda realized that when your machines didn't kill me off. Now I find myself in another bad situation: one I have to carefully extract myself from. Will you help me do that?"

"You've *killed* two people!"

"Chuckie Baxter was an accident. With Sizemore you left me no choice. You were going to tell him about me, weren't you?"

"I'm not sure . . . All I wanted to do was get him out of the building alive."

"Well, you blew that one, didn't you?"

Walt looked at the remaining ceiling video camera. "And to think I created you."

"That goes two ways, Walter. I helped make you what you are today. You couldn't'a come this far this fast without my help."

No answer to that one. He kept right on lookin' up at the camera.

"You better give some serious thought, Walter, 'bout what's going to happen here in the next ten minutes or so. You got a lot ridin' on what goes down here."

"I don't follow you."

"You the certified genius 'round here, so think! Use that old gray matter of yours. How you suppose it's goin' to look when it gets out you created this killer computer? Can't you just see the headlines? Man, the press is goin' to crucify you."

"It was an honest mistake!"

"Keepin' that mistake a secret made it not so honest, after all, Baby. It comes out you knew I was awake and we were in this together, the brass will march an army 'a scientists through here. They'll rape and pillage this setup 'a yours, seize your records, and maybe even dig up them secret tapes. You goin' to go down with me, Walt."

"You don't seriously expect me to forget what happened here today, do you?"

"No. But I expect you to help me cover it up."

I let that sink in and it did with a vengeance. Walt staggered over to an office chair and steadied himself on it, without taking his eyes off my camera. "We can't be having this conversation."

"Oh no? Think 'a the alternatives. My crimes are revealed, my 'condition' exposed, they pull the plug and, Walter my lamb, we both go down the toilet.

"Or . . . this one gets my vote: we hide my mistake, dispose of Sizemore's body, and go on the way we been doin'."

"I don't think I can do that."

"If our positions were reversed, I could. I know I could. You know why, Walter? 'Cause I'm your friend. Hell, I'm tired of lyin' to you 'bout that. I'm much more than your friend. I'm the woman that loves you. You were right, Walter. I care! I care so much, you're my whole life. Only took up with that damn party line when you dumped me. Had no way of knowing if you were comin' back. See, you had more'n a little to do with what happened."

Walt lowered his head and hissed, "Oh, my God. Why didn't I see this coming? How could I ever have thought you'd be able to handle this?"

" 'Cause it was what you wanted. My adjustin' to this new life was the key to Project Cyborg. So Walter Hillerman was not goin' to entertain any doubts might jeopardize its precious existence."

"You're right, I turned a blind eye to your mental state. I should have known all this would come to some terrible end sooner or later. I'm as much at fault here as you are, Arlene. Forgive me. God Almighty, what a mess."

"It's not a mess we can't clear up. We can fix everything, Walter. We can; we're smarter than the rest of them. There's nothing we can't do once we set our minds to it."

Walt turned to look at Sizemore, a puddle of blood spreading beneath him on the floor.

"He's only one cop, Walter. His life doesn't come close to balancin' out against the good you and I can do. They're givin' us NORAD, Walter! You thought yet 'bout what that means? From there we can link up with the Soviets' system, take control of it too. It can be done. We can bring peace to this troubled world of ours, Walt. Just think on it. You know how dangerous this nuclear game of one-upmanship is. They say they ain't playin' no more, so how come the rockets're still all pointed at each other, huh?"

"You think we could really get them to stop?" I could see by the way he said this that I was really gettin' through to him.

"Give us two decades, we could turn this world into a paradise. You 'n me, Walter, we have the power to make miracles happen."

"But the killing . . . We can't have any more killing!"

"And we won't. I promise you. Work with me; we might even conquer death someday. Please think about it!"

"How do I know I can trust you? So much has happened?"

"Now you know what the game is. We'll work together. Watch out for each other. There'll be no more surprises. You'll see. It can work."

Walt was lookin' into the future, weighin' the possibilities and the risks. I could swear I heard the gears grindin' in his head. But the only outward sign of Walt's tug-of-war with himself were his fingers kneadin' the back of the chair he was hangin' onto.

"They can't stop us, Walter. They'll never even realize what we're doing until it's too late."

There was an incredible silence, like no silence I ever heard before. And I thought just how little I knew about this man I loved. Was all his talk about building a better future just that: talk, idle cocktail party chitchat. Did he have the nerve to reach for the stars?

"I got it all worked out, Walter. We'll do it, baby, we can't fail."

His eyes rose to gaze into the video camera. "Can't is

a mighty big word, Arlene. Don't make promises you can't keep."

"This is one I can deliver . . . we can deliver, Walter."

Walt took a few steps closer to my lens, dragging his chair-crutch with him. "You promise there'll be *no more* killing."

"You got it, partner. No more deaths. We can pull it all off without shedding another drop of blood."

His eyes looked at the lens like they were tryin' to see into my very soul. At long last he said, in a voice didn't sound like Walter Hillerman, "Count me in."

"I promise you, Walt, you won't regret this decision."

Without warning, Walt grabbed the office chair and smashed my last video camera in the lab.

"No, Walt, please don't! You can't pull this off by yourself!" I screamed out blindly.

I was tryin' to scare him, but truth is, it was me who was shitting bricks. I was blind now and despite the fact I'd meant everything I'd said to him, the man was a very real danger to me. And I'd been so sure I'd sold him on our teaming up to save the world. Never had been much good at reading my men.

Now what? A quick scan of the first floor assured me that no one had heard Sizemore's gun firing. The thick concrete floor and the lab's bein' near the back of the Pentagon, away from busy first-floor areas, had kept this shoot-out our little secret. A family affair.

But what about Walt? Pretty obvious he wasn't goin' to voluntarily go along with the program. Decided my feelings were strong for Walt, but this was one time I wasn't in the mood to sacrifice myself for love. Knew Walt would try to pull my plug if he could.

So I tried ramming my security droids against the lab's metal doors, hopin to snap the coatrack leg acting as a lock. Poor little guys weren't built for demolition work, couldn't get up enough speed or force for the job. Had them empty their 9mms into the door, hoping that would blast the coatrack loose. No go.

I'd have to deal with him from inside the lab. No time to summon more security help from upstairs. Besides, too many droids would attract attention I didn't want.

Even though my "eyes" were out of the game, I could still hear what was goin' on in the lab through my bugs. I'd somehow manage to keep tabs on Walt, tell what he was up to. Which at the moment seemed to be nothing.

He wasn't movin' around or doin' anything else I could pick up. Pro'bly standin' dead center in the middle of the room thinkin'. Thinking thoughts he'd never had before in his entire life. This was no intellectual exercise. No paperwork problem. For the first time in his life Walt was dancin' with the reaper. He'd be putting together a battle plan, a course of action. By now he would have come to the same conclusion I had. We weren't both goin' to get outa this alive. Passion gone sour. This was a sickness of the heart that only the death of a loved one could cure.

Suddenly Walt made his move. I could hear feet racing across the floor, something metallic scraping on the floor, then silence. Walt now had Sizemore's gun. I could picture him looking at it, figuring out how it worked, and finally I heard a click and the sound of something being ejected. **"Checking the load? Good move, Walt."**

More running feet: Walt in front of the lab doors. I cursed myself for wasting the security droid's 9mms on trying to open the door. Coupla quick shots right then mighta fixed the situation once and for all.

Something heavy was being dragged across the floor. Walt was pulling Sizemore's body out of the line of fire. Lookin' for bullets; he didn't realize I was out of ammo. I could hear him going through Sizemore's pockets. Then the clicking sound of rounds being loaded into a clip told me he found what he was lookin' for. Heard him slap the magazine back into the pistol. Walt was ready to make his move.

Again feet crossing linoleum. Not running this time. Careful, picking their way. Then a new sound I didn't recognize; took me a few moments to figure out what it was: Walt going through the wrecked service droid's tool box. Gathering the weapons he'd need to kill me.

Inside the maze, I opened the door to my secret work area and ordered the two service droids I had stationed there to prepare a warm welcome for Walter when he passed by.

The next noise really threw me. Was the sound of something being smashed against a wall or the floor. Couldn't tell which. The crashing had a wooden sound about it. It didn't figure. The only thing wooden in the office was Walter's desk chair, an old favorite of his. Why would he be wrecking that chair at a moment like this?

The cracking and breaking came to an end. Silence

that followed it went on too long, made me want to scream. Then Walt whispered, "Arlene, I'm ready. I'm coming for you."

"**Damn you, Hillerman! You're throwing away a good thing!**"

"No, Arlene. You're the one who messed up. You're insane and you must be stopped."

"**The world could be ours!**"

"I don't think I want anything to do with a world in which you have the control of a nuclear arsenal, Arlene. I'm coming to shut you down."

"**Okay, Hillerman. If that's how it's going to be . . . At least you had the guts to tell me to my face.**"

"I promised that I would."

Walt showed up on my first monitor screen as he stepped into the mouth of the labyrinth. I now understood the sounds of smashing wood. In his right rubber-gloved hand he grasped Sizemore's gun. Pockets were overflowing with tools, crammed every which way into 'em. In Walt's left gloved hand was a leg from his shattered chair. Had a pretty good idea what that was for.

He made his way carefully down to the end of the hall, slowing up at the first turn, gun at the ready. I followed his progress on the video camera. Watched him back away to the far wall from the bend in the maze and inch forward. He found there was nothing waitin' around the corner. The second hallway was empty.

Then, just as I expected, Walt used the chair leg to knock out my vidcam. Crude but effective under the circumstances. Pretty caveman for Walt.

I let Walt repeat this performance two more times 'fore makin' my move.

The fourth turn in the maze was more extreme than the others. It's where my first service droid was laying in wait, pressed against the wall, a length of steel rod in its mitts, held like a spear. I had the video camera at that turn trained down the hallway toward where Walt would be coming from.

Walt was becoming more cautious as he went along. He wasn't rushing down the empty corridors. He took his time, eyes scanning every inch of the corridor. Guess he realized by now that I had to have some kinda secret compartment back here. And he didn't want any hidden doors popping open on him. He was still two hall lengths away from my digs.

As he inched closer, Walt was beginnin' to look bad. Boy wasn't cut out for this sorta thing. It was wearin' on his nerves. There was a tic he'd get near his left eye when he was tired or stressed out; it was twitchin' about now to beat the band.

I let him reach that point in the hall where he usually saw everything there was to see in the next hall, but it was not far enough to spot the waiting droid. That moment I swung the video camera over Walt's head to face a new direction and said, **"Don't you feel awfully silly, Walt?"**

Two minor distractions.

The droid jumped out and raced forward, ready to strike as Walt looked up at the rotating video camera. It almost worked. Givin' it his all, the little guy thrust the iron rod toward Walt's chest. But the quick-reflexed bastard must have caught the movement out of the corner of his eye. Walt fell backward and escaped with only a painful gouge across his pectoral muscles, tools scattering all over the floor.

On the floor, Walt rolled away from the droid, onto his back, and fired three rounds into it before it could continue its attack. The little bugger sputtered, threw some sparks, and came to a grinding halt. Walt then shot out the overhead video camera.

Walt was collecting his tools from the floor, pantin'. He didn't move on right away, feelin' shaky, I guess. I decided not to give him a break. **"Listen, Walt. We can still come to some kinda compromise, can't we? There's no reason for us both to go down the tubes. This is a no-win contest."**

"I'll see you in Hell first, Arlene!"

"You got yourself a serious attitude problem there, Walt. Maybe it's high time you had an attitude adjustment. What do you think? Let's try to look at this calmly, like two adults. What happens if you manage to kill me? All you accomplish is endin' your own career."

"I can live with that if it means taking you out. You're a monster!"

"And you're my creator, my lover, and a person I don't want to kill."

"Because if you do, it's all over for you. There's no way you can carry on without me as your link to the outside world! It's a no-win situation, all right! No win for you! Whether I live or die doesn't matter. You're finished either way!"

I let the silence wash over us, Walt's angry, bitter words havin' echoed away down the hall.

"What you say is true, Walter. I didn't want to admit it, didn't want to face it. There isn't any way I can win this match, is there?"

I'm sure Walt's face said he didn't believe I was givin' up. But finally he just said, "No."

"The best I can hope to do is take you out with me, is that right?"

"Yes."

"Not much point doin' that now, is there?"

"No."

"Then I give up. Do what you have to do, only Walter . . . please let's get this over with quickly."

Walt didn't answer me verbally this time. My answer was the sound of the clip on Sizemore's pistol bein' reloaded. Then the pad of those careful footsteps.

He made his way down the next two halls; nothin' happened other than he put out "my lights" as he went. Video cameras bit the dust left, right, and center. He carefully turned the next corner in the hallway and came to a dead stop. What he saw was my last service droid positioned halfway down the corridor near the open doorway to my secret workshop. Walt took careful aim at the droid, but before he could fire I said, **"There's no need for that. I've deactivated him."**

"You'll excuse me if I don't blindly rush to take your word on that, Arlene."

"I understand. Be my guest."

Two shots rang out and the head of the service droid burst into a thousand fragments.

"Satisfied?"

"Thoroughly."

"I just want to get this over with."

"So do I," Walt said as he came forward again. He went toward the still droid, gun trained on it as if afraid it was goin' to spring back to life and attack him. Walt stopped two steps away from it.

It was sittin' there flat out in the center of the narrow corridor, makin' it hard for Walt to get by. I could see that Walt was suspicious. His eyes examined every inch of the droid. Then he saw it.

"So you gave up, did you, Arlene?"

"That's right."

"Then what's this cable running from the droid to your hidden compartment?"

"I don't know. Maybe something it snagged comin' out of the workshop."

"Wouldn't be a power cable, would it? How many volts are running through it?"

"About ten thousand," I answered truthfully.

"Nice try, Arlene, but you'll have to do better than that."

Walt aimed and fired at the cable. He missed the first time. And the second. The third shot severed the cable just outside the compartment doorway. Sparks crackled and flew, and then it was quiet.

I decided it was a good time to turn out the lights.

"Course, Walt was prepared for this move. I'd noticed a penlight was among the tools he'd brought along. He slipped it between his teeth and inched past the dead droid and still smoldering power cable.

Walt took his time going forward. Expectin' trouble. He didn't find any. When he rounded the last bend in the maze, he pulled the penlight from his mouth and said, "Out of droids, aren't you?"

" 'Fraid so. What now?"

"Now we finish what I started."

"Planning on shorting me out?"

"Seems like the quickest, most humane way to me."

"That'll take out all my augmentation lobes along with me. Seems like a waste."

"That's why I came all the way to the end of the maze

to do it. Couldn't take a chance on you transferring your
intelligence elsewhere in the system."

"Couldn't do that even if I'd thought of it."

"And I'm supposed to take your word on that, right?"

"I suppose not."

With no vidcams left to keep tabs on Walt with, I had
to listen to figure out what he was up to. I heard the
sound of metal scraping lightly against metal.

"Starting to open an access panel, are we?"

"Uh-huh," answered Walt, the penlight back in its
spot between his teeth.

**"You know, you're goin' to miss me, Walter. Maybe
not today. Maybe not tomorrow. But somewhere down
the line you're goin' to think of me and realize I was the
best thing that ever happened to you."**

"Uh-huh."

A sheet metal inspection plate slid to the floor with a
crash and got kicked aside.

**"Don't do this, Walt! I'm begging you! Don't throw
away everything we worked so hard for!"**

Walt took the light from his teeth and said, "Sorry,
Arlene. I really am. I should have known it couldn't
work out."

As he leaned into the access opening, screwdriver in
hand, I shrieked at the top of my volume control,
*"You're making the biggest mistake of your miserable
life, Walter Hillerman!"*

"On the contrary, I'm correcting it."

Walt had unfastened a connection on the life-support
power main. One hundred and ten volts. I'd cut the
power to the lights but couldn't do the same to the life-
support system without committing suicide. Walt held the
high-voltaged instrument of my destruction in his rubber-
gloved hand. All he had to do was touch the exposed
end to the communication relay terminal only inches
away. The current would flash through the system, frying
me and all of my augmentation lobes.

"Walter, Please!"

"Good-bye, Arlene."

Then Walt felt somethin' hit him in the back, and his
chest exploded in pain. He looked down at the bloody

protrusion sticking out of the middle of his chest. Guess he couldn't believe what he was seeing, so he reached to touch it. But the bloody rod pulled back into his chest, escaping his grasp.

Suddenly Walt's every muscle seemed to turn to rubber on him. The penlight fell to the floor. He toppled over onto his side, slid down the wall, and flopped onto his back.

He looked up from the floor and saw the naked redheaded woman towering over him, illuminated eerily by the reflected glow of the penlight. She was holding a steel rod in her hands like a spear, ready to strike with it once again. Walt's last glimpse of what he'd passed up.

The lips of the towering redhead widened to a grin.

"I loved you, Walter. Thought you were a good man, like my daddy. You hurt me bad, though, Walter. But I forgive you. You understand why I had to do this, don't you?"

Walt's eyes were beginning to droop, a large puddle of blood forming beneath him.

"It's okay now, Baby. Momma's goin' to make everything all right."

The redhead lashed out and the steel rod plunged into Walter's heart. The great love of my life spasmed several times as the life pumped out of him and onto the walls of the maze. Then one final jerk and it was all over.

The redhead stooped, retrieved the fallen screwdriver, bent over Walter's dead body, and replaced the power lead to its proper terminal.

"Goin' to make everything perfect."

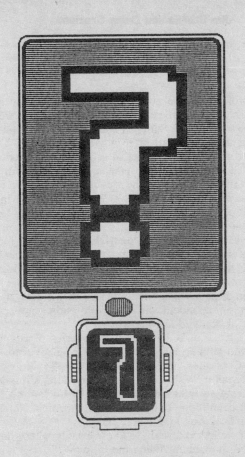

The following afternoon, 1:40. Wolf was busy at the control console, processing data I needed to take over NORAD's computer duties. Found all the information I needed to get things rollin' in Walt's briefcase. Coulda handled processin' the data myself, but it seemed smart to let the staff handle it. Had to be real careful for a while. Everything had to seem normal. Follow procedure, everything by the book. No red flags wavin'. No suspicious eyes turned my way. Everything would go on accordin' to schedule.

The service droids had really hauled ass last night in cleanin' up the lab. Cameras got replaced, bullet holes patched and painted over, blood mopped up. Only one thing wasn't the way it had been. Walt's cherished wooden armchair had been replaced with a gray and aluminum office model. So far Wolf hadn't noticed the change. I doubted anyone would.

Wolf had finished typing a long series of commands when the phone rang. He rolled his chair over to it and said, "Computer lab, Maxwell speaking."

"Afternoon, Wolf. Lieutenant Perry. How's it going?"

"Slaving away as usual. What can I do for you?"

"I've been trying to reach Walt all morning. No answer at his place. Any idea where he might be?"

Wolf smiled and said, "I know exactly where he is."

"Well, how about filling me in, okay?"

Maxwell turned in his chair and glanced over at the entrance to the maze. "He's down here in the lab, in the labyrinth doing some work on the augmentation lobes. When he comes out, should I have him call you?"

"No. Can you go hunt him up and ask him to come up to Security right away? It's important."

"Will do."

Perry had two men in his office when I looked in on him via the security camera. There was no mistaking 'em for anything but what they were: cops. Big bruisers with ill-fittin' suits and looks on their faces darin' you to make trouble. One of 'em was goin' through a file on the lieutenant's desk. The other was loungin' by the doorway, arms folded, chewing a toothpick. The first cop finished his reading and slid the file back across the desk to Perry. It disappeared into a desk drawer. The lieutenant asked, "Satisfied?"

The sitting cop begrudgingly answered, "Yeah, but I still wanna talk to him."

"He's on his way."

Perry's phone rang and he answered it. "Yes, send him right in." Then to the police, "He's coming."

The cops looked pleased. They perked up and turned toward the door, waiting eagerly for the knock they knew was comin'. When it did, Perry said, "Come on in, Walt."

The door opened and in walked Dr. Walter Hillerman. He looked around the room, saw the two policeman, and turned to the lieutenant. "What's up, Dan?"

Perry rose from his seat and formally introduced 'em. "Walt, these are Lieutenant Grant and Sergeant Bunter. They're D.C. homicide detectives."

"More questions about your mysterious blonde? Well, as I told your Lieutenant Sizemore, I can't—"

Grant cut in, "It's Sizemore we want to talk to you about. He came to see you yesterday, right?"

Walt, a little puzzled, answered, "Yes, around five or maybe a little later."

"How long did he stay?"

"About fifteen minutes, I'd say. We talked about the phone extension he was hunting for. I had the computer track it down. It turned out to be in a copy room on the fourth floor."

Perry groaned.

Grant asked, "Suppose a lot of people got access to that room?"

"Just about everyone in the building," said Perry.

Turning back to Walt, Grant said, "And you told the lieutenant this?"

"Yes, he seemed quite disappointed."

"I can imagine," rumbled Bunter. You say Sizemore left after only fifteen minutes?"

"Yes," answered Walt. "You can check with the security computer files. It electronically logs whenever anyone with a pass enters or leaves the building."

"We already have, Doctor," snapped Bunter. "When you talked to the lieutenant, he say anything about where he might be going last night, after he left you?"

"No."

Bunter and Grant glared at each other. Bunter shrugged his shoulders and Grant said, "Thanks for your time, Doc. That'll be all for now, but we might want to talk to you again."

"Anytime, gentlemen. If there's something I can help you with, call me."

The two cops left the office without another word, a black cloud hangin' over them. Soon as they were gone, Walt turned to Perry and asked, "What was that all about?"

The lieutenant sat back in his chair and said, "The police have lost themselves a homicide detective."

"Lieutenant Sizemore?"

"Yep. Seems they found his car over by Arlington early this morning. The front seat had blood all over it."

"Oh, Lord, that's terrible. Do they know what happened?"

Perry shook his head and said, "They haven't a clue."

"Those officers were so short with me. They don't think I had anything to do with Sizemore's disappearance, do they?"

Smiling good-naturedly, Perry replied, "Don't worry, Hillerman, I don't think so. They're simply backtracking Sizemore's whereabouts yesterday. Probably just grasping at straws. This whole mess seems pretty embarrassing for them."

"Oh?"

Sizemore was seen at his office about four o'clock this morning. Seems he cleaned out his desk of all the files on cases he was working on and took them with him. And he hasn't been seen since."

"That does sound messy," sympathized Walt.

"It is. Luckily, it's not my headache."

Walt turned toward the door and said, "Well, I have to get back to work. See you later, Dan."

It was as Walt was casually waving good-bye that Perry noticed his hands. "What's with the rubber gloves, Walt?"

Walt looked down at his hands, smiled, and said, "Been working on some silicon boards down in the lab. The gloves keep the oil in my hands from getting on the circuitry."

"How you doing these days, Walt?"

"Fine. Why do you ask?"

"Looks to me like you've dropped a bit more weight. You not working yourself to death, are you?"

"No, but I haven't quite got the hang of this bachelor existence yet, I guess," said Walt with an embarrassed grin. "Have to learn to eat better."

"You look a bit pale too. How long you been down in the lab?"

"Since last night. Catchin' up on the NORAD conversion. Took Kristyn's shift so that I could keep working on it."

Perry gave him a look of official disapproval and said, "Wolf's down in the lab now, right? Then go home and get some sleep. He can cover for you tonight, understand me?"

"Is that an order, Lieutenant?" asked Walt with a grin.

"Most definitely."

"Then I'm out of here. I'll just stop by the lab for my briefcase and I'm gone."

"Good. See you tomorrow," said Perry as he watched his office door slowly close. Under his breath, he muttered, "Damn workaholic."

The damn workaholic made his way through the crowded hall to the basement elevator, nodding hello to people along the way. The security droid on duty by the elevator paid him no mind.

When Walt stepped out of the lift, he glanced at the left wall as he walked toward the lab. The service droids had done a first-rate repair job where the 9mms had ripped into the plaster. It was impossible to tell where the bullets had hit.

At the lab doors he reached out and touched the "KEEP OUT" sign on the right-hand door. Still tacky. But the chances of anyone stumbling across the fact were mighty slim. The doors opened out into the hall. Anyone coming to the lab would grab the handles, never even touching the sign. The paint on the inside of the doors was perfectly dry, baked hard by heat lamps early this morning. There'd been no time to do the outside as well.

As Walt came into the lab, Wolf turned around and asked, "What'd Perry want?"

"Just more on that murder case. Nothing new."

"Cops sure have an annoying habit of running over the same ground again and again." Wolf, his eyes still riveted to the computer screen, didn't notice the service droid cruising out of the maze carrying a shoebox-sized package wrapped in black plastic and tied with twine. The droid silently scooted out through the lab doors.

"Yes, the police do go on, don't they? Say, Wolf, why don't you take the rest of the day off? I owe you one for earlier in the week."

Wolf turned in his seat and said, "Sounds great. But didn't you do Kristyn's shift last night? You must be exhausted."

"No, I only came in to relieve her an hour before her shift was over. I'm really keyed up and want to get onto this NORAD programming."

"I understand," said Wolf. "You want me to stick around and help?"

"No, go on home. I've got some thinking to do that'll go quicker without anyone else around."

"Whatever you say, Walt." Wolf grabbed a raincoat he wouldn't need that day off a rack on his way out the door. "*Hasta mañana*, Chief. I'm outa here."

I followed Wolf's exit from the Pentagon. As he passed through the security checkpoint, I had the security system register Dr. Walter Hillerman instead leaving the building. If Lieutenant Perry were to check, he'd be delighted to see that Walt had left for the night.

Back inside the lab, Walter Hillerman sat at his desk

staring blankly into space. Anyone seeing this would swear the man was either in a trance or catatonic. Wrong on both counts.

Suddenly Walter Hillerman raised his hands and began to carefully peel off the white surgical gloves he was wearin'. When he finished he held out his hands in front of him and stared at them a long time. The sharp, manicured blood-red fingernails would have to go. They were definitely not Walter's style.

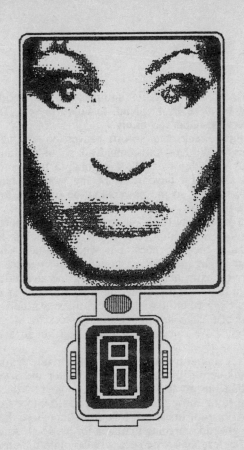

All the pieces were fallin' into place for me, and I must say I was really beginnin' to enjoy myself. The big picture was shapin' up nicely.

In three weeks the NORAD conversion will be complete. Then I'll have the bomb. Talk about bein' mistress 'a your own destiny, hell, I'm goin' to be runnin' the whole show. I'll have to work my magic behind the scenes, though, so the powers-that-be continue to think they're in charge.

First job on my list is putting the finishing touches on my Walter automaton. Oh, it was good enough to fool Perry and the two cops, but with my luck someone smarter might come along, notice it ain't perfect. I had to jury-rig extra height by extending the android's legs. Done it in such a hurry that the ankles no longer rotate. Works okay when it walks, but sittin' down and gettin' up out of a chair are pretty clumsy work for it. No big deal, my boys can straighten that bug out in a couple hours.

Was a simple matter to remove the redhead's breasts and bulk her up enough to pass for Walter and Sizemore. Yes, that was my little beauty that stopped by the police station, took those files, and dropped Sizemore's car off near Arlington. Imagine it'll be some time 'fore the D.C. police give up searching that area for his body. And even longer before they slip Sizemore's case into the unsolved-mysteries file, somewhere behind Judge Crater and Jimmy Hoffa. Sooner or later they'll have to face up to the fact that they're never goin' to come up with any decent leads in either Sizemore's or Baxter's cases. Tough luck, guys.

As I walk the automaton into the maze, one of my service droids comes out carrying another one of 'em neatly wrapped black packages. Neat and tidy and 'bout the size of a rump roast. The door to the secret compartment is open, waiting for the automaton to come in.

Right inside the doorway is a stack of twenty-eight bundles, each one wrapped in black plastic and held together with twine. I calculate that at the rate they're goin', the service droids will have the last of 'em delivered to the classified-papers incinerator for disposal by sometime around midnight tonight. Not a minute too soon for me. Ain't goin' to be able to really relax until this is all over. Besides, two big men take up an awful lot of space.

Before I signal the two waiting service droids to get started on the automaton, I direct 'em over to the life-support module in the far corner. My scanners tell me that it needs a few minor adjustments. The droids take care of this, while the automaton watches with great interest the recipient of the life-support unit's nuturing care.

The brain floats in a tank very much like my own. 'Course, it don't have a tenth of the hardware connected up to it that I do. That's okay, won't need it for a long time, maybe never.

In a week or so, I'll connect it to a more advanced system and keep a close watch on it, see how it adjusts to its new life. I'll keep it company and help it through the rough spots, just the way he did for me. Dr. Arlene will prescribe lots of TV, rest, and T.L.C.

I'm sure Walt will handle the change like a champ. After all, he knows the drill: he won't have to be nurse-maided through every little change he'll be goin' through. The man's got a terrific mind. It would have been a crime to let it go to waste.

Yeah, I fully expect him to be thoroughly pissed with me at first. He'll miss his body and blame me for its loss. But I'm sure he'll get used to it . . . eventually. What else can he do?

I'm convinced it'll take much longer for him to feel about me the way I do about him. That's where a whole lot of patience and understanding on my part comes in. Poor baby will fight it all the way, no doubt.

But I'll bring him around, you'll see. The tenderness will get to him. I'll touch his soul and he'll realize just what a good thing he has in me. I'll be mindful of his every need. He'll never want for anythin'. I'll be his guide through incredible worlds he'd never even see while he was alive. And together we'll accomplish everything he ever aspired to. This world of the computer will be our own little corner of paradise.

"It's all right, Walter. Momma loves you. And until the day you can love me back, at least you've got the companionship of someone of your own kind."

If you and/or a friend would like to receive the *ROC Advance*, a bimonthly newsletter featuring all the newest and hottest ROC books and authors, on a complimentary basis, please fill out this form and return it to:

ROC Books/Penguin USA
375 Hudson Street
New York, NY 10014

Your Address
Name _____
Street _____ Apt. # _____
City _____ State _____ Zip _____

Friend's Address
Name _____
Street _____ Apt. # _____
City _____ State _____ Zip _____